Wolfgang

Vampire's Mate Book Five

Grae Bryan

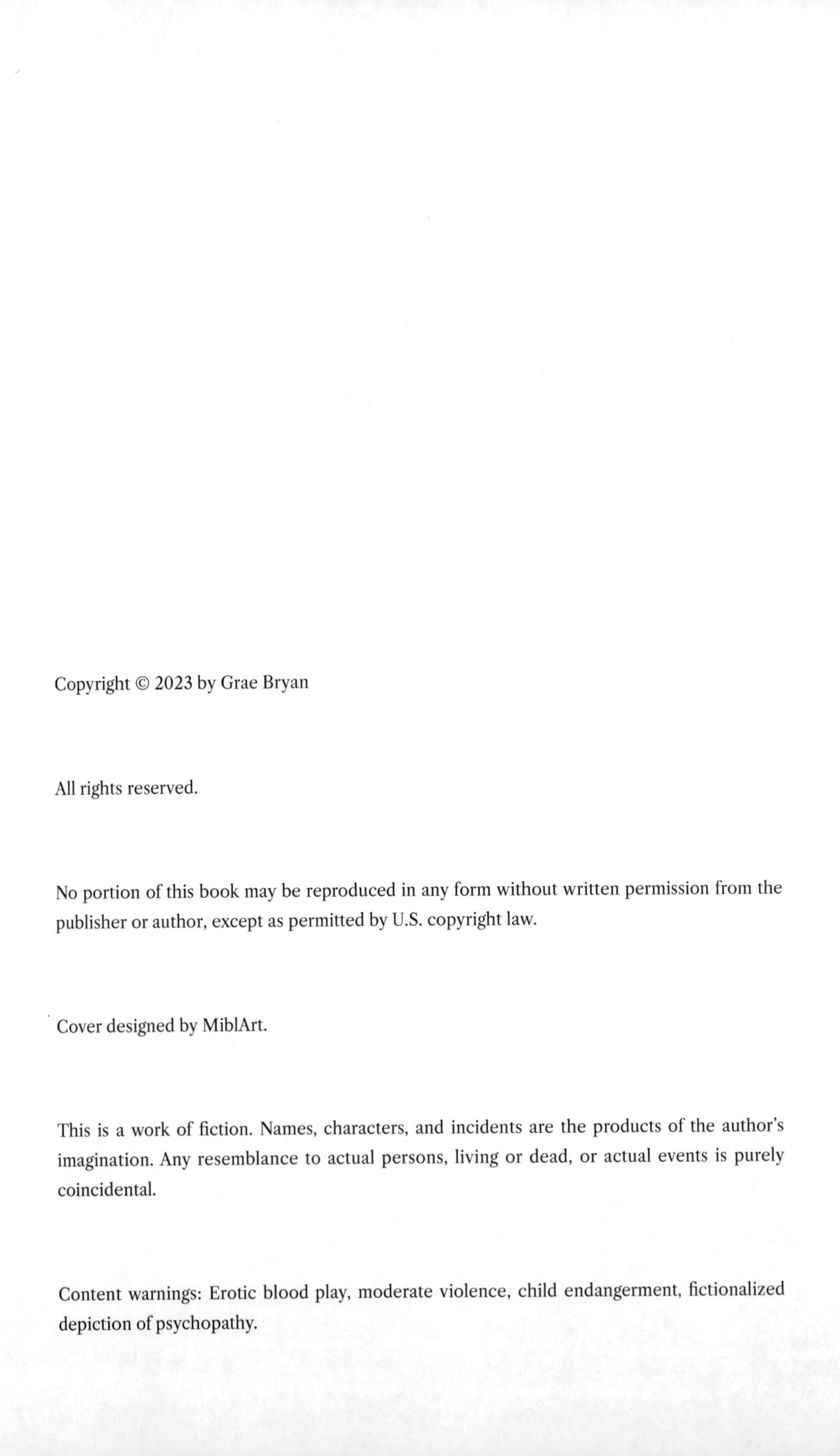

Cover designed by MiblArt.

Content warnings: Erotic blood play, moderate violence, child endangerment, fictionalized depiction of psychopathy.

Contents

Prologue

Wolfe

There was not a single part of Wolfe's being that wanted to be in Hyde Park.

He was most certainly *not* the kind of person to be charmed by its small size or surrounding natural features. He wasn't a small-town craftsman, or baker, or whatever else kind of hawker of wares that would be looking for a cozy, touristy town in which to sell their goods to self-satisfied locals and bright-eyed visitors from afar. And he certainly wasn't a godforsaken ski bunny, to be drawn in by the lure of snow-covered mountaintops.

All in all, he mused—as he swirled the mediocre cabernet in his glass, watching his guests arrive at the bar they'd oh so carefully chosen—it wasn't the type of place he belonged.

There were somehow too many humans and too few at the same time. The town had too small a permanent population to hold anything of value—no museums of note, no opera to attend, not a decent bottle of wine at any restaurant he could find—and yet it wasn't isolated enough to hold any true protection from inquisitive minds or prying eyes.

Who would want to stay here? Why would *Johann* want to stay here?

The answer, of course, lay within the very people seating themselves with Johann at this tawdry table, in this tawdry bar, ordering their tawdry beverages: Soren, the blond waif glaring daggers at Wolfe; Gabe, Soren's muscular mate *also* glaring daggers at Wolfe; then Alexei, the freshly turned mate of Johann's, an infatuated dolt of a man if Wolfe had ever seen one.

Wolfe had thought hastening Alexei's transformation would ease Johann's concerns over returning where he belonged, but he'd clearly been mistaken in that regard. He could already tell they weren't meeting with him here to discuss travel plans.

He'd underestimated the pull of friendship, apparently.

And really, of all the things to be bested by. It was almost too much to bear, for him to be at the mercy of Johann's sentimentality.

What must it be like, to be compelled by such whims as affection, devotion, love?

Lucky for Wolfe, he'd never have to know; it simply wasn't in his nature. He could be relatively fond of certain companions, sure. Possessive, even, as he was of any of his belongings. But he didn't lose all sense of reason. Not like this.

Johann *needed* to return to the den, if he didn't want a fight he couldn't handle coming his way. The little vampire had never liked violence of any sort. And the den, however odious, offered a certain protection, one that would only grow as their ranks did. With Johann and Wolfe at the helm, they'd put an end to the senseless culling of new members, allow their numbers to swell naturally.

Because if—when, really—humans wised up to what lurked among them, vampires would need those numbers. They would need the ability to declare themselves a community, a society, and not individual monsters to be put down or captured and studied.

Which was why Wolfe felt a true, sharp stab of irritation as Johann—or Jay, as he was insisting on being called (not that Wolfe would give him the satisfaction)—folded his hands on the table and stated, "I want to discuss what it would take for you to let me stay."

Wolfe kept his features even; that was easy enough, as he'd never had a very reactive face. But the answer was simple: nothing. There was *nothing* this motley little crew could do to change Wolfe's mind on this, and he'd just begun to say as much when—

There.

Wolfe tensed in his seat, his nostrils flaring. There was a scent on the air, wafting in from the entrance of the bar. Subtle, sure—it was almost completely obscured by some hideous sandalwood aftershave—but it was there. It was...floral, with a powdery note to it.

Wisteria.

Wolfe's beast—that inner part of him he always imagined slithering inside him like a snake—coiled tight in anticipation. *Something's here*, it crooned. *Something delicious*.

Wolfe's words of protest for Johann's whimsy froze on his tongue. He sat, stiff and tight-lipped, as a big blond human—the source of the scent, Wolfe would bet his unending life on it—greeted Soren's mate from afar with enthusiasm. He watched, tense and oddly bereft, as the handsome man walked off to a distant table with his companions.

"Who was that man?" Did Wolfe's voice sound hoarse to everyone else, or only to himself? Impossible to say. Either way, Soren answered his question.

A doctor, apparently. Dr. Monroe.

Wolfe wanted him. His beast wanted him. Badly enough that Wolfe found himself simply asking for him, as one of his terms, like the human was a weekly special at the delicatessen.

He was refused, of course. But no matter. Wolfe paid only half his attention to the rest of the conversation, this peace treaty they were all forming. He was barely aware of his own capitulations. Yes, Johann could stay in Hyde Park. Yes, Wolfe would serve as liaison to the den. Yes, Wolfe would most certainly still expect his monetary due.

In an instant, he mentally rearranged all his carefully laid plans. He would replace the protection of the old den with this new group. He would switch his loyalty with the ease of changing out a pair of socks.

It didn't matter. None of it did.

Because Wolfe had been preparing himself for this moment since the day he'd turned. Here it was, the person meant for him and him alone. Fate's gift. The assurance he would live forever, stable and sane, and not fall into a mindless, feral rage.

His mate.

His mate was here.

And Wolfe didn't need anyone's permission to claim him.

One

Eric

There was a red rose on Eric's front doorstep.

He paused where he stood, still in his hospital scrubs, keys in hand, breath frosting in a soft fog in front of him.

Had someone left it there on accident? Maybe let it fall out of a bouquet before they'd realized they'd gotten the wrong address for whatever heartfelt message they were sending?

But it looked so...deliberate. It had been placed front and center on his doormat. Bloodred, perfectly shaped, thorns left intact on the stem.

Eric bent over and picked it up with thumb and forefinger, careful not to prick himself. Huh. He'd never been given flowers before. And definitely not such a dramatic, singular red rose like this. It should be filling him with some kind of warmth, right? An unexpected romantic gesture at his literal doorstep.

But what he felt instead was a strange chill running down his spine.

But, then again, that could just be because it was fucking *freezing* out, the night air heavy with the threat of snow.

Eric unlocked his front door with his free hand, looking over his shoulder as he did so. He wasn't sure if he was thinking he'd catch his admirer in the act or what (and how dumb would that be, them just standing there in the wintery night, waiting for him to arrive?), but the street behind him was empty.

He stepped inside quickly anyway, throwing his keys on the hallway table as he did so, and tried to think who it could have been. Cindy? But they'd fucked like, two months ago, and she hadn't seemed too eager to repeat the experience. Philip? Except he'd told Eric just last week that he'd found a steady boyfriend and was "done hooking up on the sly." Neither seemed on the verge of courting him with floral arrangements.

Someone entirely new? That would definitely be a change of pace; Eric had never been wooed before; that was for sure. He was always the one doing the approaching, and he struck out more often than not lately, despite the fact that he was tall, blond, and built—and not that rough in the face either, in his own humble opinion. People in this town could sense his desperation, he was pretty sure. Smell his need to be touched on him or something. And he didn't quite care enough to hide it.

Because what did it matter if he was desperate, or cheesy, or smarmy? Getting rejected 80 percent of the time was better than never getting accepted at all, right? It wasn't like anyone was going to want to keep him, even if he did come off sincere.

He hadn't realized, moving to Hyde Park, just how much small towns talked. Ever since his first tentative grope at sixteen, he'd always used sex as a form of release. And it had never been a problem in the bigger cities; there was always *someone* looking for a good time. But it had taken less than six months for the population of Hyde Park to unanimously declare him a man-whore. Sleezy. Silly. Not worth anyone's serious consideration.

He couldn't even be mad about it. It wasn't like they were wrong.

Eric set the rose on the kitchen counter, thinking maybe he'd put it in a little glass with water later. First, he needed a beer. Or a shower. A beer *in* the shower, perhaps?

Before he could decide, his phone's ringtone cut through the silence. He didn't recognize the number. He debated leaving it to voice mail, but it could be one of the nurses, trying to track him down after he fucked up some order or another.

"Monroe," he answered.

Nothing.

"This is Dr. Monroe," he repeated, wondering if there was a lag on the other line.

Still nothing.

Well, fine. He hit the end call button, tossing his phone on the counter next to his flower, only for it to ring again immediately.

He answered it without looking, his tone overly jovial to hide his irritation. "Dr. Monroe here. How can I help you?"

"Well, isn't *that* a pretentious way to answer the phone."

Fuck. Fuck, fuck, fuck. If he'd known who was on the other line, he would have had his shower beer (or three, or four) before answering. Eric pressed fingers to his forehead, hard as he could manage. "Mom. Sorry, I thought you were one of the nurses."

"What, you don't have your own mother saved on your phone?"

"No, I—"

"And why would the nurses be calling your personal phone, anyway? What have you been getting up to?" His mother's tone was laced with suspicion. As if a nurse calling him on his cell was the clue she'd been looking for that he was some black market doctor / drug dealer.

Eric kept his tone light. "I'm not up to anything, Mom. Just a mix-up. What's going on?"

"I can't call you and see how you are?"

How was this conversation going so wrong so fast? Why was it always like this? "You can. Of course you can. It's just— It's Friday. You and Dad don't have plans?"

"You don't want to talk." He could actually *hear* the pout through the phone.

"I do!" He really didn't. A headache was already forming between his brows, growing stronger with every second he remained on the line. But he kept his voice as carefree as he could. She could sense irritation like a shark sensing blood in the water. "How are you, Mom?"

"I could be better."

Of course she could. And Eric listened as she told him all the many ways she could be better. If his father weren't such a flirt ("But that's just how you men are, isn't? Certainly didn't skip a generation, now did it?"). If her health were better ("Not that you ever ask"). If her so-called friends weren't such duds ("Can hardly hold a conversation. Reminds me of you as a teenager. Head full of air").

He made the appropriate noises. He laughed when he felt she expected it. And just when he was considering upping his shower beer to a shower whiskey, she brought it back to his least favorite subject.

"How's work?"

"It's good," Eric lied, like he always did. "Really good. The other day, I had this patient—"

She cut him off. "Have they asked you to stay as an attending yet?"

The headache was now a stabbing sensation, like a knife had gotten stuck behind one of his eyeballs. "It doesn't really work that way."

"If only you hadn't taken those gap years." By gap years, she meant the years between undergrad and med school he'd been working as a grunt in a research lab specializing in lung cancer treatment. *A waste of good training years*, she'd told him. "Nancy's son, he was barely a year into his fellowship when the hospital told him they were *dying* to keep him."

"Tom's in a totally different specialty, Mom," Eric pointed out, unable to keep the chipper edge to his voice anymore.

For once, she didn't seem to notice. "Well, it's not like you're a neurosurgeon. You're a—what do they call it?—a hospitalist?"

"Intensivist, Mom. I cover the ICU. The most critical patients."

"Certainly not *operating* on anyone."

"No," Eric sighed, well and truly defeated by the conversation. "Certainly not that."

There was a muffled voice on the other end, and his mother's tone switched immediately to one of carelessness. "Oh, that's your father. I have to go. You'll call me this weekend? And don't forget to up the monthly deposit. We want to redo the guest bathroom."

"Sure, Mom."

Eric hung up the phone, infinitely more drained than he'd been at the end of his twelve-hour. That was some gift she had. Fucking energy vampire.

His eyes landed again on the mysterious rose, intensely red against the white of the marble kitchen counter. With a bitter laugh, he swept it into the trash. He'd been right before; probably someone selling door-to-door had dropped it. It wasn't meant for him.

Because why the fuck would it be meant for him?

It was only when the harsh spray of the shower had him hissing, his pointer finger stinging hotly, that Eric realized he'd cut himself on the thorns after all.

Chugging his third coffee of the day—taking advantage of the one whole minute of silence where his work phone wasn't ringing like crazy—Eric reminded himself he only had three more hours left of his shift.

That was only...one hundred and eighty minutes to go.

And look, now it was 4:01. Only one hundred and seventy-*nine* minutes to go. He was practically done already.

His phone's ringer cut through the blessed silence then, because of course it did.

"Monroe," Eric answered, somehow managing to speak midswallow.

"Sup, man. It's Brent with emergency." The emergency docs always spoke like they were chill climbing bros. Which was accurate, actually. Half of them were exactly that. "We've got one for you."

"Sure thing." Eric forced an equal amount of friendly enthusiasm into his own voice. "On my way."

Two minutes later, his coffee was drained and he was trudging down to the ER, taking the stairs this time because he had to get in the exercise when he could these days. Sitting on his ass was harder to get away with after hitting thirty-seven; that was for sure. He could just imagine his mother at the next holiday, poking his stomach and asking when he'd added the spare tire.

She'd do it too.

So stairs it was.

He found Chloe, the night charge, at the nurse's station. Eric did a little double-take at the sight of her, wondering for just a second if he'd gotten confused and it was actually four in the morning instead of four in the afternoon. "What are you doing here in daylight hours?"

Chloe sighed dramatically, her eyes on the computer. "They begged me to come in early, and I caved. Don't remind me. But anyway—" She pointed to a bay, still not looking at him. "Tag, you're it."

Monroe rested his elbows on the counter and leaned in, delaying the inevitable in his very favorite way: mindless flirting. They hadn't called a code, so he probably had the time. "Chloe, darling. Have you left that husband of yours yet?"

"As if I would *ever*," she scoffed, typing furiously.

"Shame." Eric tapped a finger on the counter. "I wanted to nab Marcus for myself. I'd be eating that man's banana bread for breakfast, lunch, and dinner. Twenty-four *seven*."

That finally had her lifting her gaze, a small smirk gracing her lips. "I can't tell if you're being weirdly sexual or talking about his actual baked goods."

Eric grinned, pleased he finally had her attention. "I *feel* weirdly sexual about his baked goods; I can tell you that."

"Stop trying to poach my husband," she ordered with mock severity.

"I'll stop trying to poach him when he stops looking so damn fine."

She cocked a brow at him, pursing her lips. "I know what you're doing."

Eric straightened his spine, not at all chastised but aware his time was up. "Fine. Bay twelve, you said?"

"That's the one. We're thinking septic shock. Blood cultures were positive, and his pressures tanked the minute he walked through the door."

"You already got the drips started?"

"Well, duh. He hasn't coded yet, has he?"

"Intubated?" Technically, he should be in the patient's chart or hounding the ER doctor for these details, but he knew Chloe would have the same answers. Woman ran a tight ship.

"No. But you'd know that if you just...you know, actually went in there yourself."

Eric gave her a salute, just because. "You're the best. You can keep your husband. For now."

She gave him an ironic nod of thanks, already back to typing away.

"I'll put in the transfer orders so you can get him to the ICU, free up a bed for the next one."

"Oh, joy."

He walked away from the desk, his mood just a touch brighter than it had been five minutes ago. Chloe was one of the few people who actually *liked* Eric at this hospital, at least as far has he could tell. Not just as a doctor but as a person. That was probably due to the fact that she'd already been married when he started there, and he'd thus never tried to hit on her with any real intention.

He knew better now, after a thoroughly painful education, than to sleep with the people he worked with. But when he'd just moved to Hyde Park?

Well...he'd been lonely, okay?

Eric had just finished assessing his new patient—surprisingly alert for the four different blood pressure medications going through his IV—when his phone went off again.

"Monroe."

"Room ten's family wants an update." The voice on the other end—he recognized the caller as Carol, one of the ICU nurses, even though she didn't give her name—was brusque.

Fatigue made Eric stupid. "You haven't updated them already?"

"I have," she answered fiercely, clearly irritated with the question. "They want to talk to the *doctor*. That's you."

Fuck, Eric hated this part. The very reason he preferred his night shift rotations, even if they fucked up his sleep schedule something mighty. Fewer family members, fewer uncomfortable updates, fewer tearful conversations about realistic expectations.

It was always fine, in the end. If he walked into a room wearing his white coat, everybody acted like he was God. But that was...worse, somehow. It always made him feel like a fraud. Like one day he was going to slip up and say what was always lurking underneath: *I don't care. I don't fucking care. I don't want to talk to you; I don't want to reassure you. I just want to do my job well, and fingers crossed your family member doesn't die. I know I should care more, but I don't.*

Or that one day, they'd just...see it. He wouldn't even have to say anything at all. They'd just see he wasn't any good, not really. Not on the inside. They'd ask for another doctor, someone like....King. A man who was golden without even trying—who was surly just as often as he was charming, but no one ever seemed to mind.

Eric was never surly with anyone. He covered up his failings with an open gregariousness he always hoped would keep people happy and off his case. He always had a smile or a joke ready. Sometimes it worked, and sometimes people just seemed to hate him anyway.

But the reckoning didn't come today. Today the family members listened respectfully and thanked him profusely, one of them even grabbing his hand to shake it, grateful tears in their eyes.

He didn't take a full, proper breath until he was back in the dictation room, going over patient charts alone. *This* part he liked okay. Running through the labs and vital signs, figuring out what was out of whack with his patients and why.

It wasn't like he was a bad doctor. Not really. He knew that much.

He was just maybe a bad person.

When he got home, more exhausted than he had any right to be, tempted to sleep away his next three days off, there was another rose on his doorstep.

Eric looked over his shoulder, at the street behind him, just as he'd done the first time. At this point, he was beginning to think it was a prank.

But it didn't really matter, did it?

He picked up the flower and took it in with him. He found a small, clear glass in the kitchen and filled it with water. He placed the rose inside. He put the whole thing on his bedside table.

Because he could pretend, just this once. Pretend there was someone out there, wanting to make him feel special. He could pretend he had a person out there, just for him.

What could be the harm in that?

Two

Wolfe

Despite what recent, impulsive decisions could possibly lead some people to believe, Wolfe was someone who knew the importance of planning, of preparation, of setting the scene.

And what scene was more important than one's future home?

"And here we have the fourth and final bedroom. The closet in here is somewhat limited compared to the primary bedroom, but certainly nothing to sneeze at either."

Wolfe walked well ahead of the clacking heels of the voluptuous real estate agent, sizing up the old Victorian on display at his own pace.

It was furnished horrendously, the current owners clearly trying their best to force a modern look on a house that was simply begging for an old-fashioned touch. Wolfe truly didn't understand the current fascination with the Scandinavian aesthetic, this exaltation of the bland and the stiff. If one's furniture was going to be uncomfortable, it might as well *look* sumptuous.

Still, the bones of the house were solid. Four bedrooms upstairs, with a downstairs office, a sun-soaked sitting room, as well as a dimly lit space that could be repurposed into a proper library. It was adorned with plenty of lovely wooden built-ins and hosted an ample backyard backing up to forest service lands and hiking trails.

And hiking trails meant, of course, plenty of sturdy hikers who could be compelled inside for dinner.

It was, he had to admit, perfect.

And available immediately. Or it would be, after the right compulsion.

Wolfe turned on his heel, obliging the real estate agent to halt in her tracks. "May I have another look at the en suite?" he asked, tilting his head in a way that suggested he'd like to do so alone.

Young Miss Wilson took the hint. "Of course. I'll be right downstairs." She had the self-satisfied look of someone who could scent a sale, but Wolfe couldn't begrudge her the smugness. Not when he was so pleased with what she'd found for him.

He watched her descend the stairs and then meandered down the hall to the largest bedroom. The walk-in closet was indeed impressive, room enough to fit his own ample wardrobe and leave room for another's. The bed frame the current owners had chosen would have to go, of course. And he'd need to call painters in as soon as possible.

He could picture it all perfectly. A soft sage color on the walls. A California king with a forest-green comforter dominating the space.

And a blond head of hair spread out on the pillow.

Wolfe allowed himself a rare, true smile.

Yes, it was all going to be absolute perfection.

Boring. This is boring.

Wolfe's smile fell, his lips pursing in irritation. His beast had been unbearably petulant ever since it had realized there were much more enticing pursuits in this town. It had no concept of patience, of planning. Of the two of them, only Wolfe had the sense to know practicalities had to be dealt with; a proper living situation needed to be considered top priority. And, luckily for them both, Wolfe was in a position to take care of it.

Well, really, luck had nothing to do with it. He hadn't completely wasted the months Johann had been away. Wolfe had moved some finances around, stashed enough away that this little mansion would be no strain. None of it was anything compared to the nest egg coming his way soon, but it was a start.

Shall we make things more interesting for you? he asked his beast, peering briefly once more into the en suite bathroom. The tub there was more than adequate, large enough to fit two grown men easily. He took a moment to straighten his hair in the mirror, pushing the light-brown strands back into the appropriate side part. It wouldn't do to look slovenly for such a momentous occasion.

No answer from the impatient thing inside him. It was still pouting.

No matter. Wolfe knew how to draw it out.

"Miss Wilson," he called lightly, stepping back into the bedroom, making some mental measurements while he was at it.

He waited for the clack of her heels on the stairs, smoothed the temporary comforter with one hand as he heard her approaching down the hall.

"Yes, Mr. Volker? Would you like to see the backyard again?" she offered, stepping into the bedroom, paperwork that hadn't been there before now notably in her hands. Clever woman, going in for the kill.

"No need." Wolfe waved a hand, encompassing the space around him. "I'll be taking it."

"Oh?" Miss Wilson's smile was sharp and victorious, but she still managed to feign the appropriate surprise. "How wonderful!"

"Yes, quite. But there is one more thing." Wolfe approached slowly, allowing his human face to retreat and his beast to come forward.

Poor Miss Wilson's eyes widened, and she took a step back, toward the door.

"Wha—what?"

Under normal circumstances, it might have been amusing to see her run, but Wolfe didn't want the hardwood floors scuffed by her heels. This was their new home, after all, his and the good doctor's. So he laced his voice with compulsion as he met her frightened eyes. "You're not afraid, Miss Wilson."

Her retreat stopped in an instant, her tense features slackening immediately into complacency.

It was always such a rush, changing someone's mind against their will that way. It was a shame it didn't work on other vampires.

"Come here," Wolfe commanded softly.

Miss Wilson stepped in front of him.

"Give me your wrist."

She lifted her arm.

Wolfe rested her forearm on his open palms, then bit in with sharp teeth, warm copper filling his mouth.

There. He thought rather than spoke the words, as his mouth was occupied. *Isn't this better?*

But his beast only huffed at him in annoyance, even as it greedily drank down what was offered.

Petulant creature. Wolfe knew what it really wanted, why it was turning its nose up at what was a perfectly delicious human. And really, that was fine.

There was only one thing either of them had wanted since the week before, when their whole world had turned on its side.

They wanted their mate. And they would have him, soon enough. But first, some reconnaissance.

Wolfe would not be caught unprepared.

Wolfe's future partner was frustratingly hard to get a read on, even after days of watching him from the shadows.

A few things made perfect sense. His being a doctor, for one. Of course Wolfe's fated companion would be intelligent; that was a given. He was physically appealing as well. Tall and sturdily built, with a surprisingly boyish face for a man pushing forty, topped by a wonderfully golden head of hair, one that would suit him even better if it were allowed to grow out just a touch longer.

He was also, Wolfe had surmised, a bit of a slut. Or at the very least, tried to be.

Despite his long shifts at the hospital, the good doctor had gone out three of the five nights Wolfe had been keeping an eye on him, clearly trying to pick up a good time for the evening. Although he didn't seem too terribly disappointed when he failed, always smiling congenially at whoever had just turned him down, buying them another drink even as he left them to their own devices.

Why they always seemed to turn him down was a bit of a mystery to Wolfe. Perhaps Dr. Monroe had developed a reputation in such a relatively small town. Perhaps they all simply preferred brunettes. Or perhaps it was due to a certain...air of desperation about him. One that Wolfe, muted as his own empathetic tendencies may have been, could sense even from afar. One that was incongruent with the doctor's good looks and superficial charm.

Although, to be honest, Wolfe personally found that sort of neediness appealing, at least in this instance. It would make the act of bonding that much easier, if the doctor was desperate for connection.

But even so, Dr. Monroe attempting to sleep with half the town didn't necessarily preclude a neglected partner waiting in the wings, so Wolfe had left a little present: a single rose. To see who, if anyone, the good doctor would call to thank.

It was a bit silly and perhaps dramatic, as far as fishing for information went, but that didn't negate the delicious symbolism of his offering.

And his future mate deserved a gift, whether or not he was aware of its origins.

But in the end, the doctor hadn't called anyone. Which was lucky for his apparently nonexistent, hypothetical partner, as Wolfe would hate to jeopardize his standing in the town by killing one of its humans right off the bat.

It was odd though. In the absence of a partner, Wolfe had expected his human to be intrigued, possibly amused by the flower. But Dr. Monroe had looked not only confused but almost *frightened* by the gift.

Yes, Wolfe mused, after picking the lock on the good doctor's front door for the fifth time in as many days (and really, would it kill the man to invest in some semblance of a security system?). *Very hard to get a read on.*

He felt it was even truer after making his way into the doctor's bedroom. Because there, on the bedside table, sitting in a sad little smudged glass, was the second rose. Wolfe's chest surged with some unfamiliar emotion to see it standing there. He'd left this second one as a lark, really. The poor human had seemed so absolutely confused by the first one that Wolfe had been compelled to offer another. He hadn't expected him to keep it, not after trashing the first.

Perhaps Wolfe should have left a proper bouquet, then. That little singular rose was hardly a fitting courting gift.

Not here, Wolfe's beast grumbled, interrupting his musings. *Our mate is not* here.

"Well, you knew he wouldn't be, you foolish creature," Wolfe reasoned, opening the bedside table drawer to find—not surprising in the least—a mess of condoms and a half-empty bottle of lubricant.

Want him.

"In time." Wolfe meandered over to the dresser, on which the offensive bottle of sandalwood aftershave was sitting. He considered for a brief moment tossing it in the trash. But such an act, if noticed, would surely scare the human more than anything. Best to tackle the topic of suitable colognes later, really.

Frightened.

Wolfe froze, fingers just brushing the glass bottle. "Excuse me?"

You're frightened.

Wolfe scoffed, turning on his heel to inspect the contents of the doctor's closet. He wasn't frightened. He was *never* frightened; it wasn't an emotion with which he was even remotely familiar. Lack of fear was one of the defining characteristics of his...special condition, in point of fact.

He was simply being cautious, getting the lay of the land before he approached.

And he was right to be concerned, wasn't he? It was a complicated matter, how best to approach someone to offer immortality when it came with the condition of being bonded forever to someone who didn't quite feel things the way others did. Someone who was possibly unable to offer true love and affection.

He could lie, of course. Easy enough to do. But there would eventually be a fallout, and that would be annoying to deal with. A bonded pair was supposed to be able to feel each other's emotions, or lack thereof. Wolfe wouldn't be able to fake it, not with his future mate.

And really, it was good he was doing a little digging first, wasn't it? Because this humble abode simply would not *do.* The two-bedroom hovel might be enough for the doctor on his own, but the closet size alone was reason enough to invest in something grander.

He stood in the dismal closet, toying with the neckline of one of the button-downs hanging there, indulging himself by brushing his nose against the fabric. There it was, that wonderful scent: wisteria.

Wolfe's cock twitched as he inhaled deeply. It was a new, strange side effect, ever since he'd first laid eyes on his mate in the flesh. He was always on the edge of arousal, like some foolhardy teen.

It was surprisingly irritating. Lust had always been easy enough for him to ignore before, when it didn't suit his purposes. He could be celibate for long stretches of time without feeling like he was missing anything. But here he was considering unzipping his suit pants and stroking himself to completion, layering his own scent all over the good doctor's clothes.

Staking his claim.

He wouldn't, of course. He wasn't some wandering pervert. But the temptation was there.

Which was reason enough to leave the bedroom before he did something to inconvenience himself. Like shatter that godforsaken aftershave all over the carpet (carpet everywhere, yet another reason to change locations).

His phone buzzed in his pocket, but he left it where it was. It was sure to be Tobias, checking in again on Wolfe's progress bringing Johann home. Wolfe would have to make an unpleasant phone call sooner rather than later, but it was hard to focus on that when he had his tantalizing human puzzle to work out first.

He almost wished Tobias would follow on his heels after all. It would be incredibly satisfying to wring his head right off his neck, just for all the annoyance he'd caused Wolfe with his little "check-ins."

He reluctantly released his hold on Dr. Monroe's sweater, stepping out of the closet and taking a deep breath. He was tenser than he should be, less controlled than he liked. He might not be *frightened* like his beast so foolishly accused, but he was losing his patience with the slow approach.

Should that concern him, seeing as how it had been less than a week?

Unlikely. Wolfe's unerring self-control hadn't failed him yet, not since he was a child. Others may not always agree with his choices, but they were *his* choices, each of them.

Wolfe smoothed his suit jacket lapels and made his way into the kitchen. The refrigerator was once again pathetically stocked with mostly takeout containers past their prime, as it had been when he checked in a few days ago, but that seemed fitting enough for an overworked ICU doctor. It wasn't like proper diet was a subject worth addressing, not when what constituted essential intake for Dr. Monroe was about to change quite drastically.

As he closed the refrigerator door, Wolfe's attention caught on the wall next to it. There was a calendar hanging there. One he'd somehow missed last time.

He smiled to himself as he looked at the entry for the next day, written in red ink, like a blood-tinged invitation. "Well, well. it looks like our dear doctor has an appointment tomorrow. Tell me, would you like to see our mate up close and personal again?"

For the first time in days, his beast purred inside him.

Three

Eric

Eric walked into the softly lit parlor of Serenity, a certain tightness in his chest loosening for the first time in days.

This was undeniably his favorite part of the month: his standing massage appointment. It was a gift he'd been giving himself the past year or so. An hour with Brenda—a six-foot-tall amazon with the hands of a goddess—working every knot out of his overburdened body.

The desk clerk—he thought her name was maybe Kacey, but she wasn't wearing her badge—smiled at him in that blank professional way service people sometimes did as he walked up to the desk.

"Dr. Monroe," she greeted, her voice oddly flat, missing its normal Valley girl–adjacent lilt. "I'm afraid Brenda isn't available today."

Eric's stomach fell with disappointment. He *needed* this today. He'd been striking out like crazy lately, not able to find anyone to go home with him. There was a tight pressure in his chest and gut that wouldn't go away with any amount of self-pleasure. He needed this chance to be touched, to be...soothed.

Truth was, even when he was fulfilled sexually, the massages were something else: a physical release where no one was expecting anything back, where there was no opportunity to make a fool of himself with potential rejection. He could close his eyes and just feel *good* for once.

And now he had to wait another week for it?

Before he could spiral too hard, Maybe Kacey went on in that blank way, "But we have a substitute for you. Someone new on our staff, if you're willing."

"Oh." An embarrassing amount of relief flooded through him at the offer. "That's fine, then."

She nodded, rising from her chair and stepping out from behind her computer. "I'll take you to your room."

Eric followed behind her, noticing absently that her movements were oddly stiff. It looked like he wasn't the only one in need of a masseuse's touch. He considered suggesting she take advantage of her employee discount and book one, but even he knew that would be pushing the limits of polite conversation, so he just smiled gratefully as she ushered him into the small, dim space, where soothing flute sounds were already pumping out of the room's speakers.

"If you'll get undressed to the level of your comfort, he'll be right in."

Eric's level of comfort was completely nude, so he stripped down, folding his clothes neatly on the chair in the corner before sliding facedown under the cool sheet, grateful the massage table's warmer was already going. He fit his face into that weird hollowed-out pillow thing, blinking at the familiar, ugly patterned carpet and wiggling until he felt his body was more or less aligned.

He was barely waiting any time at all before there was a gentle knock on the door. "I'm ready," he called out.

Eric heard the quiet creak of the door opening, then the soft rustling sounds of someone getting situated in the room. A scent washed over him, one he didn't recognize from his past visits; they must have gotten some new essential oils. It was something citrusy, and the name of it was on the tip of his tongue. He'd had a candle with that scent once, he was pretty sure.

Bergamot, that was what it had been called.

"That smells good," he murmured, more to himself than to the nameless masseuse.

"Does it?" The soft, deep voice sounded almost amused, although Eric wasn't sure why. Change that to mass*eur*, then.

"Um...yeah?"

The bottom half of a pair of legs appeared in Eric's vision. Soft black pants, like Brenda usually wore, paired oddly with—were those dress shoes?

Eric chuckled, his muscles already feeling miraculously looser with the combination of the relaxing music, the soothing scent, and the promise of a professional touch any moment. "You don't get uncomfortable, standing all day in those?"

The dress shoes disappeared from view. "I believe it's *your* comfort we should be concerned with today, Doctor."

Oh. That was definitely a British accent, careful and clipped. It brushed over Eric like a finger down his spine, causing a strange shiver to run through him, despite the warmth of the table.

What the hell was that about? Did he have a thing for accents now? He never had before. He was pretty easy with his preferences, to be honest. Maybe he was becoming more particular in his old age. The thought almost had him chuckling again.

"Tell me," the masseur continued, seemingly unaware of Eric's completely inappropriate response to a few accented words. "Any particular areas of trouble?"

Eric tried to focus his thoughts back on the matter at hand. "Um, my neck and shoulders kind of always bug me. I guess I hunch at the computer."

"Mm. Charting on your numerous patients?"

"Um. R-Right." What the fuck? How would he know that? Except, duh, the man had already referred to Eric as "Doctor." Eric had gotten a discount at this place because of his employment at the hospital; it wasn't like his profession was a secret. The receptionist always called him Dr. Monroe, never Eric. Hell, they were a small enough town, if you discounted the tourists—half the population called him that.

He'd been so weirdly paranoid lately. This massage was definitely a necessity.

"We'll see what we can do about that discomfort."

Any worry Eric had that this stranger wouldn't be able to achieve the same magic he was used to with Brenda was immediately put to rest the moment the man dug his fingers into Eric's shoulders.

Eric moaned. He actually *moaned.*

"Fuuck." Oh shit. That was rude. "Sorry. I mean— You have strong hands."

"The better to tend to your needs." The voice sounded amused again, although it was a subtle note, nowhere near mocking.

Fair enough either way, when Eric was making a fool of himself. Maybe he should shut up right about now and just let the masseur do his thing. And really, he did it so *well.* Eric was quickly putty under his hands, making the most ridiculous noises. But fuck, this dude knew how to work a knot.

He moved gradually from Eric's shoulders, down his spine, seemingly unconcerned with the sounds coming out of Eric's mouth, kneading in a way that had Eric wanting to arch like a cat. "With this physique, it can't just be sitting at the desk that has you so sore, hm?"

Eric's current moan stuttered into silence as he took that in. Was the guy...flirting? But no, that British voice sounded so cool, so detached. Professional as hell. Eric cleared his throat. "Um, yeah. I try to stay in shape."

"Mm. Physical health is so important. Often underrated by the very people who tend to it in others."

Yeah, definitely not flirting. Or not any flirting Eric was used to.

The masseur dug his fingers into Eric's lower back. "And the pressure's all right?"

"The pressure is amazing," Eric sighed. "Everything you're doing is amazing."

Okay, yeah, definitely time to shut up. He sounded like a schoolgirl with a crush, not a massage client. So Eric did, remaining quiet except for the occasional uncontrollable moan, or the few times he had to answer the man's questions about sore spots, pain threshold, etc.

Eventually the masseur started working on Eric's legs, undoing tension there Eric hadn't even known he'd had. He was starting to feel close to drugged, that bergamot scent wrapping around him, relaxing him almost as much as the man's touch. This was heaven. Absolute heaven.

The only problem—and it was definitely becoming a problem—was that they were getting to the point in the massage where Eric was going to have to turn over, and he was—

Well, he was *achingly* hard.

Fuck. He didn't normally have this problem; it wasn't like the massages were a sexual thing for him. But the guy kept talking to him in that sexy fucking accent, asking him if he felt good, if the pressure was okay, and the room smelled so goddamn tasty with the new incense or whatever the hell it was and...his hands. The man's magical fucking *hands*.

The masseur—and why hadn't Eric asked him his name? It would be weird to do it now, this late in the process, right?—must have felt him tense.

Those hands paused on Eric's calf. "Is there a problem, Doctor?"

"N-No," Eric mumbled, grateful he was facedown and the man couldn't see his burning cheeks.

"Ah." The small noise seemed to be loaded with understanding. But the man couldn't know, could he? What he was doing to Eric without meaning to? And then a warm, heavy palm settled on Eric's lower back.

"Time to turn over now, Doctor." The instruction came out husky, almost a growl.

"Um."

A soft stroke of fingers down his spine, like a reassuring caress. "Don't fret. It's a natural physical response."

Okay. Fuck. So he did know.

How did he know?

Eric cleared his suddenly dry throat. "It's not, um, usually an issue for me."

But he did as he was told anyway, turning over under the sheet and blinking up at the ceiling in the dim light. His erection was clearly tenting the fabric, and embarrassment flooded him, but they were both guys, and the man seemed to know how it was sometimes. Not a big deal, right?

Long-fingered hands appeared in his line of vision, adjusting the sheet along Eric's chest, but he kept his eyes averted, not ready yet to look at the guy's face.

"Perfectly natural," the masseur repeated. "I could even assist you with it, if you like."

Eric swallowed hard. Was he offering...?

He turned his head to the side, for the first time fully taking in the man who'd been working magic on him in the dim light. He was a little shorter than Eric maybe, just reaching six feet, and dressed all in black. Light-brown hair slicked to the side. A sharp, almost severe face, with cheekbones you could cut yourself on. And his eyes...they seemed to almost glow red, but that must have been a trick of the light.

"Um."

At his hesitation, the man spread his hands—surprisingly elegant, for how sturdy they'd felt on Eric's body—in a placating gesture. "Or not. Relax, Doctor. I'll just do my job, then."

Why did it sound like an inside joke, the way he said it?

Eric closed his eyes, more tempted by the guy's offer than he should be. He'd never had a "happy ending" before. Wasn't that just, like...paying for sex? That was—

He'd never done that before, not ever.

No, he'd just finish out this massage, then go home and jerk off like the pervert he was. He shut his eyes again as the masseur started again on his legs, seemingly determined to turn them into jelly by the end of the session. Eric kept his eyes closed and his lips pressed tight, trying to contain the weird noises he'd been letting out before, refusing to look at the evidence of his own weakness.

But...his problem definitely wasn't going away, his erection taunting him as the guy worked him over, kneading Eric's thighs, then his calves, then his feet. At least he'd stopped talking to Eric in that sexy voice.

Eventually the man let go of his feet and moved up, presumably to work on Eric's shoulders again. But as he did so, he brushed a finger along Eric's side in one long, smooth glide, causing Eric's eyes to shoot open and his hips to jerk up before he could stop them.

He was doing it on purpose now, right? Turning Eric on?

But the masseur's face was impassive, professional as ever. So Eric closed his eyes again as the masseur started kneading at his neck, standing over him at the head of the massage table. And Eric couldn't help it—he started imagining what it would be like, for those strong hands to lower the sheet slowly, to grasp his straining erection with that firm grip.

He bet the guy would be confident, still professional, almost cold. And even so, it wouldn't take long. Eric was already so turned on. Just a few strokes of the masseur's hand—maybe his thumb would play along the head. Maybe if Eric was really good, stayed very still, the man would even bend over him and put his mouth on it—

His cock jerked again, and it took everything in him to keep his hips still.

Fuck. He had to stop thinking like this. He needed out of this room. He'd always known he was a horndog, but Jesus Christ, this was next level.

In a case of perfect timing, the masseur patted his shoulder. "All finished, Doctor."

Thank all that was holy. Eric cleared his throat for what felt like the thousandth time. "Th-Thank you. That was amazing. And I'm sorr—"

"No apologies necessary. As I said, perfectly natural."

Normally Eric would lie there on the table as Brenda left the room, feeling all newly peaceful and zen with that fucking flute music, but he found himself sitting up abruptly, before the guy even had a chance to lower the table back down, just so he could bunch the towel around his hips and protect what little was left of his modesty.

Too little, way too fucking late.

The room was small enough that the masseur was barely a foot away, staring at Eric with that impassive look. His eyes weren't red at all. They were a light brown.

This was where Eric would normally try to turn on the charm. The guy was attractive enough—even if he kind of reminded Eric of that one Bond villain, the one whose eye wept blood sometimes—and he clearly knew how to use his hands. And he had actually shown some sort of genuine interest, which was more than Eric could say for anyone else recently. But he felt weirdly unmoored, incapable of smarming his way through a pickup line.

"I'm sorry," Eric said instead, feeling completely pathetic. "I never caught your name."

"Does it matter?"

Eric's stomach dropped with his words, and the man's lips quirked at his obvious dismay. For all his reassurances about normalcy, he seemed to revel in Eric's discomfort in that moment.

But before Eric could ask him to lower the massage table and let him get dressed, the masseur took a step toward him. "There is one thing you can do, Doctor. Straighten up for me."

Eric straightened from his slouch, not sure where this was going. Was he going to get a lecture in bad posture?

But the man sidled even closer, an almost predatory look in his eyes. "Tilt your head. Show me your neck." His words were commanding, but his tone was mild as ever.

Eric did as he asked, weird as the request was. Did the guy have some kind of neck fetish? It would really only be tit for tat if he did, considering how horned up Eric had been for the entire massage. He couldn't begrudge the man a little neck ogling, could he?

The masseur leaned in, and that bergamot smell Eric had been drooling over the past hour intensified. Had it been him this whole time, and not incense or essential oils at all? He didn't even have time to process that before the tip of the man's nose was brushing against his skin. Eric shivered. He was still hard as hell, and his erection didn't seem like it was going to let up anytime soon.

He tilted his head back to steal a glance at the guy. Maybe he didn't need to make a move at all. Maybe he could just lean forward the slightest bit, and then they'd be, like, kissing, right? And if the professional part of this interaction was over, what could it hurt?

Except—

"Holy shit." Eric immediately startled back, falling onto his hands on the massage table. "What the—"

The masseur's eyes weren't brown anymore. And they weren't fucking red either. They were black, all black.

But the other man just met his eyes like nothing was wrong, blinking slowly at him. "You're not afraid," he told Eric, calm and clear.

"What's going on with your—?"

"Shh." The masseur leaned in again and pressed a soft kiss to Eric's neck.

Eric let out a breath. Okay, that was...okay. That was nice, even. Maybe the guy had some kind of neurological condition, and when he was turned on, his pupils just, like...took over his whole eyeballs. That could be a thing, right? (*No, idiot, that's definitely not a thing.*)

Another kiss. Eric relaxed a fraction more. But then there was a sharp, stabbing bite of pain at Eric's neck.

He leaned back hard, tearing away from the source of it. "What the fuck?"

Um. Okay. It wasn't just the eyes now. Fangs. Those were fangs peeping out between the man's soft pink lips. And that was definitely Eric's blood dripping off a pair of goddamn *fangs.*

What the fuck was happening?

The masseur smiled at him, his lengthy incisors bright red. "Just a little taste," he murmured. He licked a drop of blood off his lips. "You're not afraid," he told Eric again.

What. The. Fuck. "I *am* afraid," Eric countered, and it came out weirdly petulant, almost bordering on shrill.

He was afraid. Sort of. Mostly he was confused as all hell and worried he'd had some kind of stroke, or maybe he'd fallen asleep on the massage table and was now dreaming some weird, sexual vampire fantasy.

Confusion passed over the man's face, followed quickly by irritation. "Why—?"

And really, *why* was a good fucking question. Like, why was Eric sitting still, studying the man's expressions? If he wasn't dreaming, then he needed to get the fuck out of here. He scrambled to get off the table—it was still raised high off the floor, making the action harder than it should be—but a strong pair of hands gripped his shoulders.

The masseur made Eric meet his eyes again. "You're not afraid," he repeated.

"Get the fuck *off* me."

"I—" The guy seemed at war with himself, leaning in toward Eric one moment and moving back harshly the next. Eric tried to shake out of his grip, and the man fucking *growled* at him.

Eric wriggled with more purpose. "Did you just growl like a fucking jungle cat?"

"Ours," the masseur bit out in response.

Eric paused in his struggles, thrown off by the odd statement. "Excuse me?"

"Ours," he repeated, his voice no longer refined but harsh and guttural. "*MINE.*"

The man tugged him closer, Eric's scalp stinging as he gripped his hair. Eric couldn't be sure, but he thought he heard a whispered, "Forgive me," before that sharp biting pain ran through him again. It didn't last long though. The pain. Pleasure followed in a rush after, lighting up Eric's nerve endings like a goddamn Christmas tree.

Was Eric really so fucked up that even being bitten by a weird, demonic massage therapist turned him on? Maybe he needed to make a therapy appointment next.

And then the man was drinking his blood, Eric was pretty sure, judging by the gulping sounds and the fact that he was losing both strength and consciousness fast.

His last thought before something warm was dribbled into his mouth and his veins caught on what felt like actual, literal fire was, *This massage wasn't as relaxing as I thought it would be.*

Four

Wolfe

This was not how it was supposed to go.

Wolfe had only wanted a little taste of connection, a chance to meet his future mate in a low-risk environment, get his eyes and hands on him properly, most likely compel him to forgetfulness afterward.

And it had started out just as he'd intended. It had been easy enough to compel the masseuse into taking an unexpected day off, then to compel the front desk girl into thinking him a replacement for the day.

It had all been a bit of fun, a way to pass the time until he could come up with a proper courting strategy. It wasn't that he *couldn't* stay away from the delicious human—that sort of helplessness would be absurdly out of character—it was just he didn't want to. And why should he? Why should he resist such a choice opportunity to feel out fate's intended match for him? And his beast had been all for it—any excuse to be close to their mate.

And then, with his handsome, muscular human under his hands, so responsive to Wolfe's touch, to his very scent, he hadn't been able to resist a different sort of taste. The doctor had refused his sexual advances; that was fine. But his beast had wanted a little sip. *Blood of our mate*, it had urged. *Bound to be sweet. So sweet.* And really, Wolfe had been just as eager. They'd have a little drink, compel the doctor to forget, and plan their next move.

All part of the chase. Part of the fun.

But now here he was, wrestling his damned beast for control.

Stop drinking, he ordered in his head, his mouth too full of blood to speak. *You're draining him.*

But the stubborn creature wouldn't cooperate, just kept filling their mouth over and over with the rich, coppery blood of their intended mate. Their hands were on the smooth skin of their mate's broad, muscular shoulders, holding him in place now that his body had gone slack.

This had never happened before, this loss of control. First, the wretched thing wouldn't compel the doctor properly—and never since his earliest days as a vampire had Wolfe ever failed at compulsion—letting him panic and struggle needlessly. And now it wouldn't stop drinking.

Ours, it kept repeating, the mantra ringing through Wolfe's skull like a bell. *Our mate. We'll have him.*

Wolfe had always thought, if it came down to it, *he* would have the ultimate control over their body. He was the one with the restraint, the resolve, the humanity (however pared down his personal version of humanity may have been). But he'd never had to test it. Not really. He and his beast were usually in harmony. They both enjoyed a bit of bloodshed, the thrill of the chase, but the beast usually listened—even if it didn't agree—to Wolfe's insistence on discretion.

But now it wouldn't stop *drinking*. Wolfe could smell the first real frissons of fear coming from their mate—Dr. Monroe had been more confused than properly afraid before—now that he was losing consciousness fast.

You're going to kill him.

Going to turn him, the beast countered.

And what else could Wolfe do but agree? It was too late to take any of it back, even if he had wanted to (and did he really want to?).

He lifted his head from their mate's neck—his beast allowed it now that it could sense his capitulation, of course—and bit into his own wrist, dribbling the blood into the doctor's slack mouth. He held the human tight as he began whimpering with the pain.

"Shh," Wolfe soothed. "Shh. It will be over soon."

What was done was done. His beast purred its satisfaction.

Our mate.

It was a matter of minutes, compelling the front desk girl to forget—*now you're cooperating*, he grumbled to his beast—and carrying the limp form of the doctor to his car. He'd wrapped him in a robe he'd found in the small massage room, grabbing his clothes for later—no time to struggle with dressing an unconscious man right now.

It was a good thing he'd put such a rush on finding a house, now that his timeline had moved up considerably. There was no telling how long it would take for the doctor to wake, but at least Wolfe had the guest room set up, as the painters for the main bedroom wouldn't arrive until the next day.

Wolfe buckled their seatbelts—no sense in getting pulled over by some bored, small-town cop and having to waste precious minutes compelling his way out of it—and took the opportunity to study his unconscious passenger up close, in the bright light of day. He really was a handsome creature, his full lips soft and almost pouty in sleep. And the way he'd stared into Wolfe's eyes, cock hard and cheeks flushed with embarrassment, so clearly tempted to ask for release, even from a stranger.

Delicious, every bit of him: his face, his body, his blood, his poorly hidden eagerness to be handled.

Yes, fate had chosen well. Just as Wolfe had always desired.

A fierce spike of possessiveness ran through him as he looked at that handsome face, and his lips curled almost against his will. Wolfe had him now. His mate.

Now he just had to figure out how to keep him.

He sighed, slotting the key in the ignition and turning his focus to the road. He didn't often (if ever) feel real regret, a fact for which he was grateful—a useless emotion, really—but now he did feel a certain...irritation that things had gone this way.

"You know he's going to wake up frightened," he mused out loud to his annoyingly content beast.

Our mate.

"Christ on the cross. If it were physically possible, I'd wring your neck."

Wring your own neck, it countered smugly.

"Now you have a sense of humor, do you?"

The drive was over quickly, and Wolfe was so busy fighting with the voice inside his head that he missed the figure standing in his new driveway until he'd already wrestled the doctor from the passenger seat into his arms and was heading toward his front steps.

"What did you *do*?"

The growling accusation caught Wolfe by real surprise, and he turned with a start to see a tall figure glowering at him. Black hair, fierce blue eyes. One of Johann's new friends, Roman.

Wolfe quelled his shock quickly and nodded in greeting, repositioning the limp doctor in his arms. He had his human's clothes pressed between them, and he didn't want any of it to fall onto the dirty ground. "Good afternoon. I'm afraid you're on private property. I'm going to have to ask you to leave."

Roman was staring in horror at Wolfe's precious cargo. "You were meant to be helping us. And now you killed a human? In our town?"

"I'm sorry, are you the mayor of Hyde Park?" All right, Wolfe could admit his response was utterly childish, but he was quickly becoming so incredibly *irritated*. And possibly a little high off the adrenaline of what had just occurred. It may have been terrible timing, but that didn't make it any less of a rush, feeding from his mate for the very first time, watching the human life drain from his body, readying him for his transformation.

To his credit, Roman didn't quite roll his eyes at Wolfe's words, but he came awfully close. "You should know better than that. This is our territory."

Wolfe sniffed. "And *you* should know better. He's not dead. He's in transition."

"A fledgling vampire wreaking havoc. Even worse." Roman reached out his arms, stepping forward when Wolfe stepped back. "Hand him over."

Just like that, Wolfe's beast was out, and a growl escaped his throat, ringing through the afternoon air. "Do. Not. Touch. Him. He's *mine*. My mate."

Roman looked appropriately startled, his dark brows reaching almost to his hairline, which was the slightest bit gratifying given he generally had an unflappable air to rival Wolfe's own, when he wasn't letting his protectiveness over his mate get the best of him.

With considerable effort, Wolfe pushed the beast back, hoisting the doctor's slack body up so his head was resting on the curve of Wolfe's neck. The scent of wisteria filled his nostrils. There, that was better. He nodded to Roman. "So I think you'll find, by our kind's customs, I have full rights to him."

"He has a choice in the matter."

Not if Wolfe had anything to say about it. But he inclined his chin in false agreement. "Too true. But as he hasn't woken yet, he's under my protection until he does." He turned on his heel. "Good day."

He strode to his front door, pleased that the other vampire didn't try to follow him. He wanted his doctor safely in bed before he attempted any physical altercations—or better yet, to avoid them altogether. It wouldn't do to jeopardize his mate's safety while he was still in a delicate state.

He locked the door behind him—a matter of principal rather than real protection—and brought his mate up to the spare bedroom before placing him gently in the center of the bed. He folded Dr. Monroe's clothes neatly and set them on the bedside table. Then, after a moment of thought, Wolfe slid the man's underwear up over his hips, under the robe. Humans could be very particular about modesty, and Wolfe didn't want Dr. Monroe thinking anything untoward had happened during his transition.

He'd need to make a quick phone call to Tobias, officially letting the den know of his change of loyalties and that Johann was no longer an easy target. He'd been putting it off long enough. But it wouldn't do to have any lingering complications hanging over his head to deal with, not when his freshly turned obsession would be needing his time and attention.

The good doctor. His mate. And, as they were now intimately acquainted—after all, what was more intimate than an exchange of blood?—perhaps it was finally proper to be on a first-name basis.

"Eric," Wolfe said out loud, tasting the name on his tongue. "My Eric."

Five

Wolfe

Given how in one another's pockets the Hyde Park friend group seemed to be, it came as no surprise when, less than an hour after the encounter with Roman, Wolfe's doorbell rang.

He'd passed the time since his phone call with Tobias staring intently at his mate's face, not even bothering to change out of his borrowed clothing (and how convenient, that he and Brenda had been roughly the same height and build). He was trying, and failing, to figure out the exact moment of his loss of control. Was it when he'd bitten Eric, punctured that tender skin and opened the floodgates? Or when he'd touched him for the first time, laid hands on those broad shoulders? Or perhaps from the very first moment Wolfe had seen him and his beast had recognized what it was he meant to them?

Beast aside, Wolfe supposed he'd always especially liked things that belonged to him and him alone. As a child, he'd never wanted to share, hadn't seen the point of it—not his toys, not his treats, not the attention from adults he occasionally required. He'd reacted with violence when forced to do so, until he'd reluctantly learned the consequences of that aggression from his parents, who'd been quick to punish and even quicker to order others to do it for them. Adults were bigger and stronger than children, was what it came down to, so it didn't do to give them a reason to exercise that might.

Wolfe had learned at a very early age that manipulation was best, and the more subtle he could be, the better.

He'd started honing those skills with the members of his household staff, then perfected them at boarding school. He'd been a star pupil to the professors and a holy terror to the other children, a reputation he'd earned within days of his arrival.

Nobody had asked him to share after that.

And now here was a person, an entire human being—soon-to-be vampire—that belonged solely to him. Gifted by fate.

Was it any wonder he was so fascinated? Was it truly a surprise, when his patience had started out threadbare as it was, that the beast had been able to dig its claws into those holes and take control?

Perhaps not. Perhaps it had all been inevitable.

So while the doorbell ringing was not surprising, it *was* unwelcome. What right did anyone else have to interfere with what belonged to him? But it was necessary for Wolfe to remind himself of the bigger picture. To live the unnaturally long, protected life he envisioned, he would need security, connections, and funds. And for that, he needed community. *This* community, if he wanted his due half of Johann's billions.

So he reluctantly left the spare bedroom with his transforming mate inside it and opened the front door to find Johann standing there, dressed in another one of his atrocious sweatpants numbers. A quick glance past his small frame confirmed Roman was still on the property, along with his pretty mate, the nurse. Alexei lurked as well, and even from afar, it was clear he wasn't pleased to be separated from Johann, even for a few moments.

Wolfe was annoyed to note he now understood the sentiment.

"Johann," Wolfe greeted mildly. He wasn't quite sure what impulse exactly had him feigning ignorance of the purpose of their visit, other than the simple desire to see if he could pull it off. "How may I help you?"

But the other vampire wasn't having it, his little face already scrunched in anger. "Wolfgang." He made Wolfe's name sound like a scolding.

Wolfe didn't like that one bit.

But he didn't let his annoyance show, other than a slight flattening of his lips. "I'd invite you in, but I'm afraid now's not the best time."

Wolfe had always liked Johann well enough. He was polite, he was more observant than people gave him credit for, and he treated Wolfe's psychopathy for what it was—namely, a psychological condition rather than a moral failing. But there was no way in hell Wolfe was allowing anyone—ally or not—into his home when his mate lay there, vulnerable and unconscious. At least not until he had a proper plan of action in place.

Johann continued to look at him like he was the source of some great betrayal. "I thought I told you we wouldn't be that kind of den."

As if what Wolfe had done was anything like the practices of their old den: kidnapping random humans, turning them with the misguided hope they'd be happy to serve whatever master had chosen them, then disposing of them when they so often didn't work out. It was all wasteful, tedious, and unreasonably risky, but Wolfe had never been in a position to change anything without risking his own neck in the process.

"I beg your pardon?" He didn't let his offense at such an accusation show.

He was ready to continue this ploy of mild confusion right up until Johann threatened to cut him out of the pot, crossing his arms in some subconscious effort to physically intimidate Wolfe (a laughable impulse). "I'll leave you out in the cold, Wolfe. No money. No den. No nothing. I don't like liars."

And what Johann's body language couldn't achieve, his words certainly could. Wolfe was forced to go through the indignity of explaining his own actions to another, as if he answered to anyone other than himself. "I only wanted a little taste. The blood of a mate is supposed to be especially sweet. I tried to compel him. My beast would not...cooperate." Wolfe ran a hand through his hair, which had become decidedly mussed in the massage room scuffle and was not nearly up to its normal standards. "So I did what had to be done."

Johann's face scrunched even tighter. "And what are you going to do with him now?"

"He'll stay with me, of course."

He thought he did a fair job of keeping his continued irritation to himself, right up to the point where Johann reiterated Roman's earlier absurd assertion. "But that's not your decision."

Why did people keep insisting on this fact? They were categorically *wrong*. Whether Wolfe's transforming mate knew it yet or not, they were already bound. Eric belonged to him, body and soul, gifted by fate itself. Wolfe and his beast had known it from the very first sighting; everyone else could either get in line or face the consequences.

And there should have been a way to point that out to Johann calmly—dispassionately, even. Instead—

"He's *mine*," Wolfe found himself growling. His beast was ready to pounce, to swipe little Johann off their doorstep and rip apart any of his friends who dared come to his rescue.

He was losing it, clearly.

Wolfe had always—*always*—handled Johann with kid gloves. There had never been any reason to act otherwise. The cloyingly sweet vampire was traumatized to the point where only the smallest amounts of decency and surface-level kindness were required to guarantee his friendship and loyalty, a fact that Wolfe had always taken full advantage of.

Still, not even Johann had the right to try to remove Wolfe's mate from his grasp. No one did.

But Johann stood his ground—despite the growl, despite the rage he must have seen on Wolfe's face—an act Wolfe might have admired if he weren't so irritated by it. "That's his choice, Wolfe. You know that."

Did he?

He'll choose us, Wolfe's beast insisted, its hackles raised by Johann's verbal challenge. *He will.*

Wolfe said as much to Johann, and when he still insisted one of his party be allowed inside to verify that, Wolfe came as close as he ever had to snapping his little friend's neck, just to teach him a lesson.

But that would be counterproductive, especially with the three other vampires lurking in the background, watching their every move. So Wolfe did something he despised.

He compromised.

"When he awakens, *one* of you may speak with him."

Johann, beaming like Wolfe had offered to make him Eric's vampire godfather, immediately offered himself up as liaison, an offer which Wolfe immediately refused. "No. You're too tainted by trauma. You'll frighten him unnecessarily."

It was true. There was too much baggage there—if Eric showed even the slightest bit of fear, Johann would be trying to rescue him in an instant. Neither was Alexei the appropriate choice, seeing as how Wolfe had taken his human life by force a little over a week ago. No, Johann's mate wouldn't leave the necessary positive impression.

But Roman's lovely nurse mate, Danny... He and Eric worked at the same hospital. Perhaps it would be comforting for Eric to see a familiar face. And comfort would be good, would increase the chances Wolfe's mate would agree to stay without coercion. Danny was also happily mated to Roman, despite unfortunate circumstances surrounding his transformation. He would be perhaps more inclined to encourage another happy union, even if Eric's first knee-jerk reaction upon awakening was one of fear.

And if not...

Well, Wolfe would have to come up with some alternative plans of action.

"Your nurse friend with the lovely eyes. When the good doctor awakens, they may speak. Will that appease you?"

He resisted yet again lashing out when Johann insisted on them all coming in the morning, rather than waiting for Wolfe's call. It would be inconvenient if Eric didn't wake before then—less time for Wolfe to get into his head without their interference.

But ah, well. These were the consequences of acting on impulse.

Still, that was plenty of capitulations for the moment. It was time to return his attention to where it belonged.

"Now if you'll excuse me," he said, already in the act of shutting the door on Johann's startled face. "I have some preparations to make."

He stood here behind the door for another few moments, listening as Johann returned to his friends, as Danny agreed to speak with Eric in the morning, as Roman suggested Wolfe may be more trouble than he was worth. An annoyingly astute observation, really. Wolfe could only hope Johann's sentimentality for their past decade of friendship would buy him some time. He just needed things to...settle a bit.

"See what you've done?" he taunted his beast as he turned to the stairs. "Now they'll be trying to take him away from us."

We won't let them, his beast insisted, hackles rising yet again.

"No," Wolfe agreed, ascending the steps. "We won't."

Wolfe had plenty to do. He had the painters to call and defer, Tobias to check in on (he didn't trust that little weasel to leave them alone as promised), financial preparations to make.

But despite his list of tasks, he nonetheless found himself wandering up to the room where both he and his beast wanted to be. He drew up an armchair next to the bed and began making his calls from there, never taking his eyes off the figure resting so peacefully.

It was foolish to worry. No one was taking Eric away from him.

No one.

Six

Eric

Eric woke violently, his eyes opening in a panic to stare at an unfamiliar ceiling, his hands already moving along his body to check for injuries.

He remembered pain. So much pain. His last conscious memory was of thinking he'd been literally burning alive, from the inside out. He was half-afraid all his hands were going to encounter was a shriveled, charred husk.

But what skin he could reach with his fingers felt intact. And he didn't actually hurt now. Like, at all.

He was in a bed, he was pretty sure. It certainly felt soft enough underneath him, not like the firm massage table at all. But it sure as shit didn't feel like his *own* bed (the sheets were way too silky, for one), which was why he was having trouble taking his eyes off the ceiling to look around. Because he really wasn't sure he was going to like what he saw. He might completely freak the fuck out, actually.

"You're awake."

Eric shot up with a start, turning at the same time to see *him* at his bedside, massive book in hand.

"*You*," Eric spat out, fingers clenching in the absurdly soft sheets.

The Bond villain or masseur or whatever the fuck he was arched a brow at Eric's vehemence. "That's right, I never did introduce myself properly," Psycho said with a polite, insincere smile, as if he hadn't been literally eating Eric alive just a few—had it been minutes? Hours? *Days*?—well, some amount of time ago. "My name is Wolfgang Volker, but you may call me Wolfe."

And that really confirmed it: he even had a Bond villain name. On top of that, he'd exchanged his black loungewear for some absurd maroon crushed-velvet suit. Total villain attire. And he wanted to be on a first-name basis? "I'll call you the fucker that *bit* me."

The polite smile turned into a sly, self-satisfied smirk. "Mm. Yes. And how delicious you were."

"Um." Well, what was Eric supposed to say to that? Except the obvious. "It hurt," he accused, mortified to note that his voice came out petulant again, like that of a child getting an unexpected shot at the doctor.

"It wasn't the bite that hurt you but the transformation."

"Transformation, what—?" But Eric dropped the question, distracted. There was that bergamot scent again, stronger than before, and so weirdly appealing.

Smells good, Eric thought. And something, some...presence...inside him, rumbled its agreement.

What. The. Fuck?

Eric stiffened, trying to figure out what exactly was going on in his own brain. His own body. He felt oddly compelled to follow that scent. To bury his face in it. To...lick the source?

No, that was fucking crazy.

He barely dared to inhale as he watched the villainous fucker—Wolfe, and if he wasn't lying, the name certainly suited him—cock his head, clearly clocking Eric's change in body language. "Do you feel it?" he asked, the picture of mild, academic curiosity.

"Feel what?" Eric asked warily.

"The new part of your being." And yeah, the guy's general expression may have been mild, but his light-brown eyes were filled with a weirdly intense gleam. "The inner beast awakening."

Eric tried to laugh it off, but his throat only made a strange, strangled sound. "That sounds like some werewolf shit."

"I'm afraid not." Wolfe's nose wrinkled in distaste. "The shedding alone would be a nightmare."

Eric refused to find that funny. He pointed an accusatory finger. "You had *fangs*. Like a vampire."

"Yes. Quite like a vampire." The tiny, amused smile Wolfe gave him made Eric want to smack him. Or... He didn't know what else.

Again, licking was a possibility.

No. Jesus, what was wrong with him?

He pressed a palm hard to his forehead, trying to will his brain back into sense. "Okay, I get it."

"Do you?"

"Mm-hmm. Yep. I had a psychotic break."

"Did you?" Wolfe set his massive book on the bedside table, lacing his fingers over one crossed knee, like some TV psychiatrist. "And do you have a history of delusions?"

Eric shot him a savage look. "No."

"Hallucinations?" Wolfe asked. Eric shook his head, and Wolfe clucked his tongue. "Come now, Eric. You're a doctor. You know better."

A strange jolt of electricity ran through Eric when Wolfe used his given name. He was always—*always*—Dr. Monroe in this town. If someone liked him, or tolerated him especially well, he was just Monroe. But no one called him Eric. No one except his mother, and she didn't usually say it with any sort of fondness.

And no, Eric didn't have any history of delusions or hallucinations, but his mind clearly wasn't in the right place if he was focused on the man who kidnapped him using his first name all nicely.

"We don't have much time," Wolfe said, scooting his chair even closer. And Eric should be nervous about that, right? This guy had attacked him. Drank his blood, even, if Eric's memory was to be believed. And yet some part of Eric—that weird, new, rumbly presence in him especially—wanted him even closer than that. That same weird part of him felt like they should be...touching, even. Like, maybe touching a whole lot.

His dick twitched at the thought. *Don't you fucking dare*, he ordered it.

"Very soon," Wolfe continued, either oblivious or uncaring of Eric's internal dilemma, "some...friends of mine are going to be checking in on you. They might try to convince you to leave. They might perhaps tell you I'm a psychopath."

Now Eric did laugh, a dry, humorless chuckle. He didn't need anybody to tell him this guy was a psychopath. The evidence spoke clearly enough. "That sounds about right. Are you even a real massage therapist?"

Wolfe pursed his lips, either in displeasure or to repress a smile. "I can tell you truthfully I did not intend to turn you so...suddenly. My beast would not cooperate."

Eric's brain skipped right over the "beast" part of that. He'd been kidnapped by a delusional psychopath; that was fine. Well, not fine. Terrible, actually. But said psychopath was allowing potential rescuers to come visit Eric, so maybe he wasn't completely set on this abduction being a permanent thing.

Only...the way Wolfe had phrased that. "But you did intend to...turn me? At some point?" Eric asked. He figured "turning" must be code for kidnapping. Just a regular, ordinary kidnapping. Nothing strange or paranormal going on over here, folks.

And what about the blood drinking? And the burning feeling? And this new, weird presence in your brain, the one that's very pro-licking when it comes to said kidnapper? Eric ignored those thoughts. Those were bad, unhelpful thoughts. He was a rational person. He was a *doctor*, goddamn it.

Wolfe leaned forward, and it took everything in Eric to resist swaying toward him in turn. "We are bonded, you and I."

"Because you...turned me?" Eric kept his spine stick-fucking-straight, not giving an inch to that ridiculous urge to be closer.

Wolfe gave a single sharp shake of his head. "I turned you *because* we are bonded. Made for each other. Destined by fate."

See? That was some stalker, kidnapper, psycho, serial killer shit. And Eric really needed to get his fight-or-flight response on board. His body was way too weirdly relaxed for the situation he was in. "Are you going to hurt me again?" he asked, hoping to jog his own brain into realizing that was an incredibly likely scenario and to *be afraid, be very afraid.*

But Wolfe shook his head again. "Never. You are...precious to me."

Of all the confusing things Eric had heard these past ten minutes, that was the most confusing of all. Eric had never been precious to anyone before. That probably proved more than anything that this man was delusional as all hell.

So why did Eric want to crawl into his lap?

Maybe...maybe if they just held hands for a second?

But Eric was saved from his own unhinged self by the distinct chime of a doorbell.

Fierce annoyance and a hint of anger crossed Wolfe's face, quick as lightning, before they faded in an instant, his expression back to placid neutral.

There. *That* was why Eric should be frightened, right? This guy may have seemed all calm and collected on the outside, but he clearly had hidden depths.

But Eric still couldn't find the right emotions for it. It was like some lizard brain part of him felt safe in this guy's presence. Despite the biting, the delusions, and the apparent kidnapping.

Which only served to prove that Eric's brain couldn't be trusted right now.

Wolfe rose from his chair in one smooth motion. "I need to answer that."

Eric waved a hand. "Go right ahead."

"Remember," Wolfe said, pausing at the door, "I will never harm you. And I would rip every limb off any creature who tried."

Eric stared. Was that supposed to be comforting?

As soon as Wolfe left, Eric scrambled out of the bed, noting peripherally he was wearing some weird robe. But at least he had his underwear on underneath. He crossed over to the room's largest window, checking to see how wide it would open.

Because if Wolfe was willing to let someone convince Eric to leave? Perfect.

But either way, Eric was getting the fuck out of there.

Eric's rescuer was not who he'd been expecting.

"Little King?" Dressed in street clothes—jeans and a hoodie, with some sort of messenger bag across his chest—dark-brown curls in a messy halo around his head, there was King's little brother, Danny, an ER nurse Eric knew peripherally from around the hospital. A good-looking kid, although Eric had never personally hit on him, not wanting to get clocked in the face by an overprotective Gabe if his advances were unwelcome.

"Hi, Dr. Monroe." Danny's smile was kind, maybe a little sad. He definitely didn't look as panicked as he rightly should, considering the situation.

Eric shut the window he'd been fiddling with. It wasn't going to open wide enough for him to fit through anyway. "You're here to get me out?"

Danny gave him a strange half nod. Not exactly reassuring. "If that's what you want." And wasn't that cryptic as hell? "But we need to talk first. Do you want to sit?"

Eric shook his head. He was feeling...agitated, all overheated and tingly, like his skin wasn't quite fitting right. It was a strange sort of agitation though. Like from the outside, in. Which didn't make any sense, but he didn't know how else to describe it. He still wasn't frightened exactly, not like he should be. But he didn't think he could sit still either.

Danny sat in the chair by the bed instead, taking a deep breath afterward and letting it out slowly. "Do you understand what happened to you?"

Eric tugged absently at the fabric tying his robe together. "That fucker bit me, knocked me unconscious, then kidnapped me."

Danny's already big brown eyes grew even larger, but he nodded slowly, as if that tracked perfectly. He cleared his throat. "And do you remember what his face looked like, when he bit you?"

How was *that* the focus right now? Not, "*Oh my fucking God, he bit you, are you kidding?*" But Danny had a point. Eric thought back on that moment in the massage studio. "Um...weird. I thought— For a minute, I thought..."

"Was it anything like this?" And there, under the bright daylight streaming in through the window, right in front of Eric's stone-cold-sober eyes, Danny's face...changed. Just like Wolfe's had, back at Serenity. The pupils took over those big brown eyes completely, turning them fully black. Danny's lips parted to reveal pointed teeth.

And all Eric could do was stand there. "Holy fucking *fuck*."

Danny winced, a surprisingly human expression on such a weirdly not-quite-human face. "I'm really sorry. I know this is an abrupt way to do this, but I'm not sure how much time Wolfe is willing to give us. He's clearly already very...protective of you. So, um, brass tacks: vampires are real. Wolfe is one, so are Gabe and I. And now...so are you."

Eric was vaguely aware he was shaking his head frantically. "Nope. Nuh-uh. No way." But he could *see* it. Danny's face was right in front of him. He could reach out and touch those fangs. And he remembered that bite. The gulping sounds. Wolfe's freaky eyes and fangs.

Danny gave his head a slight shake, and his face went back to normal, just like that. "You can do what I just did too. Do you feel, like a...presence inside you? Just, um, relax. Let it out."

Eric could waste more time protesting. He could go the denial route for sure. But he could feel it...something different inside him. Something strange and covetous and starved.

There was a standing mirror in the room, right next to the closet; Eric placed himself in front of it. He could feel that presence, like a shifting shadow behind his eyes, under his skin yet intangible at the same time. So just...let it out.

He ended up staring at himself for a good minute before turning helplessly to Danny. "I don't know how to let it out. I don't know how to relax."

"I have something that might help." Danny dug into the satchel around his chest and pulled out a brown paper bag, casually fishing out a blood bag from inside.

"Are you serious right now?"

Danny shrugged, like carrying around pilfered sacks of blood was no big deal. "Just look at this and think of how hungry you are."

"But I'm *not* hungry exactly. Not for food, I don't think. Or blood, I guess. I'm...restless." *Want Wolfe back* was the crazy thought that zipped through his head. It didn't even sound like his own voice thinking it.

Danny nodded, calm as ever. "Then focus on that restlessness."

Eric did, turning back to face the mirror. He thought of how ill-fitting his skin felt, how badly he wanted to be...soothed somehow. How he had a sneaking suspicion he knew exactly *who* he wanted to do the soothing. How if he just asked, he was pretty sure he could get exactly what he wanted. As he did so, he felt some of that internal pressure release, and then his face—his own fucking face—changed, just like Danny's. Just like Wolfe's.

It was weird as hell, seeing himself look that way, seeing his murky green eyes go all black like that. He watched his reflection as he lifted a finger, touching one of those fangs. It sliced through the tip easily, blood welling. And then, just as quickly, the wound closed up.

"Whoa."

Danny was smiling, looking...proud? "Yeah, there are some benefits. Healing is one of them. Also strength. Speed. Never aging. Et cetera, et cetera."

"Why—" Eric asked, pulling at an eyelid to get a better look at his eyeball. Completely black, all the way through to the very edges. "Why did he...?"

He could see Danny shifting uncomfortably in his chair through the mirror. "Um, well... He thinks you're his mate."

"Mate?" Eric turned away from his reflection, felt his regular features slide back into place as he did. It was a weird, slippery sort of feeling but not all that unpleasant.

Danny took another deep breath, clearly preparing for a bit of a story, and then Eric listened, hardly daring to breathe, as Danny explained a completely unbelievable truth. As this ER nurse who had never seemed anything but human told him about unending life spans, feral vampires and fated pairings, his own bond with his fated vampire mate.

When Danny was finished, Eric stumbled blindly back to the bed, sitting heavily on the edge of it, trying to take it all in. It turned out if enough shock pumped through his limbic system, he could sit still after all. "So I have to stay with him. It's, like, destiny?"

"Well, no, you don't *have* to, but..." Danny shifted in his chair again. "New vampires—unbonded ones—tend to be very unstable. If you leave Wolfe—if you run from that stabilizing connection—I don't know what that would mean for you. And if you *are* a danger to the people here, we'd have to...contain you."

"So I get to choose one form of captivity or another."

"You're *not* a captive," Danny said adamantly. "He can't force you to stay in this house. He can't make you do anything you don't want to. Do you want to leave right now?"

He should. Eric should 100 percent want to leave this house, return to his apartment (cold, empty, no bergamot anywhere), and never look at that psycho vampire fucker again. But he couldn't make himself say the words. He pressed his palm to his forehead. "Fuck, I don't know. I'm angry. I'm confused. But he— He smells really good?"

Danny nodded calmly once again, as if that made perfect sense. As if someone smelling really good was reason enough to stay. And then, since talking about crazy things like they made perfect sense was apparently what they were doing now, Eric confessed, "Um, so I feel really agitated right now. Distracted. But like *I'm* not feeling that way. Like it's coming from...outside me?"

Danny's eyes widened in realization. "Oh. *Oh*. Shit. Um, yeah, that's another part of the bond. Feeling each other's emotions. Which might be kind of...strange. With Wolfe."

Eric thought back to what Wolfe had told him they'd say about him. "Because you think he's a psychopath?"

Danny gave a half shrug. "So Jay says, at least... It's not like most vampires are the pinnacle of empathy and self-control though."

"You and I both know there's not any sort of official diagnosis for that though. Antisocial personality disorder, on the other hand." Eric paused, finally registering the rest of what Danny had said. "Wait— Jay the barista? He's a vampire too? How many *are* there of y—of us—in this town?"

"With you, it makes eight."

"How is there not more press around this? Like the missing persons alone, right?"

"Wait, what?" Danny sat up straighter as he seemed to realize what Eric was getting at. "Fuck. No. We don't *kill* people, Monroe. You bite them, you make them forget, you move on." He reached out a hand, gripping Eric's forearm in reassurance. "I promise, getting turned isn't the end of the world. There will be sacrifices, sure. And I'm sorry for how it happened it you. But you'll get to know all of us. It won't be so bad." He sounded halfway convinced he was telling the truth.

Danny let go of Eric and dug another paper bag out of his satchel. "Here. This will do for now, until Wolfe teaches you how to hunt. *Without* killing," he stressed.

Should Eric be embarrassed that he'd thought he had to kill other people to eat and he'd just...accepted it? But he was overwhelmed and confused, and weirdly enough...he still really wanted Wolfe back.

He took the paper bag from Danny. "Um, can you—?" He stopped himself, unable to finish the sentence.

"You want to stay," Danny guessed, empathetic as all hell, as per usual, at least as far as Eric had seen at the hospital.

"I guess. Just—just to try. If he keeps his fangs to himself from now on."

Danny cleared his throat. "You might change your mind about that part. But yeah, okay. I'll send him up." He gave Eric a slow smile, clearly relieved at Eric's choice. "Welcome to the family."

And weirdly, for how off-putting literally every other thing Danny had said since coming to the room had been, that part didn't sound so bad.

Apparently all Eric had needed to do to be accepted in this town was give up his very life.

Seven

Eric

When Wolfe knocked politely on the bedroom door before opening it not as politely immediately after, Eric was still seated on the bed. He was no longer even slightly tempted to go around fiddling with the windows, because apparently physical escape was pointless and might end with him murdering people (and besides that, the freaky fact that escape seemed to be, deep within him, completely unwanted).

So Eric sat there and took the vampire in—*really* took him in—for the first time, not as a detached professional, not as an unhinged kidnapper, but as a...potential partner?

As a *mate*?

The idea seemed so preposterous. And yet the moment Wolfe set foot inside the bedroom, something in Eric finally unclenched, for the first time since Wolfe had left him there. That restless agitation he'd been feeling from the outside—from Wolfe, according to Danny—finally eased as Wolfe looked him over in turn, a weird, covetous glint to his eyes.

And that inner part of Eric—that new, slinking, starving presence—finally seemed to relax. Well, *relax* was a relative term. It changed its focus from *Want Wolfe back* to *Want to be touching Wolfe right this minute.*

Eric could understand, even without the weird bond part. His "mate" (he still couldn't seem to take that word seriously) wasn't exactly classically handsome, but he *was* striking. High, sharp cheekbones. Those strange eyes, brown in some lights and almost red in others. He was slighter and an inch or so shorter than Eric, but he held himself with the kind of steely posture that made boarding school instructors so intimidating.

Aristocratic—that was the aura he gave off. He even had a pocket square all artfully arranged in that crushed-velvet suit pocket.

Meanwhile, Eric was wearing a terry-cloth robe.

That didn't seem to matter to Wolfe though. He was looking Eric over like he was something edible, and it was doing weird things to Eric's junk.

Come to think of it, he sort of *was* edible. Or at least he had been. Did vampires bite each other?

Eric met Wolfe's eyes and drew in a sharp breath as a wave of... something...washed over him, from the outside, in again, through their bond. A fierce sort of possessiveness that made all his nerve endings light up.

It was a little shocking in its intensity.

"Jesus," he breathed.

Wolfe held still in the doorway, not a hint of that insane possessiveness showing in his expression, other than the gleam in his eyes. He hid the inner crazy well, this guy; that was for sure. "Did the young nurse overwhelm you?" he asked, searching Eric's face for his answer.

You overwhelm me, Eric wanted to say. *How much you seem to want me for no reason overwhelms me*. But that felt weird to admit out loud. Especially when the guy didn't really want him, right? It was just their inner vampire bits—their inner beasts, Wolfe had called them—connecting to each other or something.

When Eric didn't answer him, Wolfe tipped his chin at the blood bag next to Eric on the bed. "You haven't fed yet."

Eric shrugged. "It's cold." He didn't know how he even knew he had a preference for warm blood. It was just a feeling. The cold blood felt...wrong.

"Come, then. We'll heat it up." Wolfe turned in the doorway, presumably to head to the kitchen downstairs.

Eric considered staying where he was. He could enact some sort of hunger strike until any of this seemed remotely real. Or until Wolfe finally apologized for scaring him, for changing his life irrevocably without even asking.

But that day might never come, right? He tried to think back on his old psych classes in med school. Could Wolfe even feel guilt for what he'd done?

Eric had no idea. So he followed, blood bag in hand, docile as a fucking lamb.

It shouldn't be surprising, really. Eric had seen this before, from an outside perspective: patients or families—ones who had just received some unexpected, horrible diagnosis—experiencing a strange period of calm, one where the information was just too huge to properly process.

He supposed he was in shock, more or less.

Add to that the strange satisfaction he felt coming from this new inner beast at Wolfe's presence, and Eric was just...surprisingly chill.

He wondered how long that would last.

He stood dumbly and watched as Wolfe removed a saucepan from one of the cabinets, his movements all very precise—graceful, even. When Wolfe held up a hand, Eric placed the blood bag into it, watching as Wolfe sliced through the plastic and poured it into the pan.

This was weird, right? This was the weirdest fucking thing to ever happen to him, and he had once seen an attending reach into someone's open chest cavity and massage their heart for CPR.

But he may as well use this opportunity to get some answers. "So you didn't intend to turn me?"

Wolfe spun to face him, one hand still on the saucepan handle. "I did not." When Eric only stared, he gave a small sigh, stirring the blood with a wooden spoon before continuing. "I wanted to observe up close, I suppose. I wanted a taste."

Eric ignored how the blatant sexual undertones of that statement made his spine tingle and his cock thicken. His horny fucking body couldn't be trusted, and the word *observe* triggered something in his brain. That feeling of being watched, standing on the porch. "The roses," he said. "That was you?"

Wolfe nodded but didn't bother to elaborate any further.

Well, at least that explained why Eric couldn't figure out who the culprit was. He hadn't really had "fate-designated vampire stalker" on the list of options, now had he?

He rubbed at his forehead. It was starting to get tiring, this pull to be closer to Wolfe on the one hand, his general pissed-off-ness on the other. "Tell me why people call you a psychopath."

Wolfe stirred his blood calmly. "Because I believe I am one."

"You've been officially diagnosed with ASPD?" Eric asked skeptically.

Wolfe shot him an almost amused look, the corners of his mouth tilting up only the slightest bit. "I haven't. But there are characteristics. I'm perhaps not as impulsive as some of my like. Too aware of the consequences from a young age. But I've always been different." He started ticking off symptoms like the items of a grocery list. "Lack of empathy. Inability to form emotional attachments. I don't generally feel fear, not that I can remember, at least. And I don't feel guilt."

There it was. "So you don't feel bad about what you've done to me?"

Wolfe cocked his head, clearly considering his words. "I regret the challenge it will bring to our further connection."

"You should be a politician, the way you talk." Eric supposed he should be grateful Wolfe wasn't sugarcoating it and lying to protect his feelings. But rather than gratitude, the anger he'd been having such a hard time locating rose to the surface, strong enough to make his muscles quiver. Wolfe *didn't* feel bad. At all. and maybe that wasn't his fault, if guilt wasn't something he was capable of. But it sure did leave Eric feeling shitty, that so much had been taken from him in one single moment, and his fated, destined boyfriend couldn't give less of a shit about it.

If Wolfe was aware of his anger, if he felt it through the bond, he didn't show it. "You should eat" was all he said, pouring the heated blood into a wineglass of all the fucking things.

Eric found himself reaching automatically for the glass, shivering slightly as their fingers brushed during the exchange. With warm blood in front of him, he realized he *was* hungry. It was just kind of secondary to that other feeling, that itch to be close to Wolfe, even when anger had him bristling.

All the while, Wolfe maintained unblinking eye contact. Eric could feel it even as he lowered his own gaze to study the red liquid. He was about to drink blood. Human fucking blood.

And what was more, Wolfe clearly wanted to watch him drink it. Maybe he wanted to see the change come over Eric. Maybe Wolfe's inner beast wanted to meet Eric's, the way Eric's inner beast seemed to be yearning every second to be closer to Wolfe.

But all that did was make Eric not want to show him. The anger was still going strong, speeding his pulse in a way where he could *feel* his heart pounding. That Wolfe could change Eric's life so suddenly and be so completely goddamn unperturbed about it? Hand him blood in a wineglass like he was offering him a particularly lovely Chianti? That fucking sucked. It wasn't fair.

So Eric protested the only way he felt he could. "Don't look," he ordered.

Wolfe's only show of surprise was a slow blink. "I'll close my eyes."

Did he really think Eric was that easy of a mark? "No. Turn around."

The flash of irritation—both on Wolfe's face and through the bond—proved to Eric that Wolfe *had* intended to cheat. No guilt, right?

Eric raised his glass and motioned with one whirling finger for Wolfe to do as he asked. The amount of pleasure he took from the huff of irritation he got in return was kind of absurd.

Once Wolfe had his back to him—surprisingly broad shoulders, for such a slender man—Eric let his vampire face back out the way he had in that room with Danny. It was even easier here, with Wolfe in front of him and the coppery scent of blood in the air. Eric's beast *wanted* to come out.

Eric took a large swallow. Because hey, if he was going for it, he was going for it all the way.

And oh, that was good. Like, really fucking good. It reminded him of the first real meal after a really long shift, one of the ones where he didn't get a chance to eat any lunch at all. Satisfying on a whole different level.

He drank the rest down quickly, trying to figure out how he felt about it. He still didn't feel quite...sated. He wasn't hungry anymore, but there was still that...itching under the skin. It was really, really hard to push the beast back down. It wanted to reach out, wanted to run their fingers along those broad shoulders, to breathe in that bergamot smell. To fucking bathe in it.

No. We are not doing that. We are mad *at him.*

Eric could almost hear the beast's huff of irritation at those thoughts. But it retreated eventually, Eric's regular face shifting back into place. And Eric just stood there, empty glass in hand, not sure what to do next.

Wolfe's shoulders twitched, the only sign of his impatience. "May I turn around now?"

"Oh." Eric reached up, just to double-check that his teeth were back to normal. "Okay. Um, yeah."

Wolfe frowned at him slightly when they were face-to-face again. "Your vampire face is nothing to be ashamed of, Eric."

"I'm not." It wasn't like Eric had processed any of it enough to be ashamed about anything.

"I see." Wolfe's gaze traveled over every inch of him again, slowly enough that it was practically a physical sensation, and eventually a small smirk graced his lips. "You wished to deny me something," he surmised.

Eric glared at him. "Why does that make you smile?"

Wolfe's smirk deepened. "I haven't seen that side of you yet. Petty."

"How many sides of me can you possibly have seen?" Eric asked, feeling petulant again. Just how long and how closely had Wolfe been watching him?

Wolfe half shrugged a single shoulder. He looked aristocratic even doing that. "Only the surface levels, I suppose. A friendly people pleaser, desperate to be liked. And yet no one truly close in your life, despite that desperation. "

Well, ouch. It stung a bit, the accuracy of those words. But there wasn't any cruelty in them; Wolfe didn't seem to be intending to wound, just calling it like he saw it.

"But my pettiness makes you smile?" Eric asked, all sorts of confused.

Wolfe reached up a hand, as if to cup Eric's face. Eric was half-certain he would let him. "All parts of you are precious to me. Because all parts of you are mine." Wolfe lowered his arm. "I look forward to seeing each layer uncovered."

Sweet mother of Mary. Eric swallowed hard as the bond pulsed, dark and covetous. "Uh...yeah," he rasped. "I can feel that."

Wolfe cocked his head. "That you are mine?" he purred, obviously delighted at the thought.

"No. Jesus. I can feel your psycho possessiveness, through the bond thing."

"Ah, yes." Wolfe seemed no less displeased by that.

I want to touch him. What the fuck? Was that Eric or his beast talking? *Could* their beasts talk to them? He had so many more questions, but he didn't think he had the energy to ask them. He was just...exhausted.

He pressed two fingers to his forehead. "I'm kind of...tired?"

Wolfe's brow furrowed the slightest bit. "You shouldn't need much sleep as a vampire. But perhaps it's the new transition, wearing you down."

"Well, I'm gonna lie down again," Eric said, putting his glass in the sink (Wolfe could have clean-the-blood duty) and turning to leave the kitchen. He stopped in the doorway when a thought came to him. "Where do you sleep?"

Wolfe clucked his tongue regretfully. "Our main bedroom is unfurnished at the moment, as it needs to be painted first. I'm afraid I had to delay the professionals due to your transitioning state. For now, where you awoke is the only furnished bedroom."

Eric resisted the urge to scream. Was this guy really trying to pull some only-one-bed crap on him right now?

At Eric's pissy look, Wolfe capitulated with a gracious nod. "But if I need to rest, I will of course do so on the sofa downstairs."

"You bet your biting ass you will," Eric grumbled, heading back to his bedroom, ignoring the way the beast inside him sulked at the increasing distance between them.

Maybe when he woke back up, it would all have been a dream.

Something told him he wouldn't be so lucky.

Eight

Wolfe

Wolfe's mate was most assuredly pouting, for lack of a better word. Off in the spare bedroom all by himself, tossing and turning without Wolfe by his side. Wolfe could hear the subtle rustling of Eric's restlessness, as he settled himself in the sitting room with a massive tome on the American political system (he always thought it best to have a handle on the inner workings of whatever country he found himself in).

Wolfe had felt it, back in the kitchen: Eric's yearning. He would bet his finest suit that his doctor wanted nothing more than to touch him, to be near him, to be claimed by him. The new beast within him clearly knew who he belonged to, even if Eric's more logical brain had yet to catch up to it.

But apparently Wolfe's mate was a stubborn one, under all that surface gregariousness. And who could really blame him? It had been a fairly shocking twenty-four hours by anyone's estimation.

Wolfe flicked through his pages listlessly, finding it uncharacteristically hard to focus when the so much more interesting puzzle was just upstairs, hiding from him. Eric wasn't frightened—or he wasn't sending anything through their bond that Wolfe could recognize as such—but he *was* angry. Wolfe could feel the hot pulse of it, delicious in its insistence. But what was anger other than the first step toward acceptance? And Wolfe supposed he had the young nurse to thank for that. As irritating as it had been, having to suffer through Johann's group of meddlers insisting on interviewing *his* mate, the conversation had clearly served to help convince Eric of the reality of his situation.

Wolfe had caught snippets of it, as he'd sequestered the others in this very sitting room. Danny had explained things neatly enough, from what Wolfe had been able to gather. And he hadn't overplayed the psychopath hand to scare Eric off.

And the injustice of the whole affair had been made just the slightest bit sweeter by the delicate threads of *want* Wolfe had been able to feel coming from his mate while they'd been apart, twining around Wolfe's own agitation and need.

Eric could pretend all he wanted. But as soon as Wolfe had left the room, Eric had wanted him near again. Just as he wanted Wolfe near *now.*

And yet, despite that, here they were, in separate rooms, that beautiful body hidden away from him, just as Eric had hidden his vampire features from Wolfe's gaze. To be denied the closeness they both so clearly wanted in this transitional time, just to soothe Eric's newly awoken temper...

It should have been annoying. Infuriating. Too much to bear.

Especially with Wolfe's own beast clamoring in his head, mindless and yearning. *Time to claim our mate. Take him. Bite him. Fuck him deep.*

The thing was absolutely relentless in its new one-track focus.

And really, Eric had looked so delicious sitting on their temporary bed, his blond locks disheveled, his robe barely managing to contain that gorgeous, broad chest, with its smattering of blond fuzz. He'd been hungry and irritable and out of sorts, and Wolfe had wanted nothing more than to pin him down and bite every inch of him.

Alas, it hadn't been the time.

But Wolfe couldn't access the proper irritation for his plight. Instead, he found himself oddly intrigued, almost delighted by this turn of events.

Eric was—on the surface, at least—a people pleaser above all else. He was the kind of human who wanted to be wanted, liked, desired—even if only for a single night at a time. For him to be so petulant with Wolfe, commanding him...

Wolfe's lips twitched at the memory. "Turn around" indeed.

It was all a sign of Eric's subconscious trust in him. Eric knew, somewhere deep in that willful soul of his, that Wolfe wouldn't reject or leave him, no matter what games he played.

Was Wolfe's cock currently straining in his slacks, achingly hard with the knowledge that his tempting mate was so close yet so unreachable? Of course it was. Did he want nothing more than to kick in that offending bedroom door and claim what was rightfully his? In every part of his rotten soul.

But, recent events aside, restraint was Wolfe's gift, at odds with a psychopath's usual impulsivity. It was a point of pride for him, really. And he had to admit their new bond was already tenuous, what with the traumatic way in which it had been forged. It was concerning that Eric was so exhausted after having just woken as a vampire, for example. Wolfe could only conclude it had to do with the doctor's resistance to consummating their bond, either by touch, affection, or intercourse.

But to tell his dear doctor so would be fruitless: Eric would only think Wolfe self-serving. Conniving, even. And he wouldn't exactly be wrong, even if it didn't apply in this instance.

So Wolfe would be patient. He would wait for this petulant creature to come to him.

He'd waited patiently for an entire century already.

The women were back again.

Wolfe knew the pair was already aware of him—had probably registered his presence long before he'd registered theirs—but they kept up their study of watching the crowds go by. They were fashionably dressed in their dramatic coats, and Wolfe could smell the money in their clothing, as he had with every bit of their attire he'd seen the past few nights.

Envy gnawed at his gut. He should by all rights be wearing clothes just as fine. Not this single drab suit, pressed so carefully for repeated use.

Wolfe sidled up next to the park bench. "Looking for your next prey?" he asked, keeping his voice low enough not to carry past his intended target.

The taller of the pair, a pale, curvaceous woman almost matching Wolfe in height, with chestnut waves cascading down from under her chapeau, tilted her head up to look at him. "Pardon me?"

"Your next prey," Wolfe repeated, gesturing to the people walking past on the path, some few kilometers away. "Your dinner."

The first woman looked to her partner, a petite woman with luminous dark skin and matching ebony curls who had kept her eyes on the crowd during their exchange, a small smirk gracing her lips. "You were supposed to be keeping watch," the chestnut-haired woman accused, managing to sound more fond than angry.

The smirk grew to a mischievous grin. "I was, Sybil darling. I knew he was there." At Sybil's shocked look, she let out a tiny, tinkling laugh. "What? I liked him. There's something odd about him. Positively gives me the chills."

*Sybil narrowed her eyes. "*I'm *the only one who should be giving you chills."*

The petite woman rested a reassuring hand on Sybil's arm. "And you do, darling. He's just intriguing is all. I thought I'd let him have a little peek."

Wolfe cleared his throat, polite but pointed, eager to get to the matter at hand. He gestured with his chin to Sybil. "You were hurt last night. That man lashed you with a knife; the wound healed immediately."

Sybil shot a reproving look to her partner. "Oh my, so you really let him see everything*."*

Wolfe pressed on. "You told him to stop being afraid, and it worked. As if you tricked him somehow."

The women continued to gaze at each other, ignoring him.

"Can you die?" Wolfe asked, unwilling to be deterred.

It was the petite woman who finally answered, to Sybil's chagrin. "We can, technically, but it takes an awful lot."

*Sybil threw up her hands. "*Daphne. *Really."*

"What?" Daphne giggled. "He's curious. And we can always make him forget later."

They could, couldn't they? He'd been right.

These women had money. Proximity to immortality. The ability to manipulate others with just a few words. Wolfe felt a pinch of true excitement replace the envy in his gut, something he hadn't felt in a very long time, not since his parents had lost their fortune. Since he'd been left out in the cold despite a lifetime of careful, contained behavior.

He was bored of it. Bored of keeping himself under such tight control without reward. And with nothing left to him? Not even what was supposed to have been his due? It was only a matter of time before he was going to snap. And then he'd be risking prison or a hanging. Consequences. It was all about consequences.

It was time to change the stakes.

"How did you come to be this way?"

Daphne looked to Sybil, a flirtatious pleading in her gaze. It took only a moment before Sybil sighed and waved a hand, giving her tacit permission. Daphne rose in her seat to peck her on the cheek, then turned to Wolfe with a cheeky smile. "We were turned into what we are by another like us."

There it was. Wolfe stepped closer. "And you can do the same?"

Sybil let out a sigh, her fingertips toying with the ends of her heavy waves of hair. "I don't like the direction of this conversation."

A pity she felt that way, but no concern of his. "Turn me," he ordered, unable to bring himself to make it a request.

Daphne only smiled, but Sybil laughed at him, low and mocking. "You have no idea what you're asking. Have you already forgotten what you've seen?" She gestured to the passing crowds. "You'd need to regularly consume human blood to survive."

Wolfe nodded. "Fine."

"And you wouldn't age."

"Excellent."

"Meaning," *Sybil stressed, as if he were one of the dim-witted masses and hadn't followed that thread to its logical conclusion, "you'd have to leave your family behind, abandon your position in this world."*

"Not a problem."

Sybil leaned forward in her seat, seemingly intrigued despite herself. "You might kill, when you're starting out. You'll be out of control. You'll most likely take human lives."

Should he pretend remorse over that fact? But Daphne, for her part, was looking him over with a knowing gleam in her eyes. He wasn't so sure she'd be fooled. For once, Wolfe chose the plain truth over manipulation. "I'm not particularly bothered by that."

"What a little monster," Daphne crooned approvingly. It seemed he'd chosen correctly. "Maybe we should *turn him." At Sybil's look, she shrugged prettily. "I've always wanted a child."*

Sybil looked Wolfe over with distaste. "He's a fully grown man. And a creepy one, as you said."

"Still."

Sybil frowned at her paramour. "He won't be like we were when we turned. He doesn't have a mate at his side."

"A mate?" Wolfe asked, not willing to let them deny him on a technicality. Would they really refuse to turn him because he didn't have a wife? He could get a wife.

Daphne smiled winningly at him. "A beloved, just for you."

Sybil let out an exasperated noise, apparently displeased with that explanation. "Our kind. We're given a...matched spirit, you could say. Fate designates us a person, to spend our extended lives with. If we can find them. If not, this path won't end well for you. You'll go feral. You'll be put down like a rabid dog."

Wolfe would like to see them try. Still, best to be cautious. "How long do I have to find them?"

"Hard to say. Decades? Centuries? It varies."

The imprecision was frustrating, but Wolfe could manage. He had faith in himself above all else, including fate. "And how will I know?

"You'll just...know. They'll be yours, and you'll know it." She exchanged a disgustingly loving look with Daphne, who preened under the attention.

Wolfe took a moment to ponder it. He hadn't intended to factor anyone else into this transformation. But there was something to it, to the thought that there was someone out there, someone for him. Someone just *for him.*

He looked to the pair in front of them. He'd seen them in action; he knew the two of them were bloodthirsty, maybe even cruel. But they still had companionship, acceptance, devotion.

He could have that too. He could have everything.

His resolution strengthened.

"Turn me," he said again, trying his best to make it a request and not a demand. "I'll find my mate. You have no need to doubt me."

The two women shared another look, wordlessly communicating. And Wolfe would have that one day, wouldn't he? Then Daphne turned to him and smiled. "Come back tonight, little monster. We'll give you what you need."

Wolfe left the park with long, eager strides, triumph running through his veins. He'd known there was something off about the pair from the first moment he'd seen them. And he'd been right to follow them that night. It was destiny that he'd seen what he'd seen.

And now he had the perfect path in front of him. Longevity of life, eternal youth, eventual fortune (because how long would it really take to earn back his family's wealth, when he had whatever supernatural manipulation these women had displayed?).

And a person just for him, someone to keep for always.

Wolfe wondered what they'd be like. He wondered if they'd really see him—each one of his dark corners—and accept him anyway.

Well, they'd have to, wouldn't they? If it was fate. Destiny.

His smile grew as he walked down the path. Yes, everything was going to be perfect.

Nine

Eric

Eric flopped back onto the bed, trying to see if lying on his stomach felt any better.

He just couldn't get fucking *comfortable*. He was exhausted but couldn't keep his eyes closed. Everything ached, or itched, or...something. He'd stripped out of the robe, down to his underwear, but the sheets felt too heavy on his skin one minute and the room's mild air too harsh the next. And he kept feeling like his fangs were popping out against his will, but every time he reached up to touch, his teeth were blunt.

The weird, new presence inside him was just as restless, twisting and turning within him in a way that almost felt tangible, even though Eric was pretty sure it didn't quite work that way. That didn't stop him feeling like the dang thing was going to split his skin open.

It needed something. *He* needed something.

He needed soothing. He needed that scent.

He needed his fucking *mate*, apparently.

Eric groaned aloud in frustration, flopping onto his back and casting his limbs out, grabbing at his phone on the bedside table. The time told him he'd lasted barely an hour before giving in.

Too goddamn bad. He couldn't keep going like this.

"Wolfe!" he called out, his voice surprisingly hoarse, as if he'd been screaming rather than lying there in silent agony this whole time.

To the bastard's credit, Wolfe didn't make Eric wait; he was opening the bedroom door in seconds, almost as if he'd been sitting down there just *waiting* for Eric to swallow his pride. And judging by the triumphant gleam in his light-brown eyes, that was exactly what he'd been doing.

"Don't look so smug," Eric griped, not making any move to sit up. He'd already lost the battle, so why bother trying to hide how pathetic he was?

"So accusatory." Wolfe's voice was mild as ever, but his gaze was already hungry. It roamed over Eric greedily, the weight of it like a physical touch across Eric's bare chest, lingering for long moments before it moved down to the evidence of Eric's stubborn fucking arousal.

Because that was the other damning, humiliating aspect to this thing: Eric had been hard this entire goddamn time. He'd even tried to rub one out in the beginning, hoping it would help him sleep, but it had done nothing but work him up more. Release had kept evading him, just out of reach.

How could someone be this turned on and this uncomfortable at the same time?

It didn't help matters that Wolfe spent way too much time eye-fucking Eric's bulge before finally meeting his gaze again. *Pervert.*

Wolfe's lips twitched like he'd heard Eric's insult. Maybe he had. Maybe that was another creepy aspect of their bond no one had seen fit to tell him about. Who fucking knew, at this point?

"What do you need from me, pet?" Wolfe asked.

"I'm horny," Eric complained, stating the ridiculously obvious, too irritated to be coy or address that humiliating term of endearment. "Like, disturbingly horny."

A flash of possessive satisfaction rushed through the bond, quick as lightning. Eric clenched his teeth in frustration. This guy really had no shame.

"Mm. The new bond at work, I would say." Wolfe was clearly trying to form a sympathetic expression, but he was doing a piss-poor job of it. He looked more like the cat who'd gotten the cream. "Would you like me to touch you now, darling?" he offered. "I think it would help your...condition."

Oh, you'd fucking like that, wouldn't you?

Eric wanted to tell him to fuck off forever, but he couldn't take any more of this feeling. "No touching," he answered, trying to relax his jaw and keep his teeth from clenching so hard—he was going to break a molar or something. "And don't call me darling. Just...come here. Come closer."

Wolfe nodded genteelly. "As you wish." He stalked toward the bed and stopped right at the edge of it, where he stared down at Eric, patient as a snake coiled in the grass, waiting for its prey.

But it was better, having him there. Eric could catch a hint of that scent now, comforting and arousing at the same time. But it still wasn't close enough.

"Sit," he ordered, feeling his own form of smug satisfaction when Wolfe obeyed him easily, lowering himself gracefully until he was seated on the mattress beside him.

Eric leaned in closer, breathing deeply. Oh, there it was. Bergamot, with a strange metallic edge he didn't remember from the massage room. It didn't detract from it at all though. It was exactly what he needed. Eric groaned, his cock pulsing in his briefs.

Why did this creepy fucker have to smell so good?

Wolfe's gaze was roaming hungrily as ever. "Are you sure you don't want me to touch you?"

Eric shook his head frantically. He had a feeling if he let Wolfe touch him, there was no going back. He was already addicted to the guy's scent, to his presence—what would having Wolfe's hands on him again do to him?

The words that came out of Eric next felt like they were coming from someone else. "I want you to lie down next to me. And I want to touch myself with you here, while you keep your hands to yourself."

It was maybe the strangest request he'd ever made of someone. In every other one of his numerous sexual encounters, he'd always been conscious of his partner's pleasure. Anxious over it, almost. But Wolfe didn't deserve that courtesy, right? He'd upended Eric's life. It was *his* fault Eric was this horny, frantic mess. He had to take responsibility for his actions, and in this case, that meant doing exactly what Eric wanted.

But Wolfe didn't seem at all put off by the selfishness of Eric's request. He just shifted his fully clothed body down until he was lying next to Eric on the bed, then turned to his side, propping his head on one hand, his gaze molten as it caught Eric's.

"Like this, darling?"

Eric didn't protest the endearment this time. He was too busy tucking his thumbs into his waistband, ready to free his aching cock. But he paused one last time. "This is okay, right?"

He didn't know what made him ask. It wasn't like Wolfe deserved his courtesy. But even psychopaths needed consent, right?

Wolfe only smiled at him, the expression softening his sharp face. "Mm. More than okay. Whatever you need, precious mate, I'm here to provide."

Well, that couldn't be right. Not when Wolfe had admitted barely an hour ago that he didn't form emotional attachments.

But Eric couldn't care about that now. Wolfe was into this, at least enough for Eric not to feel like a total pervy jackass. He pulled down his briefs, kicking them off the bed. His cock stood hard and proud, the tip an angry purple, his shaft feeling swollen and abused from his earlier attempts at self-pleasure.

Eric turned his head again to catch Wolfe licking his lips. "Why, Doctor. You've been absolutely blessed."

So had Wolfe, if the impressive bulge in his suit pants was anything to go by. The thought had Eric grasping at his jerking cock. He wanted to tell Wolfe no talking, just to be a dick, but the sound of that smooth, steady voice was doing nice things to his insides, so he let it be. For now.

He started stroking himself, hard and fast, wanting to get this over with. It still felt...not quite right. But it helped, having Wolfe there, breathing him in. Maybe Eric would close his eyes, and it would be just like he was at home—

Eric startled as Wolfe's fingertips brushed his arm. "Hey! I said no touching!"

"My apologies." Wolfe removed his hand immediately, placing it on the bed centimeters from Eric's heaving chest. "But I think you should slow down, pet. This is the effect of your beast wanting contact. Connection. Power through frantically and you'll be back in this state before you know it."

Eric stared at him. "Are you lying to me right now?"

Wolfe looked calm as ever, his head pillowed on his hand. "I'm telling you my suspicions. I can't say for sure. It's not as if I've had a mate before."

Eric studied that placid face, trying to figure this guy out. He'd have thought Wolfe would want this over with too—it wasn't like he was going to get any physical satisfaction out of it. Except he seemed content to just drink Eric in, like the sight of him alone was enough to sustain him. It was almost enough to make Eric blush, the intensity of that admiration.

Staring at Wolfe—those brown eyes that gleamed red far too often, those sharp cheekbones, those lips that looked way too soft for such a stern face—Eric's muscles loosened bit by bit. With every ounce of tension eased, those soft lips twitched up further. Wolfe was pleased; Eric could feel it.

Eventually, Eric relaxed the tight hold on his cock.

"There you are, darling," Wolfe crooned, as if Eric had completed some monumental task. "Now why don't you try teasing the head? Make yourself feel good, pet."

Eric did as he said. He brushed over his leaking tip with his thumb, shuddering at the light contact, never taking his eyes off Wolfe as he did so. Was this what hypnosis felt like?

Wolfe hummed his approval. "And does that feel good?"

Eric nodded dumbly. It did. It felt really fucking good.

Wolfe broke eye contact to stare at Eric's cock. "Were I allowed to touch, I'd ask for a taste."

Eric frowned and shook his head again, but he was no longer frantic. He muscles were all loose, relaxed. "No touching," he whispered.

Wolfe's gaze returned to his. "Of course, darling. I wouldn't dream of disobeying. Now one long stroke, base to tip."

Eric's hand followed Wolfe's orders without his conscious thought. Eric breathed in deep at the same time, that bergamot scent enveloping him completely. His back arched off the bed as he did it again. And again.

"How's that feeling, pet?"

Wolfe was going hard with the endearments. Eric wanted to tell him off for it, but it was doing it for him. All of it was: the pressure of his own hand on his tender cock, the intoxicating smell of Wolfe surrounding him. Sure, he could be Wolfe's pet. His darling. Just for the moment. Just until Eric came.

Which might be any second now. Eric moaned, his hips thrusting off the mattress. His balls were heavy and aching, his hand slick from his own precum. "I don't think I'm going to last as long as you think I am."

He'd been too pent-up at the get-go, too in need of release. Too twisted up and horny, and also, it was like he could feel Wolfe's desire adding to his own. Could people feel lust through the bond? That was just... What was he supposed to do with that?

Wolfe tsked at him, which shouldn't have been sexy, but apparently anything that came out of his mouth got Eric going. "A pity. You're so gorgeous like this. You should see yourself. There's nothing like a big, strong man trembling and needy. Absolute perfection, pet."

Eric threw his head back with a groan, turned on by the humiliating words in spite of himself. "Shut up."

Wolfe stopped talking, but Eric could feel him smirking. Like Eric's petulance amused him.

He went back to stroking himself, finding a compromise between the furious pace from before and the slow teasing Wolfe so clearly wanted from him. Long, languid strokes, catching the head with his thumb every so often.

He found himself inching closer to Wolfe, not quite touching but breathing his air, their faces too close together to even maintain eye contact. It wasn't enough. He needed more. "Kiss me," he pleaded, uncaring how desperate he sounded.

Wolfe's eyes flashed, that hint of red. From the corner of his eye, Eric saw Wolfe's hand reach up.

"No touching," he snapped, panting now. "Just kissing."

He was thankful Wolfe was merciful enough not to point out that kissing *was* a form of touching. Eric didn't need logic right now. He needed that mouth on his. He needed to fucking come.

Wolfe didn't seem to require any further prompting. He slanted his mouth over Eric's, his tongue plunging in when Eric's lips parted, not a hint of coyness or any attempt to ease him into it.

Eric moaned into Wolfe's mouth, fisting a hand into his stupid fucking suit jacket. *Yes*, the beast within him purred. Eric agreed. This was better. This was right.

He whimpered when he came, which should have been mortifying except it made Wolfe groan, an almost pained-sounding noise, as he attacked Eric's mouth with even more ferocity, devouring him once again. He didn't let up, even as Eric's cum cooled on his fingers, as his body's tremors slowly eased. Wolfe just kept kissing him. Tongue stroking. Teeth nipping.

Eric was tempted to let him do it forever.

Except as his lust was appeased, as some semblance of clarity returned, he remembered he was supposed to be irritated.

No, not irritated. Angry. He was supposed to be *angry.*

He broke off the kiss, tilting his head back when Wolfe seemed inclined to chase his lips. "S-Stop. That's enough."

Wolfe stared at him with heavy-lidded eyes, looking dazed and a little manic. It seemed to take a very long time for clarity to return to him. His lips were red and bitten too. Had Eric really done that? Messed with that cool perfection? What would it be like to see Wolfe truly undone? That slicked hair messy, roughed up by Eric's hands. No more stupid fucking suit either, just miles of skin for Eric to scent and lick and rub himself against.

"Of course, darling," Wolfe finally said, bringing Eric out of his horny reverie. Wolfe's voice was no longer smooth and steady. "Whatever you say."

Eric looked down pointedly at that impressive bulge, encased in maroon velvet. "I'm not helping you with that."

Wolfe cleared his throat, adjusting himself. "I wouldn't dream of asking."

"Good." Eric's hand was sticky. He was going to need a washcloth. Or that ugly robe. But he also needed to sleep. And with that horrible discomfort finally eased, he thought he might even succeed. "I'm going to nap now."

"Of course." Wolfe nodded absently, wiping a hand over his mouth, somehow making even that gesture look classy. "Build your strength, darling."

Eric was tempted—just for a moment—to ask him to stay. Some part of him knew he'd sleep better surrounded by that scent. But he didn't want to let Wolfe win so soon, did he? Even more than that, he needed a moment outside of Wolfe's overwhelming presence to collect himself.

"So you can go now," he prompted.

Wolfe pursed those well-kissed lips in what seemed to be irritation, but Eric could still feel the soft edges of his amusement whispering through the bond. Did *nothing* piss this guy off? For a reported psychopath, he was ridiculously unflappable.

Or was that *because* he was a psychopath?

Eric was too tired to ponder it seriously.

Wolfe rose from the bed in one graceful motion, adjusting his slacks once more around what had to be a painful erection.

Eric tried to stay silent, to let him leave without another word. But he couldn't help the small "thank you" that came out.

He was rewarded with a flash of genuine surprise on Wolfe's face. "Anytime you request my presence, pet, I'll be there."

Eric tried to spot the lie in those words, but maybe his fatigue was making him gullible.

Wolfe sounded like he meant it.

Ten

Wolfe

Wolfe stared at the cooling cum on his fingertips, his back to the door of their as-yet-unfurnished en suite bedroom. He'd barely made it a step inside before he'd been fishing his cock out of his slacks and stroking himself to a hurried completion, furtive and furious, like some kind of hormonal teenager after witnessing their first porno.

But who could blame him? Eric had been simply divine back there, a glorious revelation. That big body trembling with the force of his lust, overwhelmed by his need for Wolfe's presence—not to mention his demand for Wolfe's scent, his kiss—even as he denied himself Wolfe's touch.

He was a perfect specimen: petty and stubborn and gorgeous.

And the *noises* he'd made. It had been almost a shame to cover Eric's mouth with his own, if only for the fact that it muffled all those delicious moans. What sounds would Wolfe draw out of him, once Eric gave in fully to the bond? Wolfe could only imagine a veritable symphony of whimpers, moans, and husky groans.

Want him, Wolfe's beast whined, already itching to be back with their mate.

It had been content enough at Eric's bedside, willing to suppress its urge to claim in order to witness their mate's furious fucking into his fist. But it was all petulance again now that they'd stepped away.

"We have to be patient," Wolfe soothed, feeling uncharacteristically generous after these recent delightful events. "We've frightened him enough."

He did his slacks up with his clean hand, then walked over to the bathroom to wash off his mess, using a few spare drops of water to slick back his hair, which had become very close to mussed in the act of kissing his mate.

He'd lost himself to it, in a way he never had before. Kissing wasn't usually much of a draw for him. It denoted a certain...intimacy he'd never looked for in his sexual encounters. Sex was for release, not connection. What would have been the point?

But with Eric practically begging him for it? Clenching his demanding fist into Wolfe's shirt and giving him a chance to taste those lips, indulge in devouring all those delicious, muffled groans?

It would have taken a saint to resist. And Wolfe was anything but.

He wanted to taste him again, as soon as possible. He wanted his mouth on that girthy cock, wanted to suck out Eric's cum, wanted to drink his blood all over again.

Christ. Wolfe winced at his own reflection, at the greed shining back at him in his own eyes. It wasn't the emotion itself that bothered him but the fact that he was displaying it so obviously.

He was losing control.

This new bond was both too fragile and too strong, consuming and yet unconsummated. He had no choice but to resign himself to a certain discomfort while Eric adjusted, and Wolfe did not generally see fit to abide by discomfort. But if the momentary sacrifice led to more of *that*? More of Eric asking for his presence, his mouth?

Well, then he'd simply have to bear it, wouldn't he?

Fate had provided him with an enticing creature; there was no doubt about that. But it had also presented him with a challenge. No matter. It was one he was surely up for.

Want to go back, his beast grumbled.

Wolfe was saved from answering the demand by the buzzing of his phone. He glanced at the screen, unbearably tempted to let it ring unanswered, but there could be trouble, and he'd made certain promises, ones there would be consequences to breaking.

"Johann," he greeted, turning away from his reflection.

"Wolfgang."

"Checking up on me so soon?" Wolfe kept his tone mild, but he assumed the censure was clear. He was not one to need a set of babysitters.

But trust in Johann to not grasp the nasty subtext. "Um, sort of? Why, did you need something?"

"*You* called *me*, Johann."

A huff of laughter on the other end. "Oh. Right. Well, Danny wanted me to tell you that you should coordinate any future blood theft, if you're thinking on waiting to teach Dr. Monroe to hunt."

Of all the tedious things. Wolfe allowed himself an exasperated sigh. "Eric has already been fed. The other bag will suffice for next week. From then on, he'll be hunting with me." Wolfe's spent cock twitched at the thought of his handsome mate out on the prowl, human blood coating his lips. He would be a sight to see; that was certain.

"But didn't you already steal some?"

"We only took what Danny gave us."

"Oh." Johann seemed to take a second to ponder that. "Hm."

Wolfe waited the appropriate five seconds before pressing. "Johann, please speak plainly or I'm hanging up the phone."

"It's just— The blood bank in town was broken into. That wasn't you?"

As if Wolfe had any need of blood banks. "As I've said."

"Huh. Well, I guess it could have been Tobias."

Trust Johann to bury the lede completely. Wolfe pinched at the bridge of his nose. "So you're saying Tobias came to town already. And did anyone perish in this confrontation?" If Tobias was dead, then Wolfe would have some smoothing over to do with their former den. Another item to add to his ever-growing to-do list. A large part of him hoped to hear Alexei had met his end in the scuffle—that would perhaps be an appropriate punishment for derailing his and Johann's former agreement—but he supposed Johann wouldn't be chatting so happily were that the case.

"No. No fatalities," Johann confirmed. "Soren scared him off."

"How delightful. Well, now Tobias can verify with the others that you're a protected entity."

"Pretty neat, huh? Okay, so..." Wolfe could see it perfectly in his mind's eye, the way Johann would be chewing on his lower lip right about now. "Don't steal any more blood, even if you didn't take what was already taken, okay? I've gotta go do sex stuff with Alexei now."

"Splendid." Wolfe hung up the phone before Johann could spill out any more horrifying sentences. Alexei may have been some delectable eye candy, but Johann was a little too close to familial for Wolfe to want the image of him bouncing on the mobster's cock to haunt him.

He stepped out of the bathroom, eyeing the still-empty bedroom skeptically. He did so hate to leave a room unfinished. But he thought of Eric, who seemed—judging from the sound of his steady breathing and the lack of irritated restlessness coming through the bond—to have finally fallen asleep.

He'd rescheduled the painters to arrive tomorrow. If they did their job promptly, he could have their intended bedroom put together in two days at most.

But really, would it be such a good idea to set the precedent of two furnished bedrooms before they'd had a chance to settle their petty differences? Wolfe could picture it too clearly—Eric taking over the guest bedroom, leaving Wolfe to the en suite all alone.

It simply wouldn't do.

He made another phone call. The paint job could wait another week or so.

Eric didn't come down until the next morning.

He hadn't been asleep the whole time, clearly. Wolfe had been able to hear him shifting around the room intermittently, pacing for close to an hour at one point. Nevertheless, it was almost five a.m. when he finally appeared in the kitchen.

"Darling," Wolfe greeted from his spot at the kitchen table, where he was flipping through a book of tile samples. He figured he'd redo the en suite bathroom as well—he was picturing a dark forest aesthetic for that room also. All of it a lovely, natural green.

Speaking of. Eric's eyes met his from the doorway. They reminded Wolfe of the lakes where he'd grown up, the ones shadowed by the surrounding trees. Those lakes had been dark and deep and full of secrets. Would his mate be the same?

Eric's scowl certainly said he was full of *something*. Vitriol, perhaps.

"I have to go to work," Eric said, crossing his arms over his chest in some semblance of an intimidation tactic.

Wolfe cocked a brow, flipping another page. "You're a vampire now. A soon-to-be very wealthy one. You don't *have* to do anything."

Eric paused, opened his mouth as if to ask a question, then shut it again. He marched over to the closest kitchen cabinets instead, rifling through them in search of something.

Wolfe watched him, admiring the curve of his ass as he bent to peruse the lowest cabinet. Interesting that he didn't bite at the mention of money. It would be best to strike off appealing to his greed, then, in terms of strengthening their bond.

Wolfe would just have to continue to appeal to his lust instead.

He pushed aside the tile samples, leaning forward in his chair. "Are you sure you don't wish to return to bed, pet?" he crooned. "Allow me to...soothe you again?"

He watched in delight as Eric's muscles tensed, the back of his neck darkening in a flush. Anger or arousal? Most likely both, judging from the twinges of emotion Wolfe could feel through their nascent bond.

Eric rose slowly and turned around, his scowl still firmly in place despite his reddened cheeks. "I *want* to go to work, asshole. I'm scheduled today. And Danny said I'm not a captive."

"Did he now?" Wolfe asked mildly.

"Well, am I?"

"I have no reason to stop you from going to the hospital, if you wish to."

The only sign Eric gave that he noticed Wolfe avoiding the real question was the force with which he closed the open cabinet, splintering the wood completely. Eric stared at it for a good thirty seconds before turning to Wolfe, a new, apologetic fix to his features. "Um. I didn't know it would do that."

"You're stronger than you're used to, pet. Not to worry. I was going to redo this kitchen anyway." Wolfe mentally added cabinet samples to his list of growing necessities.

"I was looking for coffee."

Wolfe inclined his head. "I didn't think of it. I'll acquire some."

"Will it— Does caffeine work with vampires?"

"We generally have no need of it. Our energy levels are naturally high, unless we've put off feeding for too long." Wolfe cocked his head, furrowing his brow in mock concern. "Why, darling, are you still fatigued?"

He already knew Eric was. He could feel the same strange lethargy in his own bones, an exhaustion born from resisting his natural urges, the ones his inner beast was now constantly voicing. *Take our mate. Claim our mate.*

Eric only scowled at him anew. "I'll just get some coffee at the hospital."

It won't help you, precious pet. But Wolfe nodded. "Of course. Shall I drive you?"

Wolfe could feel Eric's desire to say yes, just as he could feel his mate's need to draw nearer, to allow Wolfe to touch him, scent him, hold him close. It was a perfect match for the itching under Wolfe's own skin, the one he was trying to distract himself from with these horrid tile samples.

It wasn't right, wasn't natural. Eric shouldn't be leaving to sling medicine at some third-rate hospital. He should be staying by Wolfe's side, sitting on Wolfe's lap, lounging in Wolfe's bed. He should be begging and moaning and whimpering again, letting Wolfe drink down his desperate noises like a fine wine.

Wolfe crossed his legs, hiding his hardening cock from view. It wasn't the time. He needed to let his good doctor make his own mistakes first. The more freedom he allowed Eric, the sooner he would come to his senses and approach Wolfe on his own. As he had the night before.

Wolfe could only hope that would happen soon. Before he snapped completely and locked Eric in that room, kept him confined until he was *forced* to come to his senses. Which would be a pity, as it would ruin all Wolfe's hard work earning the pittance of trust he'd managed to acquire in the last twenty-four hours.

Heavens, but relationships were exhausting, weren't they?

Eric cleared his throat. "I need a shower."

"Across the hall from where you've been resting. Everything is fully stocked."

"Except I don't have any clothes." Eric gestured down to the robe he'd rather tragically placed over his boxer briefs. Wolfe had ended up tossing the shirt Eric had worn to the massage parlor—there had been an awful amount of dried blood on the collar.

Wolfe gestured in the direction of the stairs. "You'll find an assortment of clothing in your size, in the dresser."

"Creepy." The scowl was back again.

Wolfe inclined his chin in agreement, pressing his lips together to stop the smile that wanted to come out. It *was* creepy, perhaps. But his attention to detail was coming in handy now, wasn't it? He decided it best not to say so, however.

He watched Eric leave the kitchen in a huff, wondered how many hours either of their beasts would actually allow this separation. Half of Eric's scheduled shift, perhaps? Less than that?

In the meantime, Wolfe needed something to soothe this new agitation from agreeing to this ridiculous farce. He dug his phone out of the pocket, dialing Tobias's number once he heard the telltale sound of the shower going.

"Wolfe." Tobias's grating voice greeted him in a whine. "I'm already on my way back. I got the message, okay? We'll leave you alone."

"Yes. I heard little Soren gave you quite a scare. Let me just give you a message of my own."

"I already got it, okay?" Tobias hissed, seeming to think he was in a position to direct this conversation.

Poor, misguided Tobias.

"You had children when you were turned, did you not?" Wolfe tugged the book of samples closer, flipping through them again with a discerning eye. He wanted to get the green just right.

There was a long, tense pause on the other end of the line. "Wh-What?"

"Children who had children of their own," Wolfe mused. The upper left tile was *almost* what he wanted, but it was a touch too light for his purposes. “You have quite a line of descendants at this point, Tobias. A fact you’ve been careful to keep hidden from the den.”

“I— How did you...?”

“So.” Wolfe marked the tile anyway, just for comparison purposes. “If you ever come near this den again—if you threaten my new home, perhaps, or if you or your den mates try to siphon off any of Johann’s funds coming my way... Let’s just say there will not be a single trace of your genetic material left on this earth. Do you understand me, Tobias?”

Tobias’s fear was deliciously palpable, even through the phone. “Yes, Wolfe.”

“Good. Carry on with your travels.”

Wolfe hung up. He took a deep breath. There, that was better, wasn’t it? Nothing like threatening the extinction of an entire line of descendants to soothe the savage beast within.

Want our mate. Want him close.

Wolfe shut the book of samples and threw it across the room.

Eleven

Eric

Eric dove into the dictation room, slamming the door behind him.

He just needed a minute. One fucking minute, and maybe then his hands would stop trembling. He glanced at the clock on the wall, taking deep, shaky breaths. He'd made it five whole hours of his shift. Five hours where it had taken everything in him to focus on his patients the way he needed to. But that was fine. He could do seven more, right? Eight if he included the charting he was miles behind on and the report he would need to give to the oncoming doctor. Just eight measly, miserable hours.

Fuck. *Fuck.*

Starting out, he'd been worried the issue would be the blood—that he'd be distracted by it, maybe have to fight from nibbling on his own patients. But it turned out that wasn't the problem. The problem was wanting to run out the door and head right back into the arms of the asshole who'd caused all this.

He'd thought it would be better than this. He'd thought maybe some distance would help shake the hold the psycho vampire seemed to have on him, dim that restless need the beast inside him was crawling with. But it was only worse, somehow. He felt itchy and hot and irritable. And his hands would not stop *shaking*.

He clenched them into fists to stop the tremors, only for his phone to ring in the next second.

Damn it. He checked to make sure it wasn't his mother again—he had ten missed calls from her already, and he wasn't in any state to deal with the consequences of that.

"Monroe." His voice had never sounded so clipped, so irritable.

"Um. Hi, Doctor. It's Sharon from CVICU. So Mrs. Davis?"

He'd just come from that room, damn it. Eric pinched the bridge of his nose, resisting the urge to groan. "Yeah? What now?"

"I saw your order for a liter of fluid?"

"*And*?" Was every one of this nurse's sentences going to come out like a vague question, or was she going to get to the point sometime this year? "You told me you were having to go up on pressers. She's dry."

"Well, yeah. But she's in advanced heart failure. She gets scheduled diuretics as it is."

And he'd just put in an order that could throw her into fluid overload. Like he was a baby resident on his very first day. "Jesus *fucking* Christ."

Sharon's voice went ice-cold. "Excuse me?"

Eric wiped a hand over his face. He was out of line. He was so out of line he was probably going to get a call from the charge nurse in the next two minutes, chastising him for bullying her staff. "Sorry. That wasn't at you. I...stubbed my toe. I'll change it to 250 milliliters. Hold her evening diuretics. Sorry, Sharon."

"Got it." She hung up without another word, no doubt pissed at his tone. She had every right to be. He knew better than to take his temper out on the nurses. It was the cardinal rule in the ICU.

But he didn't want to *be* here anymore. He didn't want to deal with any of this. He didn't want to hold his tongue, to be cheerful and chipper and easygoing.

He wanted to yell. He wanted to rage. He wanted...

He wanted to go home.

Well, not *home*. It wasn't his empty apartment he was craving. He wanted the place where Wolfe was—that big house with a bed made up for a him and a dresser full of clothes that weren't his but were still the perfect size. That place. The one where everything smelled so good and he felt weirdly safe and the only other occupant didn't seem to mind if he was pissy or pouty or a major pain in the ass.

But no. Eric had, for whatever reason, wanted to work. He'd *had* to work. Because vampire or not, this was what he did. This was who he was. The only little bit of good he offered to the world.

And if he could just have a minute alone, it would be fine.

No patients. No phone calls. He could get this under control. He *could*.

Thirty seconds passed before there was a knock on the door.

Eric considered throwing his phone at it. "I'm busy," he bit out instead.

"Dr. Monroe?" The voice was familiar, but it wasn't the one Eric wanted to hear. It didn't have the smooth, clipped tones, the sexy accent.

Wolfe was supposed to be Eric's mate, right? His bonded soul or whatever? So why wasn't he *here*? Shouldn't he be around, when Eric was suffering? He'd said he'd be there if Eric needed him.

Wolfe was clearly a liar.

"Eric."

"*What*?" Eric snarled, yanking open the door. It wasn't until he saw Danny on the other side, the shocked look in his big brown eyes, that Eric realized he'd finally lost the battle and accidentally let his vampire face out. And apparently—judging from the cracking sound and the odd tilt to the door—broken the dictation room door right off its hinges.

"Oh my fucking God." Danny—who apparently was also much stronger than he looked—shoved Eric back inside with one push, knocking him out of the line of sight from the doorway. "You have your fangs out!" he whisper-yelled.

Eric clapped a hand over his mouth. "I didn't mean to!"

"Well, put them *back*," Danny hissed, fighting with the door to get it to close as best he could.

"I *can't*." Eric slid down into a crouch, his back against the wall. He was trying; he really was. He couldn't be wandering around the hospital with his fangs out. But it was like the beast inside him had broken free and wasn't going back anytime soon. The word *mate* just kept ringing through his head, over and over, like some sort of chant. Like it was that *thing* talking and not his own brain, and everything else was just...fog.

He was vaguely aware of the sounds of Danny, hovering over him, talking on the phone. "Where are you? Well, drive *faster*."

Then Danny was crouched as well, his face directly in Eric's line of sight, eyes full of surprisingly fierce concern. "Hey. Hey, look at me. It's going to be okay."

He sounded so sure. So confident. So caring.

"You're a good nurse, aren't you?" Eric asked dreamily, his gaze drifted off somewhere over Danny's shoulder, focused on nothing in particular. This was his life now, wasn't it? This freak-show mayhem was his foreseeable future.

"And you're way out of it," Danny said, his brow furrowed. "He should have come sooner."

"Who should have?"

Wolfe. Wolfe should have come.

But no. "Gabe," Danny said instead. "He's coming to take over the rest of your shift. But he was a ways off. I was closer, so I came to make sure you weren't— Um..."

Eric tried to focus his gaze back on Danny, the faintest hint of amusement breaking through his dazed state. "Eating the patients?"

Danny shrugged. "Well, yeah. Or whatever the hell this is."

"How did you know something was wrong?" Had Eric been so out of it one of the nurses had called Danny? But that didn't make any sense. Why would they call Danny? No one here knew they were...friends? Vampire accomplices?

“Wolfe called me. Told me to fetch Gabe. He used that word too. ‘Fetch.’ Like he’s my dog instead of my brother.”

“He did?” Warmth filled Eric’s chest at the thought. Not the “fetch” part, although that was kind of funny. But Wolfe *had* known. See? Eric had known he would.

Eric was also clearly losing his mind.

But then he heard it. The distinct tapping of dress shoes on hospital linoleum. And the sounds of Albert, one of the security guards, arguing furtively. “Sir, you need a visitor’s badge.”

“I’m not a visitor.”

Ohhh, Eric knew that voice. There it was, what he’d been waiting for the moment he’d left the house.

Albert’s voice took on a panicked edge. “Listen, you can’t be up here.”

“I believe you’ll find that I can.”

The voices grew louder; the steps came closer.

And then he was there, in the doorway, looking fierce as an avenging angel. An avenging angel in a tweed fucking suit.

Eric held his breath as Wolfe looked him over, those weird eyes shining red under the fluorescents; he let it out again as that fierce wave of possessiveness rushed over him through the bond. There was irritation there as well. Possibly even concern? But for some reason, it was that familiar possessiveness that had Eric wanting to whimper in relief from his spot on the floor.

Wolfe glanced briefly at Danny and jerked his chin to the side, where Albert was hovering over his shoulder, his gaze luckily still firmly focused on Wolfe and not Eric’s freaky face. “Deal with this one before I do something you’ll regret.”

Danny rushed forward to placate the security guard, pulling him out of Eric’s line of sight.

Eric didn’t give them another thought. Not with Wolfe crouching in front of him, so close Eric could touch the little furrowed lines between his brows if he wanted to. That lovely smell enveloped him, bright and comforting.

It was weird that he smelled that way, right? Shouldn't he smell like brimstone or something?

"Darling," Wolfe purred, his eyes traveling greedily over Eric's face.

Right. It was his first time seeing Eric as a vampire. Because Eric hadn't been able to control himself for even half a goddamn shift.

Eric didn't know what to say. He looked down at his hands, clenched on top of his knees, flooded with a new embarrassment. For his neediness. For his loss of control.

Wolfe cupped his face, his long fingers surprisingly warm. "Darling, look at me." Eric looked up. "Relax, pet. As lovely as he is, your beast can go back in now. I'm here."

Eric let out another slow, shaky breath, felt his features relax incrementally. His fangs receded, and the clenching in his chest loosened for the first time in hours.

Wolfe was here.

"How did you know to come get me?" Eric asked, his gaze locked onto Wolfe's side profile as the other vampire steered them into their house's driveway. No, not *their* house. *Wolfe's* house.

He had only the vaguest recollection of them leaving the hospital itself. Fuzzy images of fluorescent hallways, a blurry memory of Danny taking his work phone to give to Gabe in the parking lot. They'd passed some kid in the hallway—and really, who was letting their kid wander around the hospital unsupervised?—who'd looked weirdly horrified, which didn't bode well for what Eric must have looked like.

But mostly what he remembered of the last fifteen minutes was the strong, comforting presence of Wolfe's hand gripping his upper arm to guide him out, coupled with the terrifying looks the vampire had given to anyone who seemed the slightest bit likely to get in their way.

Eric had asked the question partly because he was curious—had Wolfe simply tired of giving him the pretense of freedom?—but mostly because he wasn't ready to go in yet, to admit fully that he'd taken one meager shot at independence and ended up falling flat on his fanged face.

"I felt your distress." Wolfe kept his eyes straight ahead, on the house in front of them. "I'd been feeling it since the moment you left, of course, but about an hour ago, it started to...peak. So I called your nurse friend and I came."

Eric stared at him, at those sharp cheekbones, that aristocratic profile.

Wolfe said it like it was so simple. Eric had needed him, so he had come, without Eric even having to ask. No begging, not this time.

A memory came to Eric then. A two-week leadership camp he'd been shuttled off to between his sophomore and junior years of high school. A few days in and he'd started having nausea and abdominal pain. The nurse had told him he was only homesick, so he'd called his mother instead. Told her he needed to come home, to go to the doctor. She'd refused. She'd refused for three straight days. What he'd actually needed, according to her, was that camp on his college applications. The pain had finally grown to such an intensity that the camp nurse sent him to the ER. It had been appendicitis. All the surgical consents had had to be signed over the phone because his mother couldn't "just drop everything and be there in an hour."

He'd woken up in recovery alone.

"Why this sadness, pet? You wish I had not come?"

Eric refocused his eyes to see Wolfe had turned to look at him, his head cocked.

He didn't know what to say. He *wished* he regretted Wolfe coming to pick him up, wished he weren't grateful to the very person who'd put him in this position in the first place. The fatigue he'd been feeling ever since he'd woken up was heavier than ever.

If this was what being a vampire felt like, then frankly, it sucked.

Eric pressed a palm against his forehead. "What am I going to do? We can't be apart for half a day."

Wolfe seemed to debate with himself for a minute, a strange stillness taking over his face. Then he sighed, shaking his head softly. "As lovely as it would be to have you thinking you need me so desperately, I'm afraid it won't always be like this. You're newly turned; we're...at odds. It's all very unstable."

Unstable was right. "So what do we do?"

Wolfe arched a brow. "We bond."

He said it so simply, like it was the easiest thing. Like Eric had any experience at all building a relationship that lasted for more than a few hurried, sweaty hours. "*How*?"

"How does any new relationship grow?" Wolfe waved a hand in the air. "Time spent together, conversation." His eyes gleamed with a wicked glint. "Sex."

A shock of arousal hit Eric in the belly, the fog of his fatigue shredding apart in an instant. Just like that, he was hardening in his scrubs.

What the fuck?

The unexpected arousal to such a simple word made him petulant again. "But I need to work," he insisted.

Wolfe's jaw ticked. "As I told you before, you don't."

"But I *want* to work?" It came out like a question.

Wolfe narrowed his eyes at him, obviously latching onto the uncertainty embedded in Eric's insistence, before leaning across the console, unbuckling Eric's seat belt. "Our first conversation to be had, then. Which we will have inside, in the comfort of our home."

Again, he said it so simply. *Our* home.

And Eric just...followed him inside. Docile as a lamb. He watched as Wolfe selected (after *very* careful consideration, picking up and then replacing bottle after bottle) a suitable wine, fetched two long-stemmed glasses, and ushered him up to what Eric had started to think of as his bedroom.

Wolfe set the wine and glasses down on the bedside table, sat on the edge of the bed, and patted the spot beside him. "Sit, darling."

Eric sat.

Wolfe poured the wine with all the flair of a fine restaurant's best sommelier. "So. Why do you feel you need to work? Because if it's a matter of money, we have enough."

Eric tried to think, to find the words. He came up miserably short. "It's just...what I do?"

"And they can't survive without you for a few days? If it's a matter of not losing your position long-term, it's simple enough to compel whomever necessary into giving you short-term medical leave."

Eric was having trouble focusing. Wolfe was here with him, and it was better than when he wasn't, but it still wasn't quite right. He shook his head, frustrated. "No, no. They can survive. It's not like I'm the best." He gave a bitter laugh. "Far from it."

"Are you a terrible doctor, then?" Wolfe asked the question mildly, like it didn't matter one way or another to him what Eric's answer was.

But Eric couldn't answer him. He was thinking maybe he should be in Wolfe's lap. That would be better, right? Then he could nuzzle his head right there, at the crook of Wolfe's neck, where that stupid suit stopped covering his skin, and breathe him in properly.

But that would be crazy. He had at least an inch and probably forty pounds on the guy; Eric couldn't just ask to be held like a little baby.

"CanIholdyourhand?" The question fell out of his mouth before he could stop it, all jumbled up into a single word. But it was hard to be embarrassed when fierce satisfaction gleamed red in Wolfe's eyes at the request.

"Of course, darling." Wolfe turned the hand closest to Eric palm up in invitation. "You can touch me whenever and however you like."

Eric grabbed at the offered hand. Took a deep breath. Scooted closer to Wolfe after all.

It wasn't perfect, but it was better. His head felt infinitesimally clearer.

Wolfe took a slow sip of his wine with his free hand. "So you're a bad doctor." Again, he said it so mildly.

"No." Eric swayed a little toward Wolfe, righted himself back up immediately. "I'm just not very good."

"I see." Wolfe offered the other glass to Eric, set it back down when he shook his head in refusal. "Do you lose an above average number of patients?"

"No."

"Get an unusual number of complaints from your nurses?"

"No."

"You're not advancing in your career as you should?"

"I just don't...care enough," Eric concluded, fully pathetic.

"Pardon?" For the first time that afternoon, Wolfe sounded genuinely surprised.

"I don't care like I should. I only went into all this because it's what my parents steered me toward. I've seen some doctors—like King, he can get really worked up after losing a patient. Really despondent. I never get that way. I just—I shake it off. I don't think about them afterward. I don't beat myself up. And I fucking *hate* comforting the families. I just feel like a fake, unfeeling asshole."

"Most of that sounds like healthy compartmentalization to me. I'd say it's more likely your Dr. Kingman puts himself at risk for burnout." Wolfe took another sip of his wine. "Makes him the worse doctor in my opinion."

Eric laughed in surprise. "You can't say that."

"Why not?"

"Everyone loves King. He's very..." Eric waved his free hand in the air, trying to find the word. "Likable."

Wolfe set his wine glass aside, huffing dismissively. "I don't see anything very special about him."

Meaning Wolfe saw something special about Eric? Or did the fact that they were fated make him special enough, no matter what he was like underneath? The thought should piss Eric off, but it was weirdly comforting. He didn't have to be good, or perfect, or friendly, or nice. His existence was enough for Wolfe.

How strangely freeing.

He sighed, placing their joined hands on his lap, toying with Wolfe's long, elegant fingers. If it didn't matter what he was like—if Wolfe was going to accept him no matter what—he might as well get it all out. "I was a really shitty doctor today, probably, but all I can seem to care about is my own shit. And when Danny first told me I had to drink human blood, I didn't even think about killing people. I was only thinking about myself. I think something's wrong with me. Like I lack an empathy chip."

"Mm." Wolfe seemed to take that in without judgment, as he did everything Eric said. Then he smirked. "Do you think I sit around fretting over my lack of empathy?"

"I don't know, do you?"

"I most certainly don't. There's nothing wrong with you, Eric. Maybe you're selfish." He shrugged a shoulder. "I find most people are. If I had to do the job you do, I would last barely an hour before murdering every patient on my caseload and fleeing into the night, off to find a better use of my time."

It was a horrifying statement, so why couldn't Eric find it in himself to be horrified?

Eric's head found its way onto Wolfe's shoulder, like it had a mind of its own. He didn't have the will to pick it back up. "If you lack empathy, why are you being so comforting right now?"

Wolfe's head came to rest on top of his. "But I'm not. I'm only speaking logically. It's just your anxieties happen to be very illogical."

What a dick.

"But you came for me, when I needed you."

"I take care of what's mine. And you're mine, Eric. You may take your time to adjust, you may throw fits or try to hide in your work or deny it all completely, but you're already mine. You have been since the moment I laid eyes on you."

The thought was overwhelming, mainly in how appealing it was. That new beast inside him surged in agreement, a strange feeling like a cat's purr rumbling in Eric's chest.

He forced himself to let go of that hand, to stand up from the bed. "I'm going to shower again. I feel all grimy from the hospital."

And he needed space. For just a minute, even if it was painful. Because he was realizing fully that this was real. This was happening: he was bonded to a vampire he didn't know, who drew him in and frightened him with his intensity in equal measure. Who claimed he didn't know how to care, not in the traditional sense, but was still there when Eric needed him.

And while Eric wasn't perfect—wasn't even very good—he wasn't a complete coward.

He was going to shower. He was going to take some deep, steady breaths before possibly screaming into a towel. And then he was going to get this vampire's hands all over him.

They were going to *bond*, goddamn it.

Twelve

Wolfe

Wolfe made good use of his time while Eric was in the shower. He first poured more wine for both of them, then removed his shoes as well as his suit jacket and set them both aside, undoing the top three buttons on his dress shirt as he did so.

There was a large part of him that wished to strip off completely, to stride into that bathroom and take what was his—bend that big, gorgeous body over and plunge his cock into that muscled ass, the one that had felt so wonderful under his hands in that tacky massage parlor.

Patience, he reminded both himself and the beast within him. *Patience.*

His careful approach was paying off, if they could both just rein themselves in long enough to let it. Wolfe had sensed a surrender of sorts from Eric just now. And all Wolfe had to do to keep the doctor's walls from bouncing right back up was keep the beast under control a little while longer.

It wasn't easy, with how keyed up they both were. Eric's distress had been...well, it had been *distressing*. Wolfe had never before been so unsettled by someone else's discomfort, and he couldn't say he was a fan of the feeling. He should have—if anything—felt triumphant; it was proof, after all, that Eric needed him. Payback, even, for his leaving their home and insisting on his independence. But Wolfe had only felt agitated. Helpless. Angry. He'd wanted to burn that hospital down for the offense of being the obstacle between him and his mate.

It seemed as if Eric wasn't the only one who was unstable.

But they were going to fix that, weren't they? And it seemed that it might not be as difficult as Wolfe had first imagined. Eric had responded to Wolfe's coming to fetch him like Wolfe had slain a literal dragon for him, a response completely at odds with the simplicity of the act itself. Wolfe's mate was clearly unused to receiving care of any kind.

Really, for someone who gave off the impression of an empty-headed, baby-faced playboy, Eric had been displaying a wonderfully potent mix of neuroses: a need to be liked, a need to be useful, both coupled with a deep-seated belief that he was inherently neither. That he was, for some reason, unworthy at his core.

Idly, Wolfe picked up Eric's phone, which he'd tossed so carelessly on the bed on the way to his shower. He pressed the pass code he'd watched Eric enter earlier that morning and went through a cursory inspection of his missed calls and messages.

And there. Just as he'd thought. An overbearing mother who wasn't at all afraid to insult her son in written messages. It really was marvelous, the damage a parent could do to a child's psyche, well into that child's adulthood. Wolfe wasn't sure if he wanted to tear her head off her shoulders for troubling his mate so, or send her a gift basket for creating such a toxic familial environment that even Wolfe's particular brand of caring would seem golden in comparison. He had no doubt there was some absent, unemotional, possibly toxically masculine father in the background to thank as well. No wonder Eric was so deliciously needy, greedy for affection in whatever form he could get it.

And Wolfe would oblige.

But first, he would devour.

His ears perking up at the sound of the shower shutting off, Wolfe set the phone neatly on the nightstand, next to their wine, then relaxed back against the headboard with his legs crossed at the ankles, his own glass of wine in hand.

Wolfe was incredibly pleased to see Eric hadn't bothered getting fully dressed, beads of water dripping down the bare expanse of glistening chest, his slim hips barely covered by his towel, his poor cock already tenting the terry-cloth fabric.

"Darling," Wolfe purred.

Eric stood there for a long moment, staring him down. What conclusions had his dear one come to in that shower? The bond was giving Wolfe very little to go by, other than the sweet surge of arousal and cautious tendrils of nervousness coming from his mate.

"Come here," Wolfe ordered, voice soft as silk, pleased beyond measure when Eric complied, taking long, shaky steps to the bed and stopping there, making no move to get onto the bed itself.

Wolfe took a small sip of his wine. "How gorgeous you are. Are you going to let me touch you?"

A nod from Eric, who had a delicious flush on his cheeks, either from the heat of the shower or Wolfe's praising words.

"Taste you?"

Another nod.

Satisfaction hummed through Wolfe's veins. "Wonderful. Why don't you lie down on the bed, pet."

Eric cautiously crawled over Wolfe's legs to do so. Really. One would think the man a fluttering virgin, rather than the local Lothario, with the tentative way he was following each of Wolfe's commands. No matter.

Wolfe could be gentle.

He handed his glass of wine to Eric, his lips twitching in amusement when the man downed it in one swallow. He took the empty glass from him and set it out of the way, turning onto his side and resting his head on one fist, an exact replica of their positions their first time together.

But it wouldn't be *Eric's* hand gripping that magnificent cock this time.

Wolfe let his gaze travel slowly over the glorious sight in front of him. He didn't request Eric remove the towel yet; there was enough skin on display to play with for the moment.

He started slow, tracing the muscles of Eric's shoulder with one finger before moving along to his collarbone. He enjoyed immensely the way Eric trembled beneath his touch. And when Wolfe idly circled one nipple, Eric's breath hitched noticeably.

Wolfe's lips curled. "Sensitive, are we?"

"What are you going to— I mean—" Eric swallowed hard, the sound audible in the quiet room. "What do you *want* to do to me?"

"I'd massacre legions to fuck you," Wolfe answered honestly, circling the other nipple with his finger, watching it peak. A subtle flinch from his mate, not at Wolfe's touch, but at his words. Wolfe smirked. "Why, darling, have you never had a cock up there?"

Eric shook his head, those shadowy green eyes locked onto Wolfe's, and Wolfe's stomach swooped at the thought. "But you've been with a man before," he clarified.

"Yes." Eric's voice was deliciously hoarse. "More than once." He paused, rectified. "A lot more than once."

Wolfe didn't think too hard about those who had come before him. He had no reason to mind, as long as it was all in the past.

Eric's future would be Wolfe and only Wolfe.

"Other way around, then?"

Eric cleared his throat. It was adorable, this strange shyness coming from him. "Sometimes. But mostly, just like, blow jobs. Frottage. Hand stuff. A lot of one-night stands don't want to go...there."

"Mm. Shame. You have such a beautiful cock. They should have been begging for it." Wolfe dipped a finger beneath Eric's towel, tugging gently. "Show me."

Eric undid his towel with trembling fingers. So darling, how keyed up he was. Wolfe stroked the smooth pale skin of his freshly revealed hips. "And tell me, has anyone ever tasted that virgin hole?"

His answer was a slack-jawed shake of the head.

"Fingers, perhaps?"

A slow nod.

"Toys?"

Another, more hesitant nod.

"Glorious." Wolfe let out a happy sigh. "I'm all up to speed. Now what would *you* like me to do with this gorgeous body of yours, darling? Touch it? Taste it?"

Eric only stared, but the surge of lust at "taste" was unmistakable.

Wolfe started with the neck, at the exact spot where he'd bitten him in that massage parlor. He had its location memorized, that particular tender bit of skin. He placed his lips there, kissing softly before nipping it with blunt teeth. "Your blood was the most delicious thing I've ever had the pleasure of sampling," he murmured. "Is it any wonder my beast didn't want to stop?"

The reminder clearly woke Eric from his shaky, pseudovirginal trance. He pulled back slightly to glower at Wolfe. "Don't remind me. I can feel how smug you are."

"Can you?" Wolfe closed the distance between them again, licking along the taut line of Eric's neck. "And is it any wonder? Just look at you. Who wouldn't be smug, having you at their fingertips?"

"Plenty of people."

Oh, but the hurt ran deep with this one. Wolfe could see it perfectly: a young man, whose idiotic parents were incapable of showing proper affection, searching desperately for love. Perhaps the first time he'd reached out, the desperation had been too palpable, and he was summarily rejected and shamed. He'd learned to expect only the superficial.

Wolfe grabbed Eric's chin, turning his head to meet his eyes. He wanted this message to hit home. "Idiots, all of them."

He would erase them from Eric's memory. With his touch, with his devotion. He tilted Eric's head back and dipped his tongue into the hollow of his throat, pleased with the tiny whine Eric let out in response. And then he sampled the subtle variation of flavors in each new bit of skin. There was no salt or sweat, not after the shower. All clean soap. But underneath that, that lovely scent of wisteria. Not a trace of that horrid aftershave. Which was no surprise, as Wolfe hadn't stocked any in their new home.

Generally, Wolfe would take his time. Restraint had never been a hardship for him in bed, as lust had never been all-consuming for him. But here. Now. Wolfe could *feel* Eric's need, each new tendril of arousal that blossomed so beautifully under Wolfe's touch.

His exploration was cursory at best, rushed. It was hard to take his time when every touch of his tongue or nip of his teeth pulled little groans and grunts and pants from his desperate mate. Wolfe didn't last long at all before he was moving from his position and traveling down that long, built body. He hovered over Eric's cock, delighting in the angry red color of the tip.

Eric let out a harsh breath. "A-Are you going to suck me?"

"I am." But not like Eric thought. "Turn over, pet."

If Eric was confused at the request, he didn't show it. He rolled over instantly onto his stomach, by all appearances content to let Wolfe run the show.

"Spread your legs a little wider, darling."

Oh, but he was scrumptious like this. Eric may not have been some die-hard gym bunny, but his shoulders were naturally broad, his legs muscled and lightly furred. There was strength there, more than Wolfe himself had naturally had in his human life, surely.

Wolfe ran his hands along those broad shoulders, those pale hips. He squeezed that muscled ass, earning a strange little sigh from his mate.

"You have really nice hands," Eric said, sounding almost drowsy.

Amused, Wolfe gave him another squeeze, elicited another sigh. "Wait until you see what my tongue can do."

Wolfe slid onto his belly, ignoring his own aching cock and placing himself between those spread thighs. He pulled Eric's cheeks apart, revealing the pink furl in between. He didn't hesitate. He didn't tease. He licked him in one long swipe.

"Oh my fucking *God.*"

Wolfe smirked. "How's that, darling?"

He didn't wait for a response. He licked again. No words of blasphemy from his mate this time, only a hitch of breath. Wolfe placed more focus on Eric's hole, wetting it with his tongue, teasing it with his lips. Softening it to the point where he could stick the tip of his tongue inside, exploring and stretching. The strangled noise Eric made in response was really a thing of beauty.

Here, Wolfe *did* take his time. He lost himself in devouring his mate. He was consumed by his scent, by his sounds, by the clean, musky taste of him.

It was Eric's squirming that brought Wolfe back, his hips wriggling like a fish on the line. Wolfe raised his face from his new ideal of nirvana. "Too much, pet?"

"*Wolfe.*" He said it with full, plaintive desperation. "I need to fucking come. *Please.*"

"Ah." Wolfe supposed all fun had to end at some point. He could empathize, at least. His own cock was no doubt ruining his trousers, staining them with precum. It was a shame though. He squeezed Eric's cheeks again before reaching beneath him to pull Eric's cock back between his legs, wetting one of his own fingers as he did so. Wolfe slid down further and sucked the tip into his mouth.

Eric keened. "*Jesus*."

Wolfe slid the tip of his finger into Eric's hole, sucking with more fervor. He was done with gentle. Eric let out one last, hoarse yell, and then Wolfe's mouth was filling with his salty, bitter essence, his mate's muscular body twitching and trembling under his hands.

"Oh my God. Oh my fucking God. Jesus Christ."

His mate was awfully blasphemous in his postcoital state.

But now Wolfe was reminded of his own painfully hard cock. Eric wasn't the only one who needed to come. And if Wolfe couldn't claim him fully, couldn't yet stick his cock where it rightfully belonged, then he was going to do the next best thing.

He was going to mark that gorgeous face.

Wolfe flipped Eric easily onto his back, moving up to straddle his chest. Eric's face was beautifully dazed, his eyes half-lidded, his mouth slack.

Perfect.

Wolfe freed his cock from the restriction of his suit pants. He stroked himself furiously. He had no patience for finesse, for delayed gratification. Not with his balls heavy and taut, his frame so rigid with unreleased tension he felt he might snap.

When he came, spraying his cum all over that gorgeous face, white spots danced along the edges of his vision, jolts of electricity running along his spine.

Wolfe let out a satisfied sigh, studying his handiwork. Those green eyes stared back at him, shock widening them. White dripped along his cheeks, his chin.

Eric licked at his lips, at the traces of Wolfe's cum there. "Is this your idea of bonding?"

Wolfe let himself laugh, low and mean. "Oh, darling, we're just getting started."

Thirteen

Wolfe

"I'm not sore at all."

Even though Eric was facing into the apartment, his broad back to Wolfe, habit more than anything else had Wolfe fighting to keep his lips from curling. "Well, darling, if you recall, I never gave you much more than a finger."

"Still—" Eric turned from the perusal of his apartment—his *old* apartment—to shrug at him. "It was, you know...all night."

Now Wolfe's lips *did* curl. It had indeed been all night, somewhat of a full-time job, really, ringing orgasm after orgasm from his trembling mate, bringing himself to finish maybe once for every three of Eric's own. By the time Eric had begged off, claiming oversensitivity and "serious dehydration" (impossible as a recently fed vampire, but the body sometimes took a while to adjust its expectations), the sun had been cresting over the horizon, and their mutual fatigue had officially dispersed.

It seemed their bond had begun to solidify, as intended. As evidenced by the new pep in Eric's step as he led Wolfe into his former bedroom. And by the smug, satiated little snake Wolfe's beast had turned into. Whether the stabilizing effect had more to do with Wolfe coming for Eric when he was needed or their new sexual connection, he couldn't really say. And why should he care either way? He had no intention of breaking either habit anytime soon. Or ever.

It was new, this calm contentment radiating off Eric. Wolfe stopped in the doorway of the room, assessing it. He had so far only known his mate stressed, confused, restless, agitated, or lustful (or a strange combination of all of the above). But this morning, pawing through a drawer of what appeared to be loungewear, the connection between them pulsed with something soft and sweet, like nothing Wolfe had ever experienced in his own limited emotional repertoire before.

He wanted more of it.

He stepped inside the bedroom—somehow both messy and unkempt while simultaneously underfilled and underfurnished—keeping a careful eye on his mate, ready to step in if he made one move toward the bottle of aftershave on the dresser. But Eric only finished throwing his selected heap of clothes into a duffel, then stopped, hands on his hips, a somewhat lost expression on his face. "How much of my stuff should I take?"

Wolfe stepped idly over to Eric's closet, checking if there was anything in there he might especially like to see his mate wear. "As much as you might need, to entertain you during your leave."

It had been a simple enough matter, calling in and claiming leave for a medical emergency. There were an unholy number of forms to fill out, of course. But that was a small price to pay to have what Wolfe had begun to think of as their pseudohoneymoon uninterrupted by Eric's work schedule. And if compulsion became necessary later down the line, Wolfe would make it happen.

"Like what?" Eric asked.

Wolfe cocked his head, turning from the closet. Eric seemed truly perplexed by the thought. "How do you usually entertain yourself?"

Eric shrugged. "Well, I work."

"Yes, we've established that."

Eric gestured to some texts he had piled up underneath his laptop. "And I catch up on medical research on my days off. Work out semiregularly." He glanced down at his body, then back up to Wolfe. "I guess I don't have to do that anymore?"

"Not as such."

Eric nodded. "And I go out at night. Try to get laid."

Over Wolfe's undead body. "Mm. Well, we have that taken care of already, don't we?"

Eric must have picked up on his miffed tone. He arched his brows, a new, challenging set to his posture. "People think I'm a bit of a slut."

Wolfe waved a hand. "We've also already established people are idiots."

"I do sleep around though."

"You *did* sleep around." Wolfe studied his mate, who now had his head turned away, avoiding eye contact. What exactly was Eric trying to make happen with this? Was he looking for some sort of hall pass, underestimating the fervor of Wolfe's possessive nature? Wolfe thought not. Eric clearly lusted after Wolfe, if nothing else. Was he perhaps a glutton for chastisement? No, Eric was sensitive to barbs, even if he didn't show it superficially. Or was he offering himself up for judgment before he could be blindsided by it?

Yes, that was it.

Wolfe tsked. "You know, darling, there is no inherent morality entwined with someone's number of lovers. Zero, ten, a hundred. It means nothing, if all parties were consenting. Only misguided puritan attitudes say otherwise."

Yes, Wolfe had gotten it right. Soft tendrils of relief emanated from Eric, more than Wolfe had expected.

And then Eric was no longer avoiding eye contact at all, instead grinning almost cheekily at him. "So you wouldn't mind if I upped that body count?"

Wolfe stepped forward before he could stop himself, his voice coming out harsher than he would have liked. "Not unless you also want to up the number of corpses in Hyde Park. You are *mine*, Eric Monroe." Wolfe cleared his throat, forcing himself to take a step back again. "Now collect your belongings."

It was a meager sampling in the end. Eric's laptop. The few clothes he seemed to feel some sentimental attachment to. And an assortment of medical textbooks he clearly referenced often.

Wolfe frowned at the half-full duffle. "Any other books, perhaps?"

Eric rubbed at the back of his neck, a flush darkening his cheeks. "Um, I don't really read. Or, I read a lot, but it's all medical stuff. These guys, some online journals, articles old classmates send me. I guess that makes me pretty boring, huh?"

Did Eric have a single thought about himself that wasn't mired in feelings of worthlessness? It seemed not. Wolfe cocked his head, considering. "You value knowledge and expertise. If anything, it denotes a curiosity about the world as it is, not as it might be. We'll stop at the bookstore and pick up a few nonfiction options for you. Medical-adjacent, to start. We'll see what other interests we can perk up in that lovely brain of yours."

He was rewarded with more of that soft, sweet feeling. It was so easy to bring up now that Wolfe knew the recipe. His physical presence and support, some logical reassurance against Eric's insecurities.

Perhaps relationships weren't so difficult after all.

Or perhaps it was simply that Eric was perfect for him, in all his imperfections.

And now Wolfe was becoming absolutely sentimental. He could rival Johann at this point.

Despite that sweet contentedness, Eric narrowed his eyes at him, suspicious. "Why are you being so nice to me? Like you...care." He tilted his head. "You don't care, right? Or you can't?"

The "can't" was debatable, and Wolfe wasn't in the mood for debate. He went for the simple truth. "I desire for you to be happy. Content."

"Why? To stabilize the bond?"

Wolfe crossed over to him, threading his fingers in Eric's hair and tugging gently to make sure he was listening to every word. "Because—as I believe I have made clear—You. Are. Mine. Given to me by fate herself. *Made* for me. I take care of my possessions, Eric. It *pleases me* to take care of you."

There. That would ruin this new, sweet softness between them, wouldn't it? People didn't usually like being referred to as possessions. It may have been Wolfe's particular brand of caring, but it wasn't a popular one.

But Eric only shrugged, the suspicious cant to his expression easing. "Okay. That makes sense."

Poor, emotionally neglected Dr. Monroe. But it was working in Wolfe's favor, so he let it lie for the moment. He sighed, releasing his hold and taking the duffel from Eric's hands. "What else do you do to relax, pet?"

Eric hummed in thought. "Maybe fishing? My dad took me a few times when I was a kid. We ate what we caught, which made my mom happy. She liked fresh fish."

Not surprising that even in his relaxation, Eric felt he needed to be useful to his parents. "It's winter, darling. The lakes are frozen over."

"Oh, right. Um, I don't know, then."

Wolfe directed him out of the bedroom. "You were out the other night. The first time I saw you. With friends."

Eric stiffened under his touch for a moment, perhaps with the realization of just how long Wolfe had been watching him. But it eased quickly, and he shook his head. "They were just medical reps in town. We had drinks and laughs. They left again. Not friends, just acquaintances."

It was proof enough that Wolfe was rotten, in just how much that pleased him. Ah well, he already knew his faults well enough.

But how to amuse Eric in the meantime? Wolfe would like to think the two of them together, completely isolated from the world, would be enough. But Eric was used to a fast-paced, high-stress profession. And though Wolfe would be teaching him to hunt soon enough, he didn't intend to start until the other blood bag had been used up. Waste not, want not, after all. And that would give them more time for the bond to stabilize before Eric attempted a fresh feed. Wolfe wouldn't want any unexpected complications, or to have his poor doctor arrested for murder.

Eric gave a dejected sigh. "See why I need to work?"

Wolfe tsked at him. "Just because you've been stunted until now doesn't mean you need to remain stunted."

And Wolfe wanted more of this sweet, soft contentment. What made normal people content? Other people, it seemed. Connections. So perhaps Wolfe would have to resign himself to using a few of his own.

"You remember Danny?" he asked.

Eric shot him an amused glance. "The nurse I work with, who explained vampires to me, who also saved my bacon when I was freaking out at the hospital? Yeah, the name rings a bell."

Wolfe ignored the sass. "Perfect. Well, it just so happens he hosts a regular dinner for our kind..."

The purpose of the family dinners may not have been vampire bonding, but that was beside the point. Eric needed friends. Wolfe would prefer for them to be people he already had full knowledge of. So Eric would be attending the next family dinner.

And Wolfe knew just who to ask for an invitation.

Wolfe eyed the portrait on the sitting room wall, all lush tones with a simple frame. Refined but not ostentatious, like much of the furnishing in Veronique's home. Still, to the discerning eye, it was clear the expense she had gone to in decorating the place; money had gone into it. An awful lot of money. In fact, among just the three of this heinous den's leaders lay an exorbitant sum, enough to keep an entire community of vampires in comfort for many, many years.

Which was exactly why the leaders had to go.

It should be easy enough to orchestrate, better yet with some sort of catalyst to help him along. Silas in particular had the look of one not long for the land of the sane—so much aggression there, even for one of their kind. And granted, he seemed to naturally be quite a prick regardless, but there was just a touch of...something there. He was a vampire on the road to a feral state, even if only on the first steps.

Maybe Wolfe would get lucky and Silas would tear into the other two without any prompting. Because Wolfe had done his research, over these past few years. Slowly, slyly, making sure not to create any waves. And with those three gone, it would all belong to—

"Wolfgang? You're here early. Are you looking for Vee?"

Ah. Wolfe turned from his perusal to see the object of his musings in front of him. Johann. The epitome of sweetness itself, even if his naturally sunny demeanor was somewhat dimmed by Vee's emotionally careless handling. He was carrying a tray with an assortment of fine crystal and two bottles of port, most likely for the guests after their feeding. Veronique did so love the old-fashioned methods of entertaining, never mind that the world around them was immersed in modernity. Take Johann's proper little suit, fit for a young country lord half a century ago, his dark hair slicked back severely to match.

Wolfe aimed a calculated smile at the little vampire. "It's really Veronique who's looking for me. Or, better put, on my behalf."

Johann cocked his head, wordlessly questioning, as he placed his tray on the mahogany of the bar area to the side of the room.

"She's finding a book I'd like to borrow," Wolfe explained.

"Which book?" Johann asked, apparently unable to help trying to be of service, even as he was in the middle of another task.

Wolfe wandered closer, attempting to make out the year of the port. "A collection of poems. One she claims she found transcendent. Tugs on the heartstrings, apparently."

"Oh, I see." Johann nodded as he removed the glassware from the tray, arranging it artfully. "But not yours."

Wolfe paused. "Pardon?"

"Not yours," Johann said again easily. "Your heartstrings aren't easily tugged."

Wolfe's smile fell from his lips. "Why do you say that?"

"Oh, you know. It's like you have this...mask on? Around other people. Pretending to feel what they feel." Johann turned to gauge Wolfe's reaction—perhaps realizing what he'd just said wouldn't be considered polite by any stretch of the imagination—and, at Wolfe's cocked brow, hastened to reassure him. "It's a really good mask though! Almost perfect."

"But you're not fooled?" Wolfe prompted, taking control of himself and managing a small smile, aiming to put the little vampire at ease. He had many reasons to keep Johann placated, but mostly he didn't want to scare him off before he found out how Johann had come to this conclusion. The majority of people simply assumed Wolfe was...reserved.

"Well," Johann mused, turning back to his task now that he'd reassured himself Wolfe wasn't upset with him. "I pretend a lot too. I think I just recognize it."

Oh, little Johann. So much more observant than Veronique believed, or than any other den member gave him credit for. His maker would have such a perfect little spy in him, if she were only intelligent enough to use him properly rather than delegate him to the role of some sort of pet manservant.

"You find your own emotions...subdued?" Wolfe asked, thinking that aspect of it a bit hard to believe.

"Oh, I feel lots of things!" Johann reassured him. "But Vee says there're right and wrong ways to express those things, and I usually do it wrong. So in polite company, I put on my polite face, and voilà!" He waved his hand with a little flourish.

Wolfe debated, for just a moment, pretending. It would be easy enough to lie and complain of a similar affliction. Too many emotions rather than too few.

But if Wolfe played his cards right, one day he and this odd little man were going to be allies. And shared secrets were one road to intimacy.

So he meandered just the slightest bit closer, a false expression of chagrin on his face. "I'm afraid my situation is a bit different."

Johann poured an appropriate amount of port into each glass. "Oh?"

"Have you heard of psychopathy?"

"Like a serial killer?" Johann didn't sound remarkably concerned that the answer might be yes.

"Not quite. Serial killers are more often than not psychopaths, but the majority of psychopaths aren't serial killers. Does that make sense?"

Johann nodded, setting the port bottle back down. "It does. I guess I'm a little undereducated on the subject. But that's why you pretend?"

"That's why I pretend."

Johann cocked his head, considering. "I don't think they'd mind though. The other den members. They're all vampires. And they're mean."

Wolfe let his smile grow. "They are *mean, aren't they? But people also like to think those they consort with admire them. Are fond of them. Like if not love them, even. Those things are difficult for me. And I do so much want to fit in." He allowed his shoulders to sag just a touch, trying not to overplay it. Johann was apparently not easily fooled. "You see?"*

Johann nodded thoughtfully. "I do see." He grinned at Wolfe. "Thank you for sharing with me."

"Thank you for your discretion." Wolfe had a moment of uncertainty, wondering if he'd come to regret this precedence of honesty with one so close to the key players in his personal game of chess.

But Johann clapped his hands together in excitement, more exuberant than Wolfe had ever seen him in the presence of the others. "I'll do some reading on the subject. Then next time we're alone together, I'll have appropriate questions for you!"

The laugh Wolfe let out wasn't entirely false. "How thoughtful of you, Johann."

The little vampire flushed happily, turning to attend to the arrangements of his tray.

No, Wolfe didn't think he'd regret it at all. He felt even a minute lessening of some constantly held tension, sharing a truth with someone like this. There was surely a delightful art to lies, to manipulation, to fitting in without genuinely caring for the people around him.

But perhaps some value also lay in being seen for who he was.

Perhaps he'd even found a friend.

Fourteen

Eric

Danny's house—a little yellow number close to the hospital—was fitting for what Eric knew of him: cute, comfortable, and welcoming.

Danny had greeted Eric like an old friend and then sat him down in the living room with a beer while he, as he put it, "helped Roman fuss." (Although, from the brief glimpse Eric had had of the guy—movie star good looks, strikingly bright, cold blue eyes—Eric couldn't really picture Roman "fussing" over much of anything, but whatever.)

Wolfe had abandoned him.

At least for dinner. He'd claimed Eric would have better luck bonding with the crew if he wasn't glued to the side of a psychopath, making everybody nervous, and then when Eric had been poised to protest, he'd claimed he needed to feed anyway and would join them later for dessert.

Which, okay, that should be a good thing, right? Eric was finally in a physical and emotional state where he could tolerate some space, and now here he was, getting that space. All it had taken was approximately ten thousand orgasms over the course of one night.

And great. Now his brain was replaying images of clever fingers and a wickedly talented tongue. Eric shifted on the couch, trying not to get a boner before dinner. Although, to be honest, it had been more than just the physical part that had left him so wrung out the night before.

The mate bond was really something else; that was for sure. Eric had been able to *feel* how turned on Wolfe had been, tasting him. Coupled with that fierce possessiveness Wolfe was always carrying around for him like some eternal flame? Beyond potent, to the point of completely overwhelming him.

The truth was, if Wolfe had asked to fuck him, Eric would've let him in a heartbeat. Which, big whoop, he supposed; it wasn't like he was exactly virginal. He'd just never bottomed before. He'd somehow always thought that was for pretty, twinky guys. Eric wasn't pretty, and he wasn't anywhere in the realm of twinky, yet Wolfe seemed *very* interested in getting all up in there.

He sipped his beer thoughtfully, casually adjusting himself in his jeans. Lots to consider, really. He should probably also be considering that at some point he would be joining Wolfe on a hunt or whatever. That was what he should be most concerned about, right? Drinking blood straight from the source like some third-rate Dracula? But it was hard to focus on it when the beast inside him was so unbelievably chill, other than the soft yearning that seemed to perpetually exist now—that ache for Wolfe to always be closer than he was.

Supposedly—according to Danny—Eric would start getting really hungry again in the next few days. Then maybe he'd come to better terms with his new as-yet-unexplored bloodlust.

The sound of the front door slamming open had Eric choking on his next sip of beer.

"All right, everyone, the party has arrived!"

The voice was familiar. King's boyfriend (or partner, or mate, or whatever). Soren. Why hadn't Eric realized he'd be part of the family dinner?

He didn't have much time to dwell on it before the man—or vampire, apparently—himself strode into the living room two seconds later, King a half step behind.

Soren spotted Eric immediately. "So this is why Danny insisted on moving family dinner up by three days," he drawled.

Speaking of pretty twinks. Except that crazed grin Soren often had on his face always did ruin the effect a little. The same grin he was sporting now, his artfully coiffed blond head cocked to the side as he stared at Eric, one eyebrow arched, as if expecting some sort of reaction.

Was he hoping for Eric to blush or something? They'd had one brief encounter, one that had left Eric with blue balls and a fuzzy head, and—

Eric paused, beer poised at his lips. Wait. He tried his best to hold on to the moment as he'd remembered it—hurriedly making out in an alleyway, some fumbled groping—but something else started to take its place. A memory of a sharp pain, then unbearable pleasure. But no kissing. Definitely no fondling.

He straightened up with a start. "Hey!" He pointed an accusing finger at the blond. "You *bit* me!"

Soren's grin only grew wider. "There it is. I was wondering, now that you've turned."

"Oh, thank God," Gabe groaned, wrapping a broad arm around his mate's waist. "Now we can stop pretending the two of you hooked up. It was skeeving me out."

Soren waved a dismissive hand. "Yes, yes, we all know. You're all macho and jealous, et cetera, et cetera."

Eric was having trouble getting his mouth to close properly. "You *fed* from me."

Soren tossed his head with a huff. "And?"

"And—" Eric sagged back into the couch. "Um...well, I don't know."

Soren shrugged. "Okay, well while you consider how pissed you want to be at me, I'm going to raid Roman's wine cellar." He pointed to Gabe as he turned out of his hold. "You stay here and babysit the newbie."

He flounced off, his heeled boots clacking on the hardwood floors. Eric sat, stunned, while Gabe disappeared for a minute of his own before reappearing with a beer in hand, settling himself into the armchair across from Eric.

Eric raised his bottle half-heartedly. "Cheers."

"Cheers."

"Your boyfriend bit me."

Gabe shrugged his muscular shoulders. "Technically he's my fiancé. And, well—" He pointed his beer bottle at Eric. "*Your* boyfriend drained you completely."

"He's not my boyfriend," Eric said, mostly just to be a dick. But it also definitely didn't seem like the right word. It wasn't *intense* enough for whatever Wolfe was. He was just...more.

They sat in silence for a minute, both sipping at their beers. For all that they were colleagues, and Eric had always hoped they could be friends, Gabe had never seemed to like him much. Maybe because Eric had not so subtly hit on him when they'd been starting out together.

Or maybe Eric just wasn't good enough to be friends with the golden boy of Hyde Park.

But Gabe seemed...calmer here, outside the hospital. A little less hostile. Or maybe it was having Soren in his life. He'd always been charming, seemingly without even trying that hard, but there had been something heavier roiling underneath before the unhinged blond had started appearing at his side all over town.

Was that what mates did? Helped someone be their better self? Eric couldn't imagine Wolfe helping him be a better anything. Except...

Just because you've been stunted until now doesn't mean you need to remain stunted.

Eric let the silence go on for another minute before he asked the question he'd decided Gabe might have some insight into. "So have you ever bottomed before?"

"Excuse me?" Gabe shot him a savage look, but Eric was used to those expressions from him, so he just took another sip of his beer.

"It's just, Soren seems kind of 'take charge.' Bossy. Does he top you?"

Gabe let out a heavy sigh. "You know you can't just ask me stuff like that. Jesus."

"Oh. Sure, sure." Because they weren't really friends, and everyone was only being nice to him because he'd been turned and kidnapped by someone they were all maybe afraid of. Eric grimaced, freshly aware that stuff like this was probably the reason Gabe hated him. "Sorry. I'm just kind of in new territory with Wolfe, thought maybe you'd..."

Gabe let him roil in embarrassment for another long moment before he huffed, running a hand through his hair. "I can't believe you're paired with that psychopath." He seemed to debate with himself for a minute before giving in. "Okay, so... Soren's more like a 'topping from the bottom' kind of guy. Yeah, he's bossy, but he also likes to get dicked down. Like, really likes it."

Eric nodded thoughtfully, but it was cut off by Soren's screech, sounding like it was coming from the kitchen. "Gabe fucking Christ Kingman, you did not just tell him all that."

He appeared a moment later, glass of red wine in hand, gesticulating so wildly it was a wonder it didn't splash everywhere. "Definitely no orgasms for you tonight, Highness."

Gabe rose from his chair, contrition all over his face. "No, baby, but we're hunting tonight."

"Tough."

Gabe wrapped himself around his mate, murmuring so softly that even with his enhanced hearing, Eric could only catch every other word. A lot of *baby* and *brat* being thrown around.

Eventually Soren softened in his hold. "Fine," he mumbled into Gabe's chest. "But only because *I* need it. You can come, but you can't enjoy it."

Eric kept his silence, a little worried one or both of them were going to remember he'd started this weird almost fight and turn on him. But they just settled into the armchair together, Soren on Gabe's lap. It made

Eric think of his intense urge to sit on Wolfe's lap. With Soren, it looked so natural. Would it look silly, with Eric?

Soren raised his glass at Eric. "Condolences for your mating bond."

Eric frowned. "It's not so bad."

"If he *ever* tries to make you do something you don't want to do..."

"Oh no, nothing like that." Eric blinked, surprised by the protective words. And then, because his mouth was running away from him no matter what he did, "He's a great lay so far."

Gabe snorted, raising his beer to his lips. "Not my type."

"Why not?" Eric tilted his chin at Soren. "You clearly like them scary."

Soren grinned back at him, pleased.

"Yeah," Gabe conceded, rubbing his chin onto his mate's hair. "But also beautiful."

"Wolfe *is* beautiful." Or at least, striking. And at this point, for Eric, it was kind of the same thing.

Gabe laughed. "Christ, the bond works quickly, huh? If I were you, I'd be pissed at Wolfe for at least—"

"An entire year of avoidance?" Soren cut in, a pointed lilt to his voice.

"Um..." Gabe ran a hand through his hair sheepishly. "Yeah, well, I guess it's best to go with the flow with these things. And Wolfe seems the type to be...persistent?"

Persistent was one word for it; that was for sure. Eric was hit with more memories from the night before. Wolfe almost manically wringing orgasm after orgasm from his body. Stroking with his tongue, nipping with his teeth, doing more things with one finger than Eric had imagined possible.

He cleared his throat, hoping his face wasn't as red as it felt. "Yeah, persistent is about right."

Dinner had been...strange? Weirdly nice? It was hard to decide. Everyone was being so kind to Eric, and he wasn't used to that sort of easy acceptance. And yes, maybe it was stemming mostly from pity, but he was starting to think that was better than nothing if it meant he suddenly had the makings of real friends in this town.

They'd been joined just before dinner by the adorable little local barista from Death by Coffee, Jay—someone Eric still couldn't wrap his head around being a vampire, with his doll-like features and propensity to compliment anything and everything. Like, he could be a pixie, maybe, if those existed. Just slap some pointed ears on the guy. But a vampire? And with him came his fated mate, Alexei, a big, kind of scary-looking guy, with his long blond hair in a topknot, who fit Eric's image of a biker or mobster more than something supernatural.

They had claimed to be late due to issues baking their cookies, but judging from Jay's flushed cheeks and Alexei's general air of smug satisfaction, Eric would bet a hundred dollars they'd been banging.

So it had all been fine and good, except now they were all in the living room with after-dinner drinks and peanut butter cookies Jay claimed were "only a little burned on the bottom," and Wolfe *still* hadn't arrived.

It was making Eric's inner beast restless. It was making *Eric* restless. Everyone here was in a couple, casually touching and sharing smiles and unspoken communication. Eric had never minded being the odd man out before. It was just... He wasn't this time. He *had* a mate. So where was the son of a bitch?

He half listened while the others debated which spots in the next town over were best for hunting, and became slowly aware of little Jay—who'd plopped himself on the couch between Eric and Alexei—inching closer to him.

"Hello," Jay whispered after realizing he had Eric's attention. He even gave a little wave, despite the fact that they'd already greeted each other and had in fact just shared an entire dinner together.

"Um." Eric looked to Alexei, who was listening intently to Roman explaining the recipes from dinner. "Hi."

"How are you?" Jay asked.

"I'm good," Eric answered automatically. "How are you?"

Jay's brow furrowed. "No. I mean, how *are* you?"

"Um. Still good?"

Jay gave a little huff of frustration and looked to Alexei. "It's not working."

Alexei turned easily away from his conversation with Roman. "That's because you're being uncharacteristically coy. Just approach it like you usually would, kitten."

"Right." Jay swiveled to face Eric. "I'm Wolfe's friend from our old den, which was terrible, and I hated it, and Wolfe was one of the only nice parts, at least after Soren left. But he's caused a lot of trouble since coming after me here, and I'm sorry he turned you and also sorry that it's sort of my fault he's here at all." He turned back to Alexei. "Was that better?"

Alexei dropped a kiss to Jay's head. "Perfect, sweetheart."

Jay hummed happily, then gave Eric his full attention once more. "So how are you really? Are you very sad to be a vampire? Has Wolfe been rude to you? Has he told you about the money, or is he being stingy? Because as his mate, you should be entitled to what's his. It's only fair."

"Oh. Okay. So." Eric took a second to catch up with both the barrage of information and all the questions. Jay seemed to sincerely want to know about Eric's emotional well-being, but Eric wasn't exactly all that used to discussing his feelings. It was easy enough with Wolfe, for some reason. Maybe because he didn't seem to judge Eric any differently, no matter what he said.

Eric tried to put the answers to Jay's questions into some semblance of coherence. "So I don't really know how I feel about being a vampire?

I think the reality of that is still sinking in. But the Wolfe part has been...nice?"

"He has?" Jay's skepticism was clear, and his brow was furrowed again.

Eric cleared his throat. "Well, maybe not *nice*, but supportive? He's been taking good care of me. So you don't have to worry, I guess is what I mean."

"Hm." Jay cocked his head. "You were always kind of smarmy before, whenever you came into the coffee shop. At least, that's what Alicia always said. I didn't mind it, but you look...softer? More at home in your own skin. So that's probably good."

Eric was saved from having to respond to that strange statement by the loud sounds of a debate getting more heated.

"I'm telling you," Soren was saying to Danny, "I haven't scented anything! Stop asking. I'll let you know if I do."

"Well, now both the blood bank and the hospital have been raided. If it isn't any of us, then we have to have another vamp in town, right?"

"Why wouldn't they just be feeding off people?" Gabe asked, petting Soren's arm soothingly.

"Possibly too close to feral? Or afraid of losing control," Danny mused. "Roman was using blood bags when we first met."

"Are you sure Wolfe's not lying to us? He could be stocking up and not wanting to say."

All eyes fell on Eric. He tried to resist squirming in his seat. "Um. Well, I've only fed from the blood Danny's given me. And Wolfe said he was hunting tonight, so I don't see why he'd be stocking up on blood bags. Or when he'd even have the time."

"The hospital theft was the same day he came to pick you up," Danny pointed out mildly.

Eric shook his head. "No. He came for me right away. I know it."

He had a weird flash of memory then: that kid staring at Eric in horror as they left the hospital. Had he been carrying something? But no—he was just a kid. That would be ridiculous.

Eric kept it to himself.

There was more arguing over possibilities before Soren sat up straight, scenting the air like a fucking bloodhound, a bitter smile on his lips. "I stand corrected. There's another vampire in town. Two others, to be exact."

For the second time that night, the front door opened with a loud slam. The entire room seemed to hold their breath until the living room doorway was filled by a tall, lanky man dressed all in black, his green hair in a half ponytail. He was joined an instant later by a stockier, intimidating companion, glowering over his shoulder.

Soren sighed deeply when the second man appeared. "Christ. That's what I thought."

The green-haired man grinned at them all, easy and bright despite Soren's less-than-enthusiastic greeting. "What's up, bitches? Whose head are we ripping off today?"

Fifteen

Wolfe

Wolfe slipped around to the back of the tiny yellow house (thank the heavens he'd found more acceptable real estate than *this* in this drab town), careful to keep his steps quiet enough even enhanced vampire senses wouldn't pick them up.

Protect our mate.

Wolfe didn't bother responding to his beast. He'd seen the couple—a punk-looking kid and his seemingly older companion, a casually elegant man with silver at his temples and a leather jacket Wolfe would like to see on Eric's broad shoulders—making their way up to the front door. The slight metallic scent on the wind had given them up as vampires.

They weren't from the den; that was sure enough. Wolfe would have recognized them. But that didn't stop him cursing himself for leaving Eric unattended. Here he'd been trying to be *thoughtful.*

Eric would need companionship, when his lack of aging forced them to move along. He would also, most likely—as the wounds left from his parents slowly healed—need a softer touch than Wolfe's current method of blunt logic in the face of insecurities, if Wolfe wanted to keep him content in the long run.

And that was exactly what Wolfe wanted. Eric content. Always and forever.

It had been barely a day, and Wolfe was already addicted to the new, soft sweetness pulsing down their bond. He thought he might do anything to keep that feeling coming, including the indignity of allowing Eric the space to bond with new friends at dinner.

But it was this exact sentimentality that got people into trouble. Eric was currently in a strange home, undefended. Johann and his ilk may have been more moral than most of their kind, but Wolfe had no doubt the others in the house would protect their mates first and foremost.

Which left Wolfe skulking along to the house's back door, intent on having the upper hand in surprise if not in numbers. As far as he was concerned, it was two against one. Eric had no business fighting, and Wolfe wasn't yet sure if he could count on any of the others.

And if a single hair on Eric's head was harmed, Wolfe would kill everyone in that room.

He vowed it to himself just as he opened the back door in time to catch the boisterous, "What's up bitches? Whose head are we ripping off today?"

Wolfe went for the leather-clad man behind the green-haired instigator. He had the look of a killer about him; best to incapacitate him first.

Wolfe had him in a headlock in an instant, mindful to keep his arm around his throat, where the stranger's fangs couldn't catch him.

The man growled fiercely, clawing at Wolfe's arm with both hands. "Poutain de—!"

Wolfe used the wall as leverage to keep the man still, but his eyes were already on Eric. He was there, on the couch between Johann and the mobster, spine straight with alarm but otherwise in no sign of distress. "Wolfe!" he cried out, relief and what might be concern pulsing through the bond.

Notably, however, no one else was reacting. At least, not in a way that implied they'd be joining any sort of fight. The green-haired vampire had—rather than come to his companion's aid—pulled out his phone with a wide grin, as if to photograph the moment.

Wolfe stood there, facing the living room, snarling head under one arm, his muscles tensing with the effort of keeping him still. "Would someone please tell me whether I'm holding friend or foe?" he asked mildly.

"Friend," said Danny and Johann, while at the same time—

"Foe," from Soren and Gabe.

Roman was chuckling into his glass of wine, slouched comfortably in his armchair. "Why, Lucien, I do believe you've lost your touch, letting someone creep up on you from behind like that."

Lucien snarled anew. "Roman, I swear to God."

"Jamie, is it?" Soren drawled to the green-haired punk. "I'll need you to send me that photo. I'm going to have it framed."

Danny stood up from his seat on the arm of Roman's chair. "Okay, so let's all chill out, maybe?" he soothed. "You're getting Ferdy worked up." He pointed to the corner of the room, where his heeler mutt was—despite his owner's words—curled up on a dog bed, his ears not even twitching at the commotion. "Jamie and Luc are friends, I promise. Wolfe, you can release Lucien now."

Wolfe looked down at the seething vampire, whose fangs were out. "I'm a bit concerned he's going to bite."

The green-haired one—Jamie, presumably—laughed, bright and easy. "Oh, don't worry, he's relatively tame these days. Aren't you, monster?"

Lucien narrowed his black eyes. "You're asking for trouble, ma fleur. Big trouble."

Jamie only winked at him. "Lucky me."

Not wishing to be a vehicle for the strange couple's flirting, Wolfe released Lucien from his hold, effortlessly dodging the fist the irritated vampire threw his way. He stayed as close as he dared, not yet ready to consider them free of threat. He took the opportunity to soak in the sight of his mate, who was now looking a charming mix of befuddled and relieved.

Meanwhile Soren rose from his seat and sidled up, although he stayed noticeably far enough way that Lucien couldn't swipe at him, studying the companion instead. "The infamous Jamie." Soren made a big show of taking him in, his eyes traveling over the artificially colored hair, the multiple earrings, the all-black outfit. He grinned, slow and wide. "Finally, someone *else* with a sense of style."

Jamie tilted his chin at the still-snarling Lucien. "I think Luc's got great style."

"Luc doesn't count." Soren huffed. "We don't speak of him."

Jamie's brows rose. "Except he's right here, newly freed from this dapper fucker's headlock."

"No, he isn't. Because if he was"—Soren's grin widened impossibly—"I'd have to be tearing his head off for attacking my mate and then running off like a coward."

That prompted another growl from Luc, but Jamie's hand on his arm stopped it short.

"So he's not here," Soren concluded pointedly.

Jamie nodded slowly, his own smile dimming. "Cool beans, I guess I'll just take Mr. Invisible here to a nearby hotel and let you all fend for yourselves."

Soren ignored the threat, reaching a hand out to Jamie's jewelry. "Where are those earrings from? They're gorgeous."

Jamie cocked a brow. "I'd tell you, but then I'd be breaking your rule. They were a gift. From a certain *non*someone."

Soren waited him out, clearly hoping for an answer anyway, then threw his hands up in frustration. "Fine! You can both exist! But I'm not talking to him."

Jamie smiled easily again. "That's cool. He's more fun when he's pissed off anyway."

"Says you," Soren grumbled, slinking back to place himself on Gabe's lap.

Satisfied that no skirmishes were on the horizon, Wolfe hastened over to Eric's side. He cupped his mate's face in both hands, ignoring Johann's enthusiastic wave of greeting.

"You are unharmed." It was more a statement than a question, but he felt it worth saying out loud.

"Uh." Eric's cheeks flushed a darling pink. "Yeah."

"Good." Wolfe cleared his throat, which was unusually dry, then tried it again. "Good."

He sat on the arm of the couch, his hand firmly on Eric's shoulder, ready to whisk him away should things in the house get any more tense, while Danny made formal introductions for all those who hadn't met before.

Alexei, generally quiet in a group setting, spoke up. He pointed to Lucien and Jamie. "So it's the two of you who've been raiding the blood banks? Mystery solved?"

"Psh, no," Jamie said. "We just got here. We were on a road trip, hunting a particularly slippery serial killer."

"Delicious," Lucien murmured, wrapping one arm around his mate's hip.

"And I had one of my helpful visions," Jamie continued. "Except it was kind of confusing. Like, a vampire in Hyde Park. But he was young. Like, really young." He shifted in place, clearly disturbed. "A child."

Wolfe felt Eric tense under his hold.

"Oh my God." Danny looked horrified. "Can that happen? *Does* that happen?"

Roman shrugged, looking to Lucien, who did the same. "We haven't heard of it, but that doesn't necessarily mean anything."

"It can," Johann piped up, sounding sad. "It's really frowned upon though. Like, very taboo."

Danny made a strangled noise. "And they just stay a kid forever?"

"No, they age into their adult bodies, then stop there. But I've heard it can mess with their head a bit. It's like their brains develop with their inner beasties already inside. I think it usually leaves them at least half-feral. And sometimes there are other side effects, like mutism, or feeding from animals. And they can be really hard to control. But it's hard to find people willing to put them down, for obvious reasons."

Wolfe had never heard of a child vampire in the den. He caught Johann's eye. "How do you know all that?"

Johann shrugged. "I just listened a lot, in the den."

"And you saw one in Hyde Park?" Danny asked Jamie.

"Yeah, I recognized some of the streets. I've been here before, once or twice. My buddy Colin lives up here."

Johann straightened up, eager. "My manager Colin?"

Jamie grinned at him. "You working at DBC, little guy?" At Johann's enthusiastic nod, he laughed. "Rad. Colin's chill. We grew up together. He's a Tucson baby."

"Super-duper chill," Johann agreed. "Does he know you're a vampire?"

"No." Jamie frowned. "Why would he? Wait—does he know *you're* a vampire?"

Wolfe pinched the bridge of his nose. "As lovely as this six degrees of separation is, if there is a child vampire here, it needs to be controlled. Likely, from the sound of it, eliminated."

He felt a pulse of pure distress coming from Eric and looked down to see his mate frowning up at him. "We can't kill a kid," Eric protested.

"I could," Wolfe said. And he would. From what Johann had told them, a child vampire was too unstable, too unpredictable, to be allowed. For the protection of the whole, to prevent exposure, it would need to be put down.

At Eric's deepening frown, Wolfe tried to reassure him. "Darling, he's already dead. Whoever turned him saw to that."

But Eric was shaking his head, trying to slide out from under Wolfe's hold. It was surprisingly painful, his rejection of Wolfe's touch. It left Wolfe's stomach feeling cramped in a way with which he was unfamiliar.

Danny cleared his throat. "We'll figure something else out. We'll come up with another option."

Wolfe folded his hands in his lap, allowing Eric's retreat, unsettled and uncomfortably on edge.

It was risky to wait. True, the child was starting with blood banks and hospitals, which pointed to a certain natural intelligence. But what if he moved on to people? What if he went too far and started draining Hyde Park's citizens dry?

Then there would be all sorts of trouble, including the risk of exposure.

Exposure meant danger. For himself, for his mate.

It couldn't be borne. He'd have to make plans of his own. But Wolfe was willing to let these other vampires talk in circles in the meantime.

Hopefully it would give Eric time to settle, to return to that soft, sweet state.

Time for him to return to Wolfe's touch.

Sixteen

Wolfe

It quickly became clear no one had a feasible solution to the problem. "Find the kid" seemed to be the only consensus, but—as Johann oh so helpfully informed them—child vampires apparently did not yet have the distinctive vampire scent, at least not until they grew into their adult forms. Hence Soren's inability to track another vampire in town. Yet another reason this brat was a loose cannon in need of being contained.

But of course Wolfe was a monster for saying so. It was the first time he'd truly felt Eric's censure in their time together. There had been pouting, yes. Irritation. Anger, certainly. But this disbelief bordering on disgust was entirely new, allowing a sour tinge to work its way into their bond. Wolfe didn't like it. It didn't sit well in his stomach.

Soothe our mate, his beast urged.

We can't right now, Wolfe countered. At least not like Wolfe wanted, with logical conversation and shared touch and Eric actually meeting his eye. There were too many spectators, including these two new strangers, one of whom wouldn't stop glaring at Wolfe over his mate's shoulder.

Wolfe shot the brute a mild look in acknowledgment of his ire. "You seem perturbed, Lucien. I believe I already apologized for accosting you."

"You definitely *didn't*." Lucien's glare transformed into a sneer. Yes, he was most certainly French in origin.

Wolfe cocked a brow in mild surprise. "Didn't I? How strange."

"Notice how that's still not an apology?"

Soren made a scoffing sound from his place on Gabe's lap. "Like you're one to talk about unprovoked aggression, Luc."

Luc directed his sneer at the petite blond. "I thought I didn't exist to you."

"You exist when it suits me." Soren waved a dismissive hand, then turned it back around to study his nails. "Get used to it."

Jamie laughed, a surprisingly bright contrast to his mate's glowering. "I like this one." He nodded his chin at Soren's footwear. "Great boots too."

"Thank you." Soren accepted the compliment with a gracious nod. "I officially declare you too good for him. Find yourself another mate."

Lucien growled. "I did always so regret not breaking *your* arm, Soren."

"I'd like to see you try, asshole."

The arguing continued, but Wolfe had officially had enough. The problem of the child was not going to be solved in this moment, especially with all the unhealed animosity in the air. Perhaps if the group was given an evening to vent their frustrations with one another, the next gathering would be more productive.

If not, Wolfe would hunt down the little creature himself.

He rose from his seated position and offered a hand to his mate. "I believe it's time for us to take our leave."

Eric, who'd been much, much too quiet the past half hour, blinked at him, a dazed look in his eyes. "It is?"

"Yes, darling. We have our own concerns to deal with." *We are our own concern*, he wanted to say. *We must address your disgust with me before it taints our bond beyond repair.* Instead, he gave a nod to the room at large. "Keep us apprised of the situation with the vampire brat, would you?"

Danny rose from his seat, ever the polite host. "Of course." He snapped his fingers. "Oh, Eric, I have something for you. It's in the kitchen."

Eric followed Danny obediently, and Wolfe watched them go, his patience fraying quite thin. He wanted Eric back in their home, back in his arms, back in his bed.

Wolfe felt a tug on his sleeve. He looked down to find Johann, still seated, offering him a plate. "Cookie, Wolfgang?"

"No, thank you."

Johann set the plate down, but he didn't let go of Wolfe's suit jacket. "You told me you couldn't love," he said softly, too quiet for the other arguing vampires to hear.

Wolfe shrugged a shoulder. "I believe I told you I never had before."

Johann's brow furrowed. "You tricked me, you mean."

"It's not my fault you didn't do your proper research," Wolfe countered, too irritated to use his usual kid gloves. "There's nothing to say people with psychopathic tendencies can't love."

Johann nibbled on his lower lip as he thought that over. "Why'd you let me think that, then?"

"Because you didn't want a romantic relationship, and neither did I. I thought it would help you feel more certain in that."

Johann's gray eyes met his. "You were manipulating me."

Wolfe was coming very close to losing his temper. What was the point of not hiding who he was with Johann if the little vampire was still going to act surprised when Wolfe acted true to his nature? "I don't feel bad about it," he said harshly. "Go to Alexei if you're looking for sympathy."

Johann didn't look cowed in the slightest. "Did you let Veronique die on purpose, that day in the woods?"

Wolfe said nothing. He'd always wondered if Johann would figure that out, once his grieving had passed.

At Wolfe's lack of answer, Johann nodded slowly. "You did." He rose from the couch, straightening another one of his hideous sweaters. "I think I might be very mad at you right now, Wolfgang."

"That would be well within your rights."

He watched as Johann wandered off, Ferdy on his heels. He couldn't spare the extra energy to contemplate how to placate the little vampire, not with things so askew with his own mate.

But apparently the night was not done with him.

Wolfe allowed himself one heavy, indulgent sigh as Alexei sidled up next to him. How many more unwanted heart-to-hearts was he going to have to have this evening?

Alexei crossed his arms and made some Russian-sounding grunt. "I don't like you manipulating Jay. But I *am* glad she's dead."

Wolfe pinched the bridge of his nose. "I really don't care how you feel one way or another, mobster."

"That's fine," Alexei said easily before moving to stand directly in front of Wolfe, the small amount of space between them emphasizing his unfortunate height advantage. "But be nice to Jay or we'll see just how far this new vampire strength of mine goes."

Wolfe smirked up at him. "I don't like threats."

"And I don't like seeing Jay unhappy."

"I won't apologize for Veronique's death. It was her own fault for ignoring Silas's deterioration."

Alexei shrugged his massive shoulders. "You don't need to. He'll forgive you anyway because that's who he is." He turned, presumably to follow his mate, before looking back at Wolfe. "Just eat one of his cookies next time, okay?"

By the time Wolfe escaped the cursed yellow house, he found Eric already waiting in the passenger seat of the car. "I've changed my mind about you having friends, darling."

Eric didn't answer, not even to glower. He just flipped through what looked to be a journal of some kind.

"From Danny?" Wolfe asked.

"From Danny."

Well, at least his mate was not entirely incapable of speaking to him.

"His notes on vampirism," Eric continued. "'New vampires are unstable and bloodthirsty. Except when they already have mates, then they're just super horny all the time.'" Eric chuckled, though the sound was without humor. "Helpful."

Wolfe tried to catch his eye. "What's troubling you, pet? The child?"

Eric frowned down at Danny's notes. "Yes. No. Yes. We definitely need to talk about what you said back there at some point. But... I don't know. I think it's hitting me: this is my life now. I'm not human anymore, am I? And it goes beyond this bond with you. I'm going to have, like, vampire friends, and deal with vampire problems. And one day I'm going to go hunting with you and feed from a living person. But I guess I should just be grateful some asshole didn't turn me when I was still some innocent kid."

Wolfe felt some tightness he hadn't been aware of in his chest loosening as Eric shared with him. "You don't have to be grateful at all. You're allowed to still be angry with me." *Be angry all you want, as long as you don't cast me aside.*

Eric sighed. "I'm not though. I'm kind of getting it now. You acted on instinct when you turned me. It's fucked up, but it also just...happened. I feel it with this new beast inside me, always longing to be close to you at all times. I can imagine it would get exhausting, resisting it."

"Yes."

Eric finally looked at him, a strange half smile on his face. "You talk to yours a lot, you know. Like, out loud."

Wolfe saw no point in denying it. "I suppose I do."

"Why?"

"Mine has always been vocal. And perhaps before I was turned, I was a bit...isolated. It wasn't so bad, having a bloodthirsty companion in my soul."

Eric's brow furrowed, just the slightest. "Were you really unhappy before you met me?"

"I wasn't unhappy in the slightest." Wolfe didn't think he'd ever been truly unhappy. He'd been angry with his family, frustrated with society's need for his self-control. But unhappy? He'd have to have cared more for that to be possible. As Eric's frown deepened, Wolfe conceded, "Perhaps things were a bit duller." He reached a hand to Eric's cheek, pleased when his mate didn't flinch at his touch. "I find the world has a bit more color with you in it."

"But why? You hardly know me."

Here was where a different type of mate may have been able to offer flowery words, lovely reassurances of Eric's worth. But Wolfe, as always with his mate, could only offer him the truth. "Other people may need to rationalize, may have morals or hang-ups or other things that get in the way. But I've always run on instinct. I trust myself more than anyone else. And I want you. I want to keep you. That's enough for me."

Eric pursed his lips and drew away from Wolfe's touch, clearly still doubtful.

Wolfe tried again. "If you had turned out to be unsatisfactory... An idiot, say. Irritating to be around. I would have changed my mind, were I able. But you're not. You...*please* me. You're beautiful to look at." Wolfe smirked at Eric's blush. "You're also intelligent, eager, needy in a way that suits me quite well. I believe you're also kinder than you give yourself credit for, but that doesn't mean much to me. Except it may temper my more...aggressive instincts. And I suppose I should be grateful for that."

Wolfe held his breath, waiting for a response. It wouldn't be enough, would it? He wasn't saying any of it in the right way.

But then Eric's lips were on his, kissing him unprompted. Nothing filthy, no tongue or hungry noises. Just a soft touch of his mouth.

Eric pulled away, smiling at whatever he saw in Wolfe's face. Their bond wasn't exactly sweet and soft, not like before. But some of the sourness had left it. "Okay, weirdo. Take me home."

But Eric's strange, solemn mood still hadn't lifted upon their return.

Wolfe found himself missing the anger, the petulance. Those he could recognize—enjoy, even. But this...subdued sorrow? If that was even the correct diagnosis for what Eric was feeling. Wolfe didn't know. He couldn't recognize the emotions pulsing through the bond, this new heaviness in the pit of his stomach. For possibly the first time in his extended life, Wolfe had some modicum of regret for the way he was.

He simply wasn't equipped for emotional nuance. The best he could think of, after getting Eric settled in the sitting room, was distraction. He'd prefer the sensual kind. And though barely twelve hours had passed, it felt like it had already been too long since they'd last enjoyed the embrace of each other's bodies.

His beast agreed. *Touch our mate. Taste our mate. Fuck our mate senseless.*

Talk to me when you have something new to say. But Wolfe would only have been too happy to oblige. To get down on his knees and take another taste of his mate's cock, to help Eric lose himself in pleasure. But it was hard to believe his advances would be welcome at the moment.

It had been easier in the beginning, when Wolfe had only ever known Eric's discontent. But he'd tasted Eric's happiness now. He knew the contrast, and he wanted it *back*, damn it.

His strange need for it made him wary, more cautious with his words and actions than he was used to being. He didn't want to set their relationship back any further.

So he brought out the book of paint samples to the sitting room. "Help me pick out colors for the main bedroom, darling."

Eric turned from where he'd been staring into space. "Weren't the painters already supposed to come?"

Wolfe set the samples on the coffee table, standing off to the side. "I'm afraid they were...delayed."

"All right." Eric leaned forward on the love seat, running through the samples more flippantly than Wolfe would have liked. "You really like green, don't you?"

"When it's the right green." A dark, deep green. That of shadows dancing on a lake. Eric's green.

Eric had barely been looking for a minute before he pointed to a selection. "Okay. This one's good."

It wasn't, not at all. The paint swatch he had pointed to was all wrong. Too bright, too garish. Wolfe hummed noncommittally. "I'll take that into consideration."

Well. That hadn't provided as much distraction as he'd hoped. He replaced the book with one of tile samples instead. "Now these, pet."

Eric didn't even glance at it. "You hunted tonight," he said softly, staring off into space again.

"I did."

Eric turned in his seat to look up at him. "Tell me about it."

Wolfe hesitated, if only for a moment. Was this some excuse to feel more disgust for him? Was Eric searching for more proof that Wolfe was a monster? Too bad, if so. Wolfe had behaved impeccably.

He sat down next to his mate on the love seat, folding his hands over one crossed knee. "Let's see. I dropped you off for dinner. I went to a nearby park, one dimly lit and out of the way—"

"I want to sit on your lap," Eric interrupted, the words almost running together in his haste to say them.

Wolfe found himself genuinely, truly speechless.

Eric's cheeks were flushed a dusky pink. "Nothing sexual. Just while you tell me about the hunt. I want to be sitting on your lap."

Yes. Always.

Wolfe got ahold of himself quickly. It wouldn't do to let Eric marinate in his embarrassment too long. "Of course, darling," he purred, uncrossing his legs and patting his thigh.

Eric shuffled onto his lap slowly, as if he'd never done so before. He didn't sit crosswise; he placed his back to Wolfe's front, widening his legs to drape them over Wolfe's. And then he did the most darling thing Wolfe had ever had the pleasure to experience: he grabbed Wolfe's hands, dragging his arms to settle around his waist, and refolded Wolfe's hands over his lower belly.

Eric made a soft noise of contentment. "There. Now you can tell me."

Wolfe tried to find the words again. He swallowed against a dry throat. "A-A woman came by, she was running alone. I compelled her, told her to remain calm—"

"That didn't work on me," Eric interrupted again, relaxing his broad form back against Wolfe's chest.

Wolfe's smile was hidden in Eric's hair. "No, it didn't. But my beast was less...recalcitrant this time. I fed from her quickly, healed her bite with my saliva, and sent her on her merry way."

"You don't kill to feed." It was more a statement than a question.

"I've told you that already, pet."

"But you *have* killed." Eric was toying with Wolfe's fingers. Not unclasping his hands, just petting along them, occasionally tapping them, as if to test their mettle.

It was pointless for Wolfe to ask himself whether to tell the truth. He never seemed to lie to Eric. "I have."

Eric hummed his acknowledgment. "And you want to kill this kid. If he exists."

Wolfe did not *want*. He would take no pleasure in that sort of execution. But the end result would be the same. "I won't risk exposure," he said firmly.

"Why not?"

Wolfe allowed himself one slow, deep inhale of his mate's scent, letting the wisteria relax his tense muscles. "Because I've lived long enough to know better. I was human during the First World War. I was a Swiss citizen, so I didn't fight. But you couldn't escape it either: the pointlessness and the cruelty. Then I was turned shortly before the second, and I remained in Europe throughout. I know what humanity is capable of. Death would be the least of our worries."

Eric was petting his forearms now, as if to soothe either Wolfe or himself. "Because we're monsters, you mean. Humans will think of us as monsters?"

"We do not age; we can regenerate after injury. It's my belief that we'd be taken, most likely as research subjects. There are some fates worse than death, darling. I won't risk it. And I won't let *you* risk it. I will protect us, first and foremost." Wolfe tightened his hold, reassuring himself with the firmness of his mate's form. "We're different. Humans don't take kindly to different. The others have their morals. I do not. I will do anything to keep you safe. Do you understand?"

There was a long silence as Eric processed. Wolfe couldn't ascertain much through the bond, at least nothing new, as far as emotions went.

"Jay's a vampire," Eric eventually mused, seemingly out of nowhere. "That cute little barista. He drinks blood to survive. He hunts like you do."

Wolfe did his best to contain the surge of jealousy he felt at the phrase *cute little barista*. "Yes."

"Show me."

"Show you?" Did Eric think he carried a photograph of Johann on his phone?

"The bite."

Oh, but Wolfe's beast liked that idea very much.

Taste our delicious mate?

Eric took Wolfe's silence for hesitation. "Unless...is that gross? Drinking from another vampire?"

Wolfe cleared his throat. "Not gross, no. Intimate."

A shock of lust from his mate, tightening Wolfe's own belly and making his cock twitch. Eric clearly liked that word: *intimate*. He'd had both too much and too little intimacy in his life.

Wolfe could fix that.

He could fix everything, if only Eric would let him. He'd tear down any obstacles to Eric's happiness. Touch him whenever he wanted. Reassure him when his misperceptions of self got the best of him. Allow him the time and space to learn what he enjoyed.

It could be that easy, couldn't it?

And Wolfe would even let him keep those friends. Not only because they were another barrier between them and what might harm them, but also because Eric clearly needed some sort of community, some sort of touchstone for this new reality. It burned Wolfe that he alone might not be enough, but that was normal.

Not everyone had his single-minded intensity.

Wolfe unclasped his hands. "All right, pet, stand up."

He could *feel* Eric pouting.

Wolfe smirked. "For the demonstration, darling."

Eric stood, his back still to Wolfe.

"Turn around."

Eric did as he was told. His green eyes were even darker than usual, his mate clearly aroused at the thrill of the hunt.

Perfect creature.

Wolfe rose and stalked forward. "I came around the front, too quickly for her to startle away. Eye contact is key, during compulsion." He grabbed Eric's chin with one hand, holding that green gaze to his. "There we are."

Wolfe let the beast out as slowly as he could, allowing Eric to watch the transformation up close. It made his beast preen, to be the center of their mate's attention. "When you have a hold, you reassure, you soothe." He licked at dry lips, avoiding touching his tongue to his fangs. "You're not afraid, Eric. You're calm."

"I'm not afraid. I'm calm." Eric repeated his words dutifully, as if under real compulsion.

"Perfect, darling. There are many options for where to bite. I chose her wrist. The neck can be seen as—"

"Intimate," Eric finished for him, a shiver running through him at his own word.

Wolfe smiled, slow and genuine. "Quite."

But Eric didn't offer up his wrist. He tilted his head, displaying the taut line of his neck for Wolfe's perusal. "And then you bit her," he prompted.

Wolfe hovered, inches from the pounding pulse of that delicious nectar. "And then I bit her."

He waited for the punishment, for the tease. *No touching. Don't enjoy yourself.*

But Eric remained as he was, on offer. It would be foolish to hesitate, when such a choice delicacy was on display. And no one had ever accused Wolfe of being foolish.

He bit in.

Seventeen

Eric

The bite—the exquisite pleasure of it—cut through the fog in Eric's brain, sharp and hot and sweet.

He'd known he was confusing Wolfe, had been able to feel the restless yearning coming from him, the desire for them to be in sync. He'd just needed a minute to process was all.

Dinner—and the whirlwind of drama that had come after—had driven the knife home in a way even Eric's failed shift at the hospital hadn't: he wasn't human anymore.

Like, the food Roman had made had tasted *good*, but it had satisfied nothing. All of them eating human food together was just...sentimental playacting? Eric didn't even mind that part of it so much, if it meant an excuse to gather. But the reality was he only ever had two real cravings anymore: human blood and Wolfe. He'd wanted Wolfe before the drama had started—had missed him all throughout dinner, even with everyone being so nice to him—and he hadn't even been surprised when Wolfe had appeared out of nowhere, right when needed.

There was the little fact that Wolfe seemed willing to put down a child; that would need to be dealt with, and soon. But Eric wasn't going to turn from Wolfe because of it. It was just how Wolfe's brain worked, Eric was realizing. Wolfe was *selfish*, pathologically so. But due to the bond or his possessiveness or whatever else, his selfishness now included Eric, and that made him the most caring person Eric had ever known. That care may have extended *only* to Eric, but Eric was just selfish enough in turn to not give a shit about that.

It was nice to be cared for, for once in his entire life. Cared for because of who he was and not what he could achieve.

Wolfe came when he was needed. He told Eric that he was good, that he was wanted. And he said he would keep them safe. No one had ever been concerned whether Eric was safe.

The bite ended too soon.

Eric whined in protest as Wolfe released the sharp hold of his teeth, licking at Eric's leaking wound like a contented cat.

He smelled good. He always smelled so fucking good.

Which begged the question, How would he taste?

"Let me bite you." Eric wasn't sure if he was begging or ordering, but he knew Wolfe wouldn't censure him either way. He liked Eric greedy. He seemed to like Eric all ways.

The truth of that was displayed in the heat of Wolfe's eyes, flashing red in the dim lighting. "Of course, darling. Where would you like?"

God, how was he supposed to choose? He wanted to nibble over every inch of that lithe frame, get that ridiculous suit off and see for himself which spot tasted the very best. But there would be time for that, wouldn't there? And there was a certain allure to the traditional.

Eric hastened to undo Wolfe's tie. "Well, it's my first time biting. I should go classic, right?"

"The neck," Wolfe purred, tilting his head, a mirror of Eric's earlier position. His eyes were still black, his teeth gleaming red with Eric's blood. It shouldn't be so fucking hot. "Be my guest, pet."

Eric threw the tie on the ground and let his own beast out while he undid Wolfe's top buttons, revealing the taut line of Wolfe's neck to his gaze.

Eric nosed along the soft skin there first, licked experimentally. Wolfe tasted like clean skin. Like salt. But he could smell it, under the surface.

Metallic but also...different. Wolfe didn't smell like the humans in the hospital. He smelled richer. Sharper.

Eric couldn't be sure if he decided to bite or his beast decided for him, but the next second, he found his teeth puncturing Wolfe's skin, that coppery warmth filling his mouth.

Oh fuck. Fuuuuck.

Eric was going to become addicted to this, wasn't he?

He'd been hard since the moment Wolfe had bitten him, but now his cock *ached*. It hadn't been like this, drinking that reheated blood bag blood. Was this a from-the-source thing? Or was this a mate thing? No wonder Wolfe hadn't been able to stop. Eric didn't want to ever stop.

His beast shifted and writhed inside him, gluttonous and strange yet familiar at the same time. Like a hunger he'd had at the back of his being all his life, one he'd denied and starved and kept secret. Turning had let that hunger out. *Wolfe* had let it out.

Eric drank until he felt a sharp sting in his scalp—only then did he realize Wolfe had threaded his fingers through Eric's hair and was tugging him off with impressive force.

Eric allowed it for the moment, licking the stray drops of blood off his lips, eyes heavy-lidded as they met Wolfe's sharp, red-tinged stare.

"That's enough, darling," Wolfe ordered, his voice a husky rasp.

Eric's responding no was petulant, needy. He strained against Wolfe's hold. "I want more."

"You wish to drain me dry, pet? Is that your idea of revenge?" Wolfe looked almost proud.

Eric tugged at Wolfe's lapels. "You belong to me, don't you? Isn't that how this works? You're all mine. Body. Mind. Heart. Blood."

He wasn't even quite aware of what he was saying. He was overwhelmed. By Wolfe, by his new life, by the unholy revelation that was the joy of consuming his mate's blood. He knew he was being demanding. He was maybe being crazy.

But Wolfe's eyes shone bloodred with dark, obsessive heat at his words. "Yes, darling," he purred. "You have all of me."

"And you want all of me."

Wolfe's eyes narrowed. "I *have* all of you."

Eric shrugged, tugging at Wolfe's lapels again. "You haven't had all of me yet."

It took a surprisingly long moment for Wolfe to get it, his pupils blowing wide at the realization. "Are you going to let me fuck you, pet? You're going to take my cock?"

"And if I want it the other way around?"

Wolfe perused Eric's face, his fingers still firmly threaded into Eric's hair, holding him in place, allowing only a few inches of distance between them. His bite wound was seeping blood, but Wolfe didn't seem in any hurry to close it. "But you don't, do you, pet? You're greedy for my touch. Greedy for my blood. You'll be just as greedy for my cock. Because you want to be filled, don't you, darling? My poor, empty mate. You *need* it."

Eric didn't bother denying the truth of that, his blood running hot in his veins at Wolfe's filthy words. "Yes."

Wolfe's smile was sharp. Triumphant. "I should bend you over this chair, take you right here."

Eric wrinkled his nose, his gaze straying to the embroidered chair. "This thing won't work for fucking. It looks like it was made for grandmothers to serve tea from."

Wolfe paused, taken aback. "You dislike the decor?"

"It's fine," Eric reassured him, too turned on to let this become some sort of argument. "It's...elegant?"

"I suppose you'd prefer a man cave of some kind?" Wolfe asked, his brow furrowed, clearly affronted. "One with overstuffed cushions and a meteor-sized television?"

Eric couldn't help his smirk. "Doesn't sound so bad."

"Ah." After a moment, Wolfe's expression smoothed, and a wicked glint appeared in his eye. "Warming my cock while you watch your American football, perhaps?"

A shock of lust punched through Eric, unexpected in its intensity. "What? I didn't say anything about that."

"Bent over some hideous leather sofa, your face pressed into a couch that will 'work for fucking'? Is that what you'd like, my needy darling?"

"Jesus fucking Christ." Eric was panting now, not sure if he was humiliated or turned on beyond belief.

Wolfe gave another tug to his hair, grinding his erection against Eric's own. "Come, pet. I trust you have no objections to the suitability of our bed."

By the time the short trip to the bedroom had taken place, Eric's bravado had worn off.

How the hell had he been so confident propositioning this? *You haven't had all of me yet*? What the fuck was he, some sort of femme fatale?

True, he was no stranger to hookups. The twist of two bodies, soft or hard. Condoms and sweat and awkward goodbyes at three in the morning. But he'd never been...taken. And he didn't just mean in the sense of never having been fucked. He'd never been the object of such fierce, unholy possessiveness before. Because Wolfe wouldn't be leaving at three in the morning. Wolfe wouldn't be leaving at all, would he? And he would probably chase Eric to the ends of the earth if he tried to run instead.

And it was pointless pretending it didn't thrill him, being wanted in that way. Not just for a few hours or a few nights. For always.

Wolfe slid in ahead of him as they entered through the bedroom, and Eric stood awkwardly, watching as Wolfe made his way to the bedside table before neatly removing a bottle of lube and placing it just so. No condoms.

Vampires couldn't give or receive STIs; that was what Danny's helpful little book had said.

Wolfe removed his suit jacket and turned to face Eric, deftly unbuttoning his own shirt as he did so, nodding at Eric to do the same.

Eric frowned at him from his spot in the doorway, even as his gaze followed the slow reveal of smooth, lickable skin. "That's it? We're just gonna strip?"

A small twitch of Wolfe's lips. "I'm sorry, darling. Did you need to be seduced?"

Eric didn't dignify that with a response, instead holding his breath as Wolfe shrugged off the shirt completely and stalked over, placing Eric's face in his hands.

He held Eric's gaze for a long moment, as they both breathed the same air, then one hand trailed down to Eric's neck, wrapping around the front, using the leverage to tilt Eric's mouth up toward him. "You like to be kissed, don't you, pet?"

Eric tried to keep in his moan, was halfway successful. "Everyone likes to be kissed."

Wolfe clicked his tongue. "Not everyone."

"What, you don't like kissing me?" Eric teased. He'd seen how undone Wolfe became after making out; he wasn't going to be fooled.

"I never liked kissing anyone." Past tense. Wolfe confirmed it with the next word, his gaze hot. "Before, that is."

"But now?"

Wolfe leaned in closer, pecking the corner of Eric's mouth before taking his bottom lip between blunt teeth. "Now I could happily devour you whole."

He captured Eric's mouth fully, and Eric lost himself in the kiss, in the sure strokes of Wolfe's tongue, in that firm hold on Eric's throat.

He was only halfway aware of Wolfe undressing them both with his free hand, manhandling Eric deftly while he kissed him senseless.

Maybe Eric *had* wanted to be seduced.

When Wolfe finally pulled away, he kept his hold on Eric's throat, studying his face. Eric had no idea what he looked like, but he had to assume it was some form of wrecked: his breaths were coming out in desperate pants; his cock was leaking, pressed against Wolfe's firm stomach; and he'd gone slack and pliable in Wolfe's hold, practically held up by it.

Whatever he saw, it made Wolfe smile, wicked as ever. He squeezed once before releasing Eric's neck, giving him a soft smack on his hip. "Onto the bed with you, darling."

Eric made to lie on his belly again, like he had before, but Wolfe tutted at him from where he was standing at the foot of the bed. "On your back, pet. Knees bent. No hiding this time."

Eric did as he was told. Wolfe looked him over, slow and thorough. He hadn't stopped smiling. "What a gorgeous form you have."

Eric rubbed uncertainly at his chest. "I'm not anything special."

Wolfe moved to kneel over him. "Ah, but you are. You are. There's strength here." Wolfe ran a hand along his calves, his thighs, brushing at the curls around the base of his cock. "And beauty." He trailed caresses over Eric's chest, circling his nipples. "Such broad shoulders. I had no doubt fate would select me the perfect specimen."

Like Eric was some sort of lab rat. Except Wolfe wasn't looking at him like that. He was looking at Eric like he was special, beautiful, maybe even perfect. "Why were you so sure?"

Wolfe pinched Eric's nipple, smirking at his gasp. "Because anything less would be unacceptable."

It was that simple for him, wasn't it? Like he had an understanding with the universe that he would get his due. That he deserved it, by virtue of being himself. Would that rub off on Eric eventually? Or would he simply be protected under the umbrella of that inhuman confidence, a shelter against the storms life threw at them?

He wasn't sure he cared. He was glad of it either way.

Wolfe sat back down on his knees, lube in hand, and began opening Eric up. One finger. Two. Three. It was strange, the stretch and the slight sting, but even that sting wasn't as bad as Eric would have thought. Whether that was because of his vampire body or just how greedy he was for it, he wasn't sure. But he was glad. He didn't like to hurt.

All the while, Wolfe watched him with single-minded intensity, catching each of his reactions, no matter how small. Studying him. Eric couldn't look away, even as he gasped and squirmed and moaned with each crook of Wolfe's fingers.

Wolfe would have him figured out by the end of the night, wouldn't he? He'd be able to play Eric like a fiddle whenever he wanted. But Eric couldn't exactly be mad about that. Not when it felt so fucking good.

"Wolfe," he moaned, ready for certain promises to be fulfilled.

Ready to be filled up.

But Wolfe didn't stop, didn't move things forward, just kept twisting his fingers, watching Eric's stomach muscles quiver.

What was he waiting for?

Then he caught the twitch of Wolfe's lips. Ah, right. He wanted to be begged again, the narcissist.

"Wolfe," Eric whined.

The lip twitch again. "Yes, pet?"

"Fuck me. Now."

"Always ordering me about."

But Eric didn't miss the smug, catlike smile.

Wolfe withdrew his fingers, seeming to revel in Eric's gasp as he did so. He began lubing up his cock, never taking his eyes off Eric's. But Eric couldn't help it; he let his gaze lower to what was happening below. *That* was going to be inside him. That cock, maybe a bit shorter than Eric's but most definitely thicker, the tip of it an angry red.

Wolfe cocked a brow, noting the direction of his gaze. "Are you ready, pet?"

Eric was *not* a fucking blushing virgin, damn it. "I'm ready." The words came out more breathless than he would have liked.

Wolfe slid forward on his knees, looming over Eric's supine form. The long, lean line of him was beautiful. So fucking beautiful. Eric had always found men attractive, but he'd gravitated mostly toward twinky types—anyone younger, smaller, more feminine. Maybe some misguided attempt to feel more masculine in comparison? Who the fuck knew.

Wolfe may have been slimmer and shorter than him, but he was by no means petite. There was strength there, as Wolfe would say. A certain feline grace. And that alarming, intense, obsessive possession—that sharp, greedy feeling—Eric could feel reach a fever pitch as Wolfe pressed back Eric's thigh, lining himself up for entry.

Eric's eyes closed reflexively at the sting as that fat tip entered him.

"Eyes open."

It was more snarl than command. Eric opened them again to find Wolfe closer than before, hovering over Eric as he pressed in deeper, his brown eyes darker than Eric had ever seen them. "Watch me while I take you, Eric. You're mine. Completely mine."

Eric kept his eyes wide open, breath catching as his body stretched to receive that intimidating cock. But it wasn't real pain, nothing sharp or terrible. Just that incredible fullness of his body accepting his mate, opening up for him as he bottomed out.

He's ours, hissed that new, beastly presence in Eric's psyche. *We're his.*

Wolfe started slow, watching Eric all the while, clearly delighting in every change of breathing pattern, every embarrassing noise he could get out of him, no matter how small. And Eric felt horribly, wonderfully exposed, each time Wolfe withdrew that thick cock, leaving him empty and aching until the next moment, when he was filled again.

It wasn't as embarrassing as it could have been. Not when he could *feel* Wolfe's desire for him, smell that bergamot musk thickening with his arousal.

When Wolfe picked up the pace, canting his hips in a way that had Eric keening, Eric's eyes finally closed, high-pitched moans punching out of him with every thrust of Wolfe's hips.

Wolfe didn't chastise him this time, just kept mercilessly hitting that sharp, tender spot in him. He had pressed Eric's thigh as far back as it could stretch, and had landed his torso in the open space until his body was blanketing Eric's completely, Eric's cock sliding against the soft fuzz of his stomach.

Could Eric come just like this?

He opened his eyes again to see Wolfe had finally come fully undone. His hair had come out of its careful, slicked hold. His eyes were dark and glazed, his lids heavy. He was panting, gasping, muttering, "Mine. You're *mine*."

"Yours," Eric slurred mindlessly.

It didn't seem to appease Wolfe any. Only drive him to thrust harder. "You'll come like this, pet. Just like this. With me inside you."

And apparently Eric's body—just like his mind, his heart, his fucking soul—knew who it belonged to. Because he did. Just like that. A punch of heat along his spine, then an aching, electric release that had the edges of his vision whitening out.

Wolfe groaned in frantic approval, capturing Eric's mouth as he found his own release, burying himself deep with a shudder while he sucked, bit, and bruised Eric's lips.

Minutes or hours or fucking days later, he finally released Eric's mouth.

"Oh my God," Eric groaned when he finally caught his breath. Wolfe had let his weight fall, and it was heavenly, to be held down by it. "Oh my *God*."

He felt the vibration of Wolfe chuckling.

"I don't think I can move," Eric sighed.

Wolfe pressed a swift kiss to his tender lips. "You don't have to, darling. I'll get you cleaned up." He shot him a wicked smile. "You must save your strength."

"For what?"

"For round two."

Eighteen

Wolfe

Consciousness came slower to Wolfe than he was used to. He was first aware of the warm, happy, sated scent of his mate, the wisteria wrapping around him like some sort of sweet fog. Then came the soft rustling sounds of the sheets. And then the press of a hot mouth against his upper thigh.

How marvelous. He would have thought his mate would need a bit more time for recovery. Wolfe hadn't exactly taken it easy on him, especially for a first time bottoming. It had tested every bit of his resolve to take his time preparing Eric, to wait so carefully until his mate was desperate for it.

He'd thought perhaps he'd finally be sated after claiming him, but it had only stoked the flames of Wolfe's desire. He'd had Eric twice more before wiping down the exhausted, beautiful man and letting him sleep the few hours they required.

But apparently Eric was already up for more. Wolfe waited, eyes closed, for Eric to inch along from his thigh to his hardening cock. His beast shifted lazily, contended and anticipatory both.

He got a nip of blunt teeth instead.

Wolfe opened his eyes and peered down to see Eric looking beyond delectable between his thighs, his blond hair tousled, his stubbled cheeks pink, and a delightfully mischievous tilt to his mouth.

Wolfe found himself smiling easily—how could he not, with such a perfect vision in front of him? "What are you up to down there, pet?"

Eric licked a stripe up the side of Wolfe's thigh. "You said there were lots of places we could bite."

"Mm, I did, didn't I?"

Eric nipped him again, on the tender skin where Wolfe's thigh met his pelvis, his teeth still blunt. "Here?"

"Are you hungry, pet? You know my blood can't nourish you."

Eric shook his head, his stubble tickling Wolfe's skin. "Not hungry." He paused. "Well, a little. I wouldn't mind that blood bag later. I just want to...do it again, I guess. Is that okay?"

What a beautifully greedy creature.

Wolfe leaned his head back, threading his fingers through Eric's hair—still too short, but it would grow. "Be my guest, darling."

There was a brief, sharp sting and then that lovely wash of sensation from the night before—Eric's pleasure at Wolfe's taste, Wolfe's own pleasure at the feel of the bite.

Wolfe may not have been getting his cock sucked, but this was its own form of perfection. Eric would drink, the greedy thing. Then Wolfe would direct that cheeky mouth to his cock, feed his mate essence of a different sort. And then...well, he'd simply decide from there. So many delicious choices. Suck Eric off as well? Use his hand and capture those lips again? Have Eric bring himself to completion, perhaps in front of the mirror, so he could see how gorgeous he became in his lustful state? Or possibly edge him for hours, see what desperate sounds he could tear out of him.

The harsh sound of a phone ringing broke through Wolfe's delightful daydreams.

Eric lifted his head from Wolfe's lap, his lips bloody. A vision like no other. "That's mine."

"Ignore it."

But Eric was already leaning over the bed to peer at the damned thing, most likely conditioned from years of being the doctor on call.

Wolfe could feel Eric's dismay through the bond before he saw it on his face. "My mom."

"Ignore it," Wolfe said again.

Eric's brow was furrowed, his reddened lips twisted in a frown. "But she's *been* calling. For days now. I can't just—"

"You can." Wolfe picked up the offending device and tossed it on the floor, where it slid beneath the dresser.

Now Eric's frown was directed at him. "Hey!"

"You're an adult, Eric. You don't have to answer."

Eric sat up with a huff. "And you don't get to dictate who I talk to. Or am I a prisoner after all?"

It was a laughable accusation. The good doctor had been walking all over Wolfe since the moment he'd gotten there. Wolfe tried to rein in his annoyance and stick to the facts. "I don't like what I sense through the bond when she calls." More to himself than Eric, he muttered, "She'll have to be dealt with."

His beast agreed with every ounce of its unnatural being. *Kill what hurts our mate.*

Eric eyed him with suspicion. "What does that mean?"

As their interlude had been so painfully interrupted, Wolfe rose from the bed, striding to the closet to grab his favored silk robe.

"Wolfe," Eric prompted.

Wolfe grabbed a second robe for his mate and tossed in on the bed.

"*Wolfe.*"

Perhaps he'd run them both a bath.

Eric slid to the edge of the bed, trying to catch Wolfe's eye. "Hey. Psychopath. You can't kill my mom."

Wolfe ran a hand through his unacceptably disheveled hair. "Are you so attached, then?"

He didn't understand it, this loyalty to someone who clearly made Eric so miserable. This woman who had the irritating power of ruining his mate's good mood with one measly phone call. Wolfe may have been grateful she'd created such a needy void in Eric, but she'd already played her role. He had no more use for Eric's dissatisfaction. He wanted his mate content, joyful, lustful. Anything but this strange mix of shameful and distressed.

Eric was gawking up at Wolfe like he'd come from another planet. Wolfe tried again. "I won't have you upset, darling."

"Killing my mother would upset me." Eric spoke slowly, as if to drive the point home. Like Wolfe was some kind of simpleton.

"I'll think of something." At Eric's suspicious look, Wolfe sniffed. "Something *else*, I suppose."

Wolfe moved to the vanity, combing his hair back into place. He'd simply have to work within the bounds of Eric's ridiculous sentimentality. He didn't want to know what the consequences of offing one of Eric's family members would be, especially after being asked so deliberately not to. Separate bedrooms? Separate *houses*?

Eric seemed to take him at his word and left it at that. Wolfe watched him through the mirror as he sat up and donned the robe Wolfe had left for him, leaving it untied, much to Wolfe's delight.

"What about *your* family?" Eric asked, after a minute.

"They're long dead, darling."

A pregnant pause.

Wolfe turned from the vanity with an exasperated sigh. "I didn't kill them."

Eric nodded, his belief in Wolfe's words clear on his face. "But you didn't love them."

"I didn't. And as far as I know, the feeling was mutual." Wolfe went to work picking their discarded clothing up from the floor, setting each item in the hamper. It wouldn't do to start acting slovenly now.

"They knew something was wrong with me very early on; they set up strict punishments from the beginning. Trying to prevent public embarrassment, I suppose. I quickly learned the importance of minding consequences, so I suppose I should be grateful for that lesson. And then they lost our fortune after the war, lost what was rightfully mine, what I had worked so hard to be respectable enough to earn, and I had little use for them after that."

"And then you turned, and it all went wrong," Eric said softly.

Was that what Eric thought? Wolfe suppressed a laugh. "I *asked* to be turned, pet."

"What?"

Wolfe strode back to the bed, pleased when Eric leaned against him, his head nuzzling into Wolfe's stomach, his arms draped casually over Wolfe's hips. "I found a fated pair. I saw what they had: immortality, eternal youth, the power to do what they pleased when they pleased. And, I suppose, each other. I wanted it."

"And the drinking blood thing didn't dissuade you at all?" Eric mumbled the question into Wolfe's robe.

"It did not."

Eric huffed, his warm breath tickling what skin it could reach. "You're really one of a kind, did you know that?"

"Of course." Wolfe smoothed a hand over his mate's hair.

"Jesus." Eric started laughing, a deep, husky, delighted sound. He'd laughed in Wolfe's presence before, of course—in disbelief, in surprise, in release—but this was different. Relaxed and joyful and so lovely it hurt.

All that would have been ruined, Wolfe was sure of it, if the mother had been allowed to speak with him.

Eric's chuckles tapered off, but he didn't release Wolfe from his grasp. "When you turned, did you see your parents again?"

So inquisitive today. No matter. Wolfe didn't mind answering his questions, if it kept him so content. "I did not. I changed my surname, and I fled."

Eric tilted his head to peer up at him. "Am I going to have to fake my death or something? When I don't age."

"It depends on how hard people will look for you. How much they care. Otherwise, you could simply disappear."

Eric pursed his lips as he thought. "She'd try to find me, I think, out of a need for control more than anything else."

"Then we'll kill human Eric."

"That'll be kind of cool, right?" Eric's smile was surprisingly loose and easy for the topic at hand. "Starting fresh, I mean. Although, I guess I couldn't be a doctor anymore."

Eric could be anything the fuck he wanted. Wolfe would make sure of it.

"There are ways, darling. Forged documents. Compulsion. You can be what you wish."

But Eric wasn't listening, too lost in his own thoughts. "I could move more to research, maybe."

He sounded hopeful—content, even. Wolfe stroked his hair while Eric plotted, and their bond pulsed, soft and sweet once again.

Wolfe hadn't lied when he'd told Eric he hadn't been unhappy before. But he supposed the truth was he hadn't been happy either. He hadn't known the difference.

He knew the difference now.

"So am I, like, your prized possession? Is that how you think of me?"

Wolfe mulled the question over as he soaped Eric's broad shoulders. The large ledge of the tub allowed Wolfe to sit out of the water with his back to the wall, his calves bracketing his mate as he bathed him. The edge of his robe was damp with bathwater, but it was hard to mind.

Was Eric his possession? Eric was *his*; that was certain. His to have, his to protect, his to cherish. But Wolfe had no doubts Eric was also his own person, one with thoughts and feelings and opinions. He'd made them known well enough in their time together.

"Does the thought displease you?" he asked, rinsing his hands and reaching for the shampoo.

"I don't know." Eric sighed with contentment as Wolfe started to lather up his hair. "You seem to take really good care of your possessions."

Wolfe smirked. "And you wish to be cared for, don't you, darling?"

"Doesn't everybody?"

"I don't know that I do."

Wolfe didn't need Eric to coddle him, to soothe him, to bathe him like this. He just needed Eric to...exist. To be there, at Wolfe's side. And perhaps to allow Wolfe to do those things for him, allow him to take delight in pleasing him.

But Eric seemed to take it another way. "You don't want me to love you?" he asked, uncertainty lacing his tone.

The question took Wolfe by surprise. "I understand it could be difficult to."

Eric hummed noncommittally, playing with the soap bubbles as Wolfe rinsed his head. Wolfe's beast shifted restlessly, agitated by the turn in the conversation. Now that Eric had brought it up...

Wolfe did his best to keep his voice mild and unconcerned, despite what Eric may have been able to feel through the bond. "What does it mean to you, darling? Romantic love."

"Oh fuck, I don't know. I don't have any experience of it. I guess..." Eric paused as Wolfe worked conditioner into his strands. "I guess it's wanting that person safe and happy. And then feeling safe and happy with them too. Wanting to be around them all the time. Considering their needs like you do your own. But also wanting to touch them and hold them and sex them up. Like, attraction mixed with care?"

Attraction mixed with care? Was it really so simple? Some elementary equation?

Wolfe's breath caught as Eric tilted his head back, those dark-green eyes fixed on his. "I can feel it, you know," Eric murmured. "A softening to the way you feel about me, compared to before. It's still obsessive and...intense. But it's also changed. There's care there, I think."

Now it was Wolfe's turn to hum noncommittally, as he motioned for Eric to turn around and let Wolfe rinse the conditioner. "The painters come this afternoon."

"For real this time?"

Wolfe could feel Eric's smirk, even with his head turned away. "Mm. I believe we'll finish the en suite in the next few days. And then we'll move in there. The both of us."

As far as tests of loyalty went, it was a ridiculous one. But for the first time in his life, Wolfe found himself wanting reassurance. He waited, his muscles held tense, for Eric to protest, to insist on remaining in his own, separate room.

But Eric just leaned more firmly against Wolfe's legs, his wet torso hot from the bathwater. "Yeah, sounds good. And then maybe the den thing? I know you were teasing me about fucking me over couch cushions and stuff, but it didn't sound so bad. Like, a comfy space. Not the fucking." He paused, cocking his head. "But also yeah, the fucking too."

Ridiculous. As if Wolfe had been *joking* about fucking Eric over couch cushions. And Eric may have slyly not mentioned the cock warming, but Wolfe hadn't forgotten Eric's hitch of embarrassed breath at the thought of it.

There would be time to explore that later.

"We can make you a room," Wolfe agreed. "And I may put a desk in there for myself," he added, once again keeping his voice light.

How much will you let me invade, pet? How much space will you try to claim?

Eric just shrugged those delectably broad shoulders, blowing bubble foam into the air. "Yeah, sure. But you have to agree to some atrocious-looking, extra-comfortable leather office chair. To match the vibes. No embroidered fabric allowed." And then Eric was laughing again, a deep chuckle, clearly pleased with his vision. With his orders.

Something unclenched in Wolfe, deep in the dark recesses of his soul. He should have known his needy mate wouldn't mind Wolfe near, but there'd been...a light concern, perhaps. With the bond solidifying, without that instability, Eric could take more space if he wanted to. Only, Wolfe no longer wanted him to have that space. Not even an inch.

Apparently Eric wasn't the only needy one.

And while his own possessiveness didn't necessarily surprise him, it was unsettling how much he now needed Eric to want the same.

"You know, I might have seen that vampire kid at the hospital."

Eric said it so casually it took a moment for Wolfe to realize the import. "Pardon?"

"I'm not positive. I was all sorts of confused at the time, and I don't even know why I'm stuck on it. But there was something off about him. And the days add up."

"I see." Wolfe fought to keep his hands relaxed, where they rested on Eric's shoulders. "And?"

"And I could compare notes with Jamie's vision. Help look for him, even. If he's seen me before, maybe he'd be more open to being approached. Maybe he saw I was a doctor; maybe he'll realize I could help."

So many maybes for a situation where Eric's safety was concerned. It was unacceptable.

Wolfe cleared his throat. "I suppose we could look together..."

And then Wolfe could take the child and do whatever needed to be done.

"Um..."

Wolfe did tense this time. "You wish to go alone?"

Eric scoffed. "Um, no offense, but you're a little intimidating, babe."

Wolfe froze, his fingers clawing just slightly into Eric's shoulders, attempting to process what had just come out of his mate's mouth. *Babe.*

Eric turned to grin at him, gripping Wolfe's wrist with one hand. "Didn't like that one? You are though." His thumb rubbed circles onto Wolfe's pulse point. "It's hard to tell at first, because of how you dress. But you're like, super fit. Especially naked."

What to do with this man? Wolfe did the only thing he could: he shrugged off his robe and slid down the ledge into the hot water of the tub, bracketing his mate between his knees. Eric leaned against his chest with a happy sigh.

Wolfe tried a dash of reason. "We don't know when this child was turned, darling. He could be stronger than you. He could hurt you, perhaps severely."

"But it's hard to kill me, right?" Eric grabbed Wolfe's hands, wrapping them around his waist as he'd done once before, on Wolfe's lap. "It's worth a few scrapes and bruises, if we can help him. He must be so scared."

As far as Wolfe was concerned, nothing was worth Eric scraped and bruised. "I can't believe you were concerned over your lack of empathy, pet. A proper bleeding heart, you are."

"They're just a kid."

Wolfe thought it over as he held his mate close, scenting the wisteria even through the bath products. He could let Eric search, surely. And then he would search himself. He had more experience with enhanced senses, with the challenge of a hunt. He would inevitably find the child first.

And then he would do what needed to be done. If the kid was truly half-feral, it would be a mercy.

He pressed a kiss to Eric's wet hair. "All right, pet. We'll discuss it with the others."

Nineteen

Eric

For all his bluster, Eric had no idea how a kid's mind worked, or where a vampire child potentially on the run would be hanging out. So he went with the obvious: the playground. There was one the next neighborhood over from the pretentious spot Wolfe had chosen for their home.

"Okay, time for you to go," Eric said, making a shooing motion with one hand.

Wolfe looked decidedly unimpressed at the command as he continued to scan their environment, as if this vampire kiddo was going to spring out of the bushes any second.

It would save them a lot of time if it went that way, actually.

They'd checked in with Jamie and the others, verified what they could based on what Eric could remember of the kid. It seemed to match. But so far all Eric could spy were a few moms and their young children—mostly toddlers, although there was one tow-headed grade-school kid going full hog on the monkey bars—braving the winter chill for a little outdoor time.

Wolfe's expression stayed mild as ever as he drawled, "Just so you know, darling...if this child attempts to harm you in any way, I'll rip its head off."

For the briefest, most insane moment, Eric almost said, "I love you too," in response.

Because that was what Wolfe's statement *was*, wasn't it? A declaration of love in the only languages he seemed to know: violence and obsession. And Eric hadn't been lying before, in the bath—he could feel it, this new soft, fuzzy edge to Wolfe's familiar possessiveness.

But Eric couldn't just go blurting it out when Wolfe hadn't *really* said it. Hell, judging from what he'd said of his childhood, maybe the guy wouldn't even recognize the emotion for what it was.

Except what the fuck was Eric going on about?

Because whether *Wolfe* said it wasn't the important part; the important part was that *Eric* couldn't say it. Because he couldn't possibly love someone he'd known for barely a week, someone who'd drained his goddamn blood and kidnapped him and hadn't even ever apologized for it.

Mate, insisted that weird voice that seemed to pop up sometimes now.

Thank you, that's very fucking helpful, Eric replied with full sarcasm in his own head.

He turned to Wolfe, catching his gaze fully. There was something Eric had to say that was more important than any emotional declarations. "So, uh, I know from the bond and all your sly, sneaky looks and your general past behavior that you probably want to do it anyway: kill this kid, I mean. You're going to do what you want and maybe ask forgiveness afterward?"

There was a flash of genuine surprise through the bond, one reflected in the barest widening of Wolfe's eyes. Oh yeah, Eric totally had him pegged. "And I guess you could do that," he continued. "I probably even would. Forgive you, that is. Eventually. I seem willing to forgive a whole lot where you're concerned. But if you care about me, as something more than just a possession, then please." He grabbed at Wolfe's sleeve, tugging gently. "Please, just don't. I know it's inconvenient. I know you don't want that exposure, but...please."

Wolfe stared at him impassively, admitting nothing. "Why do you care so much about this nameless urchin, pet?"

Eric shrugged. "I just do? I may not be the most considerate person in the world, but I don't want some innocent kid dead just because he's a nuisance."

"Some presumably innocent, already *undead* kid, pet." Wolfe let out a put-upon sigh. "I feel manipulated."

Eric scoffed. "This is what relationships *are*. This is what people do. They compromise for each other."

"I see." Wolfe gave Eric a hard look. "And how do you compromise for me?"

Eric pressed a hard palm to his forehead, not sure whether to laugh or scream. "Are you kidding me with that question right now?"

There was a long, tense moment before Wolfe gave the barest perceptible nod in response. It wasn't much, but Eric was certain Wolfe was thinking his words over, if only because of the little pulse of frustration flitting across the bond.

Eric caved and pulled him in for a goodbye kiss anyway, delighting in another jolt of shock from Wolfe. He was always so surprised when Eric initiated affection. And oh God, Eric was going to be initiating all sorts of things now, wasn't he? Who knew being fucked was like the greatest thing ever?

When they separated, Wolfe was smirking. "Now, darling, how are you going to concentrate on catching our little imp with these kinds of lustful thoughts dancing around that brain of yours?"

Eric's face went hot. "Shut up. You need to go now."

"I'm giving you two hours," Wolfe said, smoothing out his lapels. "Before I fetch you, return you to our home, and endeavor to find out what new, desperate noises we can ply out of you. Let the other riffraff worry about the child."

With that, he stalked off, clearly still irritated over Eric's attempt at an intervention, although he hid it well enough on the surface. Would he listen to what Eric had asked? Was he capable of curbing his more selfish instincts to keep Eric happy?

It seemed like a large gamble.

Eric registered somewhere in the back of his brain that it didn't hurt anymore when Wolfe left his side. His absence now only created a sort of subdued longing, from both Eric and his beast, rather than the mindless frenzy of the early days.

But Eric wasn't alone long before a familiar lanky form, dressed once again all in black, ambled over to where Eric was standing by the benches.

The Tucson vampire. Jamie. The one who could apparently see visions of the...future? The present? Eric wasn't quite sure how it all worked, but either way, weren't vampires weird enough already? Did there really have to be actual mind magic in the world to top it all off?

Jamie nodded in greeting as he slid into place next to Eric. "Playground," he said around the toothpick he was gnawing on. "Smart thinking."

"I thought the group was gonna let me look alone."

Jamie snorted. "Please. As if Danny isn't already casing the blood bank and the hospital. Jay put the word out with his coworkers about a runaway. Soren's trying his bloodhound thing—apparently he thinks he can find the kid through a 'lack of scent,' whatever that means. Bunch of bleeding hearts, for a group of bloodsuckers."

Bleeding hearts. Exactly what Wolfe had accused him of being. It was the first time Eric had ever received that particular feedback about himself.

"And why'd you get stuck with me?" he asked.

Jamie hopped up onto the park bench, using the back of it like its own seat. "Because *I* know for sure what the little brat looks like. And *you* seem to think he might be willing to chat with you. We're the most likely team, man. Let's revel in the greatness that is us."

Eric frowned, not sure if Jamie was being glib or sincere or some strange mix of both. "What if you scare him off?"

"Me?" Jamie tugged the toothpick out of his mouth and grinned wide. "I'm a fucking ray of sunshine, baby. Kids love me. Plus, they dig the hair." He pointed to his green locks, currently pulled back in a half pony.

Eric moved to sit on the actual seat of the bench, shading his eyes to look up at Jamie. "And what about your...mate?"

"Oh." Jamie waved a hand. "He's busy stalking your man to make sure he doesn't pull anything psycho."

Eric tensed. "He's *what*?"

"Listen, the group has certain trust issues with your boo right now, given that he keeps turning people all willy-nilly and lying to the little sweetheart Jay and also engaging in occasional kidnapping." At Eric's expression, Jamie laughed, loose and easy. "Don't worry. They'll ease up when he proves himself a little. They used to hate Luc too."

Eric thought back to Soren's *he doesn't exist* routine. "Used to?" he asked pointedly.

"Yep." Jamie responded happily, popping the *p*. "Now we're one big, happy, dysfunctional, fanged family."

Bunch of fucking lunatics was what they were. But Eric kept that to himself.

They sat in silence for some number of minutes, scanning the park. A few of the moms and their kids left, and a few more came to replace them. No sign of the kid from the hospital. Maybe the park had been a stupid idea, after all.

"So Luc's done bad things too?" Eric eventually asked, tiring of the silence.

"Oh yeah," Jamie said easily. "Big time. My monster's been off the rails before, for sure."

"And you still...like him."

Jamie shot him an amused glance. "What are we, in grade school? I fucking love him."

"Even though he's done bad things?"

"Even then." Jamie didn't elaborate beyond that. As if it was that easy. As if it didn't matter at all what Luc had done.

Eric ran his fingers over the uneven edges of the park bench, watching Jamie from the corner of his eye. "When did you know?"

"Oh. Um..." Jamie shrugged. "Way before he and I even met, probably."

Eric turned in his seat to look at him fully. "Excuse me?"

"You *know*—" Jamie gestured to himself. "The visions. I saw him, wanted him, loved him."

Eric's laugh of disbelief caught somewhere in his throat. "Isn't that a bit...fucking crazy?"

Jamie grinned widely. "Sure. But hey, last week you were human, and now you're a fucking vampire. We're all a little crazy." He cocked his head, a sly look on his face. "It's okay to love him, you know. Even if he's a psycho. It's going to be an eternity of you and him, bound together. Does that sound good to you or not? Because if it does, fuck everybody else."

An eternity with Wolfe. It was frighteningly easy to picture. Elaborate mansions with hideous, uncomfortable furniture. Soft touches mixed with possessive fire. Easy reassurances every time Eric's insecurities ran away from him. And...someone who didn't expect anything from Eric other than his continued existence. His presence alone being enough, for the first time in his entire life. Being wanted, always. Every day. Forever.

Yeah, that sounded fucking perfect.

Jamie's dark eyes lit up at whatever he saw in Eric's expression. "See what I mean? Crazy can be *fantastic*."

Eric saw it then, out of the corner of his eye. A familiar mop of messy brown hair, a pointed, elfin chin. Crouching among the trees at the opposite edge of the playground, watching the mothers and their children with the hungriest expression Eric had ever seen.

"That him?" he asked as quiet as he could.

To his credit, Jamie barely turned his head, catching Eric's energy and looking out the corner of his eye. "Yup. That's him."

Unfortunately, even as quiet as they were, vampire hearing was apparently no fucking joke, because the kid took notice of their words, startling up from his crouched position.

For one long second, he stood there, staring at Eric, right in his eyes. Then he looked to Jamie. Back to Eric...

And then he bolted.

Eric sped through the forest, the trees a blur all around him. He was fast now—light-years faster than he'd ever been in his short stint on the track-and-field team in college—which was theoretically helpful. But really, speed was useless when he didn't know where he was going. It was like the kid had disappeared into thin air, and now Eric and Jamie were just tearing through pine trees without purpose.

When they paused to catch their bearings, Jamie looked around doubtfully. "Maybe we should split up?"

Eric tried to control his panting, unsure why his vampire body even insisted on it. "Isn't that how people meet their bad ends in all the horror movies?"

Jamie's eye roll was sassy as fuck. "Dude. He's a kid. I think we'll survive."

Eric hesitated, just for a moment. He knew what Wolfe would want—he'd want Eric to have the extra protection. He'd want him unharmed and with plenty of backup.

But wasn't it more important to not lose this kid? What if they never got another chance like this?

He nodded slowly. "Yeah, we can split up."

So they did. Jamie went east. Eric went west.

He went deeper than he'd ever cared to explore in these woods—deep enough that he'd worry about finding his way back, if not for the fact that he'd learned how to use the sun to gauge cardinal directions in the Eagle Scouts his mother had made him join. Something about making him competitive for prep school.

The run wasn't exactly pleasant. The pine smelled good and all, but the winter sun had melted the snow enough to make everything a muddy mess. And maybe it still could have had some sort of scraggly charm if Eric weren't so fucking frustrated.

Where had this kid *gone*?

He stopped in a small clearing, one where the melted snow had made the world's tiniest pond. Once again, he asked himself the question: Where would he have gone as a kid? Unfortunately, the truth was he'd probably have run far, far away and never come back. If the kid had been traumatized by some vampire and then saw two more of them stalking him in a park? He'd be wise to be long gone.

God, Eric had fucked it all up, hadn't he? He'd ruined it. He should go back to the playground, let Wolfe take him home. Stop trying to be of use when he was inherently useless.

The telltale snap of a twig had Eric whirling around only to see more of nothing all around him. Definitely horror movie vibes.

When he turned back, the kid was there.

He was standing unbelievably still, across the tiny pond, maybe five feet back from the edge. Eric had probably gauged his age about right, maybe somewhere around ten years old. He was filthy up close. Had he been that filthy at the hospital? He had dirt smudging his face, his clothes, his hands—one of which was holding the limp body of a squirrel.

Eric's stomach churned. Jesus, had he drained the thing? Was it like Jay had said: the kid could eat animal *and* people blood? Some sort of vampire omnivore?

"Hi there." Eric winced at the sound of his own voice. Was that really the best he could do?

He at least knew well enough not to step closer, not when the kid looked ready to bolt again at any second, his small, wiry frame tense as hell.

The kid pushed back a matted lock of dark hair with his free hand. "Smell like him."

His small voice was surprisingly hoarse, like he hadn't spoken for a very long time. And from the way he said the word "him," it didn't sound like a compliment.

Still, it was some sort of jumping off point, at least.

"What does, um, *he* smell like?" Eric asked.

"Old pennies."

Of course. The coppery, metallic vampire scent.

"You mean the person who did this to you?" Eric clarified. At the kid's small nod, he explained, "We all smell like that. All...vampires...do."

The kid shook his head. "I don't."

So he wasn't fazed by the vampire part. Either he'd put it together himself or the sick fucker who'd turned him had already told him.

The kid took a step closer to the pond. "Doctor."

"Me?" Eric pointed to himself like an idiot. Another small nod. "Um, yeah. We can—we can be doctors."

Was this going to be some sort of "we can still be all we can be" moment? *You can be a doctor, a nurse, a psychopath with inherited wealth.*

But then the kid said the worst possible thing, holding his mangy squirrel tight. "You can fix me."

Oh. Oh shit. Eric stepped closer before he could stop himself, rubbing a hand over his face. "No, buddy, I can't. I'm so sorry. It's...permanent. The change."

The disappointment on that young face was like a knife to the chest. Eric should have lied, right? Wolfe would have lied, would have reassured him with false promises to get him somewhere safe. But Eric couldn't bear to give this poor, filthy kid fake hope.

The little guy's eyes welled up like he was going to cry, but all he did was nod again. "That's what he said too."

"The one who did this to you?" *Give me a name, kid. We'll rip his head off for you.*

"No." The child cocked his head, studying Eric through his messy hair. "The voice. Do you have it too? My imaginary friend."

Was he talking about his beast? He must have been, right?

Eric debated taking another step forward but in the end chose to stay where he was. "Yeah. Mine only talks sometimes though. Real limited vocabulary. But my—my partner talks to his a lot."

"Hard to think sometimes. Hard to talk. Always growling." The kid held his hands in claws like a cartoon monster, the squirrel swaying in his grasp. "Always hungry."

"Yeah, that sounds pretty...rough."

Then they were staring at each other, and Eric had no fucking idea what to do next. Where did he go from here? Find out where he was from? Offer to help him get another squirrel? Offer to find and kill the fucker who'd done this to him?

The kid grasped the squirrel in both hands. "I hurt Mama."

Jesus Christ. Eric was not equipped for this. He tried to keep his voice calm and level. "Did you—is your mama...is she still alive?"

"Yes. I—I stopped. Ran." The kid was twisting the squirrel in his hands. The tiny head popped right off. "I'm really fast."

"Yeah, you are. I couldn't catch you; that's for sure." Eric tried his best not to look at the newly decapitated body in the kid's hold. "How'd you know to go to blood banks? And the hospitals? You must be really smart, huh?"

"Mama was a...phlegmologist?"

Eric racked his brain for what that could be. "A phlebotomist? She drew blood from people?"

"Yeah." The kid gave him the smallest, most hesitant smile. "Phlegmbolomist."

"That's great. That's a really cool job." Jesus fuck, he sounded like an idiot. Eric had never been good with kids. There was a reason he hadn't gone into pediatrics. "So do you, uh, wanna come back with me? I can help get you food, and you could have a bath?" At the kid's frown, Eric tried again. "Or a shower?"

The kid looked down at his clothes, at his bloody hands. "Dirty."

"Yeah, I bet you've been really roughing it, huh?"

The little guy seemed to be thinking about it, cocking his head and looking Eric over, as if to search for hidden motives. But then he started tensing again.

Shit, he was going to run for sure. Of course he was. He'd been turned by some random vampire who smelled just like Eric—like *blood*—and now here Eric had been stalking him in the woods, talking about bringing him home and bathing him?

Eric prepared himself for another chase, but faster than he could process—faster than the kid could process either—there was Wolfe, right behind the little vampire, one arm wrapped around his throat.

"Well, what do we have here?"

Twenty

Eric

Oh fuck. This was not going to end well, was it? Not unless Eric did something. Should he distract Wolfe? How? Strip naked? Start talking about pretentious interior decorating?

Or maybe he didn't need to distract. Maybe he just needed to...assuage.

"He didn't hurt me!" Eric blurted out.

It felt ridiculous to say, what with how tiny this vampire child looked, Wolfe's arm wrapped tight around his neck, his little fingers clawing at the restriction.

"I know he didn't," Wolfe answered calmly, not loosening his hold one bit.

"So...you won't hurt him?" Eric allowed himself to be hopeful for one second that this wouldn't turn into a complete shitshow.

Wolfe's flat gaze met his. "Why, don't you trust me, pet?"

Eric almost laughed. Because, well, that was the question, wasn't it? The love stuff, Eric had maybe figured out. Or was at least *open* to figuring out. But *trust*?

When it came to Wolfe and his behavior with other people, definitely not. He'd do what he wanted, when he wanted, without caring for how it affected anyone else.

But when it came to Wolfe and Eric?

Yes, he did. Eric trusted Wolfe to take care of him, to put his happiness first. It may have been intertwined with Wolfe's selfish desire to feel that happiness for himself, but still… Wolfe wanted Eric content, and he must have known that in this instance that included a nonviolent solution to this particular problem. So…

"Yes," Eric answered, his gaze unwavering. "I trust you."

There was a flash of fierce satisfaction through the bond, like Eric had just given Wolfe the key to the fucking kingdom. Which he supposed he sort of had. Without trust, what else was there?

The same kind of toxic relationship Eric had with his mother, he supposed.

"My perfect darling," Wolfe purred, his light-brown eyes boring into Eric's obsessively, as if he wasn't holding a struggling, snarling grade-schooler with one hand.

Eric felt his face heat. "Um…"

The kid made a rabid growling noise, and Wolfe turned his attention back to where it probably should have been. "Now, child," he admonished. "You want to run. It's quite understandable. But that would be very foolish. You're young and scared and hungry, and you have a beast inside you that you don't understand. You're going to end up hurting someone. Most likely killing someone."

Eric started to protest—really, wasn't that a harsh thing to say to someone so young?—but he closed his mouth when the kid's struggling stopped abruptly.

"That's right," Wolfe said approvingly. "The grown-ups are in charge now. You won't be harmed." He met Eric's eyes again. "We don't harm children here."

"Hungry," the kid said, his gaze fixed on the squirrel he'd dropped in the struggle.

"And we'll get you something to eat, won't we?" Wolfe answered.

"Hurt Mama."

Eric opened his mouth to explain, but Wolfe was already on it.

"We can get you food without hurting anyone. I'm afraid squirrels won't fill you up for long. Now, if I release you, will you behave?"

The kid nodded as much as Wolfe's tight restraint would allow. Wolfe loosened his arm, letting the little vampire slide out of his hold. Immediately, the kid moved to pick up the disgusting squirrel corpse.

"Leave it," Wolfe ordered, his voice harsher than before. Apparently his new patience had its limits, and that limit was the prospect of squirrel guts on his upholstery.

But the kid obeyed easily enough, giving one last mournful look at the drained body before sidestepping the little pond and walking in what seemed to be the direction of town.

Wolfe stalked after him, tilting his chin for Eric to follow, and Eric trailed behind, trying to think what they were possibly going to do with the little guy once they got him home.

They walked on for a while, and Eric startled when he noticed the kid had sidled closer to him. At his surprised look, the kid grimaced. "You're nicer."

Wolfe scoffed at that. "What's your name, little one?"

Jesus. Eric had forgotten to ask for a name. How had he thought he was equipped to deal with sniffing the kid out when he'd forgotten to even ask for a *name* once he'd done it?

The kid shot Wolfe a suspicious glance, stepping even closer to Eric. "Riley."

"Well, Riley. Did the man who turned you harm you in any way? Other than the first bite?"

Riley frowned. "No. But I didn't like him." He glanced at Eric, as if confiding in him. "He kept saying he turned me for 'her.' To make 'her' happy."

"Who's her?" Eric asked, trying to keep the horror out of his voice. It all sounded creepy as hell. What the fuck had this kid been through?

Riley shrugged, looking back down at his feet. "Dunno. I ran back to Mama. Then I had to run away for good."

"Do you remember what the man looked like?" Wolfe asked.

Riley kicked at the dirt as he walked. "Mean face."

"And where does your mama live?" Eric asked, attempting to catch Riley's gaze again.

But when Riley met Eric's eyes with his own, they were all black. "Hungry," he growled.

Eric froze, and he noticed Wolfe stepping closer out of the corner of his eye. "Um, we'll get you food soon."

Riley didn't say anything in response. But he didn't make any move to attack or run. He just kept walking beside them, making little growls every now and then. It was like he wasn't quite all there.

"I think it would be wise to return him home now." Wolfe spoke as if Riley couldn't hear them, even though they were both flanking him. And maybe he couldn't, with whatever state he was in. "It's remarkable as it is that he's controlled himself this well for this long."

"He would have run, if it were just me," Eric said, unexpectedly bitter. "I fucked it up, scared him somehow. Scumbag, per usual."

"You are nothing of the sort," Wolfe said evenly.

Eric shook his head. "You're just saying that to keep me happy."

He got a frustrated noise in response. It was kind of cool, actually, how Eric could manage to get a rise out of his unflappable mate. Everybody had their talents, right?

Wolfe stopped in his tracks, a hand on Riley's shoulder to halt him, ignoring the little growl he got in response. His gaze was piercing, freezing Eric in turn. "If you don't trust how I feel about you, pet, trust how I feel about myself. You are my perfect match. My *mate*. So no, you aren't a scumbag, or useless, or defective in any way, no matter what you may have been raised to believe. You are, by very definition, perfect."

Eric sighed, unbelievably touched but also a bit tempted to laugh. "Was that just a roundabout way of calling yourself perfect?"

Wolfe cocked a brow. "Some would say I have my faults." He smirked at Eric's chuckle. "But you, darling. You are perfect for me."

This time, Eric did say it, unable to keep it inside. "I love you too."

The flash of pure, unadulterated shock on Wolfe's face was incredibly satisfying. Eric would have kissed him for it, if not for the dazed, vamped-out child hovering between them.

He looked Riley over skeptically. "He seems really out of it."

Wolfe started walking again, as if the declaration had never happened, pushing gently at Riley until he did the same. "We'll feed him the blood bag at home. And perhaps call Danny, see if he can bring extras."

"Isn't that gonna raise even more suspicion? More missing blood bags?"

Wolfe shrugged one shoulder. "We'll compel who we need to compel."

It was a far cry from Wolfe's original "do anything to prevent exposure." He was *helping*, beyond just the big favor of not trying to put the kid down.

As rigid as Wolfe was by nature, he was adapting. Changing. And he was doing it all for Eric.

Eric smiled to himself as they picked up the pace. Yeah, the love definitely went both ways.

They made it back home without attracting any attention, thanks to Wolfe's car parked at the edge of the forest. Jamie had caught up with them briefly, but he'd run off again with Luc to see if they could spark any visions of who had done this, given the small amount of new information they had.

Now Riley had already gulped down their one blood bag, slouching over their kitchen table, but his eyes were still all black and he wasn't talking any. Eric didn't know what to do about that. It wasn't like the kid had been mute before. But who knew what it was like, being a kid and having that hungry, beastly presence in your body?

Like, was the beast a kid too? A baby beast?

The sound of the front door flinging open had Riley tensing up, clearly two seconds away from bolting, but Wolfe's stern, "Stay put," seemed to have the desired effect, and he relaxed back, licking at the stray drops on the inside of the plastic blood bag.

Eric followed Wolfe to the front door, visions of FBI officers invading their home running through his head. He knew it was unlikely, but they were harboring a kidnapped child at this point, weren't they?

But it was only Danny and Jay, each carrying a giant paper bag stuffed to the brim. Jesus, was that all *blood*?

"We come bearing comic books," Danny singsonged by way of greeting, answering Eric's unspoken question.

"Well, praise the lord," Wolfe mocked, a sneer on his lips. "That solves everything."

"Don't be snide," Danny chastised, swishing past him with a frown, before nodding at Eric in greeting. "We also come bearing blood."

"Slightly more useful," Wolfe conceded.

Danny gave a put-upon sigh and headed straight into the kitchen, where they could hear his soft, "Hiya, kiddo."

But Jay stopped in front of Wolfe, his paper bag still in hand. "You did a very good thing, Wolfgang."

"I'm so glad you approve."

But Wolfe's sarcasm seemed lost on the little barista, who nodded happily in response. "I do. Your mate is good for you. I get it. Mine's good for me too."

Wolfe's lips twitched. "Quells your psychopathic urges, does he?"

Jay cocked his head, seeming to mull it over. "Well, I'm not sure I have any of those. But he does accept me, just as I am."

Wolfe cast a sidelong glance to Eric. "Yes. I may know something about that."

"Perfect!" Jay beamed. "You two are officially invited to the next family camping trip."

"I'll try my best to contain this overwhelming excitement."

"You do that." Jay wandered off into the kitchen, patting Eric on the chest as he passed by.

Eric moved to follow, but Wolfe stopped him with a hand on his upper arm. And then Eric was being pressed against the wall, Wolfe's breath hot on his ear, his voice the quietest whisper it could be without being too soft to hear. "Once this mass of intruders is out of our home, I'm taking you to bed, and I'm not letting you out for a month." Wolfe tugged Eric's earlobe between blunt teeth with a soft growl. "It will be my reward. For all this...good behavior."

"You want to be rewarded with another kidnapping?" Eric was going for sarcasm, but his voice came out too breathy for it to be very affective.

"I want my mate. And I want him *alone*. It's been far too long since I've had my cock inside you."

Eric did his best to suppress his shiver of desire, his breath catching at the heat in Wolfe's eyes. He didn't want to be walking into the kitchen with a massive hard-on. But fuck if he didn't want the very same thing. Their last time together felt like it had been a thousand years ago.

Danny's voice rang out from the kitchen. "May I remind you there are children present, and you two are not being as quiet as you think you are?"

"May I remind you whose house you are in?" Wolfe snarled before Eric kissed him to shut his mouth.

He allowed himself the briefest, chastest kiss he could manage—well, minus one tiny slip of the tongue—before he sidled out of Wolfe's hold, readjusting himself before joining the others in the kitchen.

He found Riley finishing off another blood bag, his wary black eyes focused on Danny, who was smiling in encouragement.

Jay was unloading his paper bag enthusiastically. "I hope you like superheroes. I borrowed these from Colin, though, so we should be careful not to get too much blood on them. And he's really into something he calls the antihero, so we have a lot of that red-suited snarky guy and also that one sharp-toothed alien snake-tongued guy who shares the other man's body, and they seem to be a couple, but also he looks a little scary for my taste." He eyed Riley with careful consideration. "Is that too mature for you? How old are you? Six? Fifteen?"

Eric opened his mouth to tell him he was wasting his time, that Riley was too focused on his inner beast to even speak. But Riley's eyes were already returning to their normal dark brown, and he was tossing his empty blood bag on the table, reaching eagerly for a comic. "Old enough for comics," he mumbled.

In less than a minute, he and Jay were settled side by side, giggling over whatever over-the-top comic-book violence they were reading.

"Okay, yeah," Eric conceded, smiling at Danny. "The comics were a really good idea."

"Psh. Duh," Danny said happily. "But, um, speaking of good ideas...what exactly are we going to do? We're all pretty well known in this town. It would be awfully conspicuous if we suddenly had, like, a half-feral ward. And Jay barely looks old enough to drink, let alone have a ten-year-old son."

Jay looked up from his comic. "Technically I wasn't. Old enough to drink, that is. When I was turned."

"You, on the other hand." Danny pointed a finger at Wolfe. "You're new here."

"I will not be raising a child," Wolfe said firmly, his eyes focused on Riley's dirty hands all over his kitchen table.

A wave of relief washed through Eric. Riley seemed...fine? But it was going to be enough of a challenge, keeping Wolfe in line for the next eternity, without the added pressure of throwing a child into the mix.

Danny looked a little shocked by the refusal, which was kind of funny, considering who he'd just asked. "But—"

"I think you'll like my solution just fine, Nurse Danny. It should be here in about two hours. Plenty of time to get this creature a little more presentable."

Riley scowled at Wolfe over his comic book.

Wolfe inclined his chin. "Yes, I'm talking about you. And you can't take the comic into the bath. It will get soggy."

Johann shuffled through the comics, selecting one out of the pile. "You can take this one. Colin has two copies, and he said you could have this one for keeps. So it's okay if it gets a little soggy."

Riley grinned triumphantly at Wolfe, as if to say, *See?* Wolfe looked askance at Johann. "Does this human manager of yours actually know there's a vampire child in town?"

Johann didn't even look up from his comic. "Why, was it a secret?"

Wolfe pinched the bridge of his nose. "Two more hours," he muttered. "Just two more hours."

Twenty-One

Wolfe

Wolfe's solution showed up right on time. And it actually knocked like a civilized person, unlike the two miscreants playing Go Fish with a freshly bathed Riley on Wolfe's elegant coffee table not suitable at all for children.

But manners apparently stopped short there, because Wolfe barely had the door open before Daphne—dark eyes shining like he'd never seen—sailed past him into the house without so much as a hello. "Is he here? Did he agree?"

Wolfe nodded to Sybil—still on his doorstep, dressed in a formfitting velvet wrap dress just this side of decent—who shot him a wink in return. "She's a bit overexcited about the whole situation."

They followed the clacking of Daphne's platforms to the sitting room. She'd paused in the doorway, her hand on the doorframe. "Well, hello there, little one."

Riley only threw her a mistrustful look from his seat on the floor, his muscles tensing as if to flee *again*, but Johann shot up immediately. "Daphne!" He rushed to embrace her, arms held wide, as if she were a long-lost sister rather than an acquaintance met only a handful of times.

Such a sentimental little thing.

But the warm welcome seemed to appease the skittish child, who unclenched his muscles and took the opportunity to peek at Johann's cards. He was decent enough looking now that he'd been bathed, Wolfe supposed. There was certainly a sort of elfin charm there, when he wasn't snarling or beheading squirrels.

But enough charm to entice a pair of would-be mothers?

Johann peered around Daphne's form—for once, he wasn't the shortest in the room, platform shoes or not—and his eyes lit up in delight. "And Sybil!"

Wolfe was forced to bear witness to more hugging, more enthusiastic reassurances of affection. It was, frankly, over the top.

"Well?" Wolfe asked when all the fawning was over, gesturing to Riley. Impatience was getting the best of him, and he was struggling to rein it in. He wanted this situation over with. He wanted all these people out of his house. And he wanted Eric *alone*, preferably on all fours, being fucked within an inch of his life.

Sybil cocked a mocking brow, her hand on the nape of Daphne's neck. "You're not going to rush us, Wolfgang. Not with this."

Johann looked at the women with dawning comprehension, his gray eyes going wide. "Oh. *You're* the solution." He turned back to Riley and Danny, who for his part was looking cautious but hopeful. "So, Riley, maybe we should go finish our game upstairs. Let the grown-ups talk."

Riley scowled at his cards. "About me?"

"Yes, about you." Ever the honest vampire, Johann. "But nothing bad. Just how to help."

Riley looked, for whatever reason, to Eric, who'd been standing off to the side, observing the whole spectacle with a sort of patient confusion. "I can't go back to Mama, can I?"

Before Eric could speak, Daphne stepped forward carefully, squeezing Sybil's hand as she did so. "Not like this, I'm afraid, little one. We're so sorry for what happened to you."

Riley nodded thoughtfully, gathering his cards and looking to his two playmates. Wolfe was hard-pressed to tell whether he was resigned to his fate or biding his time to the next escape attempt.

Danny gestured to the stairs with his chin. "You two go on up. I'll be there in a minute." He gave a small wave to the newcomers. "Hello, I'm Danny."

Wolfe couldn't help the roll of his eyes. "Yes, yes. This is Danny. And this is Eric. Sybil and Daphne, as I'm sure you both heard Johann yell quite loudly. We've all met; let's get on with it."

Danny made a skeptical noise. "Isn't it a little sexist to pawn the kid off on two women?"

Sybil laughed airily, grabbing at Wolfe's arm. "Yes, Wolfgang, isn't it?"

Wolfe gritted his teeth. "I distinctly recall Daphne expressing the wish for a child."

"Of course you do," Daphne said approvingly, tapping a finger to her head. "That steel trap of yours." She turned to Danny, the picture of sincerity. "He's not wrong. It's my one regret of meeting Sybil when I did. No younglings of our own. Unless you count Wolfe, and he's really not the most affectionate son."

Wolfe tugged his arm out of Sybil's hold, scowling at Daphne. "I am *not* your son."

"See what I mean?" Daphne cocked her head, studying Danny, acting as if she hadn't realized what he was the moment she'd waltzed into the room. "You never wanted one of your own?"

Danny shrugged. "I have a dog, so..."

"A fur baby!" Daphne clapped her hands. "How delightful."

Wolfe resisted the urge to pinch the bridge of his nose. The two women knew his tells too well, and they'd never stop goading him if they realized it was working. "Do you want the brat or not?"

"Wolfgang," Daphne chastised. "First of all, he needs to agree to it."

"I believe he will. You two have a...warmth to you."

Sybil gave a dramatic gasp. "Compliments! How absolutely maudlin of you." She fixed her gaze sharply on Eric. "Could it be this young gentleman's influence?"

Daphne took her cue, and the two began circling Eric—who'd been absolutely closemouthed during this whole ordeal because he was a perfect creature and not nearly as annoying as every single other person currently invading Wolfe's house—like a pair of sharks.

"Very handsome," Sybil crooned. "These shoulders. But still, a certain sweetness to the face."

"He should grow that hair out a bit though," Daphne mused. "It would suit him better."

"If the two of you would stop eyeing my mate like a slab of beef, I'd greatly appreciate it."

"Your mate?" Sybil pressed a hand to her chest, wide-eyed in mock surprise. "Way to bury the lede, Wolfgang."

"You don't think the vampire child in need of a home merited the lede?"

Eric was tense, clearly nervous, but he still managed a lovely smile for the women. "It's nice to meet you both. I didn't realize Wolfe had any friends. Except Jay sometimes."

"Sometimes?" Daphne's brow furrowed, rounding on Wolfe. "Have you been upsetting sweet Johann?"

Wolfe waved a hand. "I may have acted...rashly a few times since my arrival."

"He sort of kidnapped me," Eric murmured, his cheeks flushing pink when Wolfe cocked a brow at the admission.

Sybil laughed with delight. "Well, who could blame him?"

"Stop. Flirting." Now Wolfe did pinch the bridge of his nose. He hadn't had a migraine in a century, but he thought he could feel one coming on regardless.

Danny cleared his throat from his spot on the floor. "Um, so about Riley?"

"Riley." Daphne sighed happily. "He looks like a Riley."

"You think you can take care of him?"

"It will be a challenge, surely," Sybil said. "As a whole, we know very little about vampire children. Except that they have monstrous appetites. Can he feed on animals, do you know?"

Eric shrugged. "He drained a squirrel, I'm pretty sure."

"That will help." The two women looked at each other, starting a rapid-fire back-and-forth. "Somewhere woodsy, then. A large plot of land. Perhaps elk territory?"

"But close enough to civilization to find humans to supplement."

"And if he stabilizes? What of his mother?"

"Turned so young...he may forget her. With his vampire self clamoring constantly for blood, and the general trauma of what's happened. But if not, we'll deal with it when it comes."

They nodded in unison, clearly having come to some sort of conclusion, and then Daphne turned to Wolfe. "What about the son of a bitch who turned him?"

"We don't know," Eric answered for him. "Jamie and Luc plan to try to find him, if they can. They think he may still be down south, in the desert."

That was news to Wolfe, but perhaps Eric had received a text of some sort.

There was the brief clamor of stomping down the stairs, and then Riley and Johann were once again among them, moving to join Danny.

"It was boring, just the two of us," Riley said by way of explanation, observing the two women out of the corner of his eye as he dropped his cards on the table.

Wolfe scoffed. "Was it really boring, or were you busy eavesdropping?"

He received a slap on the shoulder from Daphne, who moved to crouch down in front of the child. "Hello, Riley. I know this is all happening very quickly, but Sybil and I would like to take you with us.

Somewhere far away, where the bad vampire who turned you can't find you. And we'll help you with that bottomless pit of a belly you've got."

"I won't forget Mama," Riley said firmly. Eavesdropping indeed.

Daphne only smiled softly. "And one day, when you're older, and you're not in danger of hurting her...we'll help you track her down. Does that sound all right?"

Riley pointed to Johann. "Is he coming with us?"

Johann glanced uncertainly at Daphne, who nodded. "I'll visit, when your guardians think it's safe. And we can Facetime! I do that with Jamie's sister sometimes."

Riley sighed, a surprisingly heavy sound for one so young, before grabbing the one comic designated as his. He stood from the coffee table, reaching for Daphne's hand. "Okay."

Thank the lord, thank the devil, thank whatever other entity may have been involved. These people were finally leaving his house. Wolfe moved them along, unsubtle but uncaring. It wasn't as if Riley had any belongings to pack. He and Daphne were already whispering to each other as they walked out the door, bonding in that quick way children and those fond of them were capable of.

Sybil stopped on the porch, having the gall to pat Wolfe on his cheek. "I'm so glad you've find your mate, Wolfgang. He softens your edges, I can tell."

Wolfe's edges didn't feel very soft at the moment, but he managed a small nod of acknowledgment, if only to hurry things along. But then his mouth was moving without his permission. "And did you always want a child as well?"

"Oh." Sybil sighed, her eyes on Daphne and the urchin. "I would have been fine without, I'm sure. But my love yearns to care for one, and I yearn to care for my love." She smiled conspiratorially at him. "We'll do an awful lot for our mates, won't we?"

"Keep that child far away from us. If you lose control of him, I want nothing to do with it."

Sybil gave his cheek another pat. "There's my lovely Wolfgang. Don't you worry, we'll be out of town by the morning."

Trembling with barely contained irritation and anger, Wolfe stalked to the sitting room, trying to get himself under control. It wasn't in his nature to leave a complication open-ended, especially one as likely to blow up as this child. It made his skin itch. But he'd still done it, hadn't he? And all for the man waiting for him in the sitting room, seemingly as tense as Wolfe was, most likely due to whatever he was feeling through the bond.

What was Wolfe to do with him, this insecure mess of a man who claimed to be missing proper empathy but still tried to soften the lack thereof in Wolfe?

Eric was watching him with wary green eyes as he entered the room. It was maddening. Wolfe wanted to punish him for forcing this compromise. And yet he was loath to cause his mate distress. Contentment—that was what he wanted from him, wasn't it?

It was terrible, these warring impulses, this conflict of emotions.

But before Wolfe could open his mouth to speak—and what would he say, if he did?—Eric dropped to his knees, shuffling forward until he was directly in front of him, his head in line with Wolfe's belt.

It was an unmistakable gesture. What a clever mate, offering himself up as a sacrifice. Lust stirred hotly in Wolfe's loins despite the lingering annoyance.

Eric smiled softly at him, the expression almost shy. "You did a really good thing today."

Wolfe cocked a brow. “And you think to placate me by sucking my cock?” He tsked. “I doubt your mouth is that talented.”

Eric’s smile lost its shyness, as if Wolfe had given him encouragement rather than censure. “But you love my mouth,” he teased.

And how irritatingly true that was. Wolfe was addicted to it: claiming it, nipping at it, listening to all the ridiculous things it spouted.

He’d turned into a sap.

He clucked his tongue anyway, unwilling to admit defeat. “Cocky.”

Eric reached out to toy with his belt. “Well, that’s your fault, isn’t it? For being so nice to me all the time. It’s messed with my ego.”

Another truth, at least in part. Wolfe had spoiled Eric from the beginning, hadn’t he? Given in to all his whims. And it seemed he had no intention of stopping. He’d be concerned about the ledge he’d seemed to have found himself on if not for what Eric had told him in the woods.

“Say it again,” Wolfe demanded, stepping even closer, delighting in the way he towered over Eric’s kneeling form.

Eric didn’t have to ask what he meant. “I love you.”

Wolfe’s arousal was flush with Eric’s face, his mate’s breath warm even through the layers of fabric. Eric took the hint, fishing him out of his slacks, taking Wolfe’s already hardening cock in hand.

Wolfe smirked down at him, this beautiful man. “You gave me so much trouble in the beginning. Now look at you.”

Eric stroked him before answering, Wolfe’s cock stiffening painfully in no time at all. “That’s because you deserved it.”

“And now I deserve your devotion, do I?”

He was granted a sly smile before Eric placed a chaste kiss to the base of him, running his fingers over what bare skin he could. “It depends on my mood.”

Wolfe sucked in a breath as Eric licked him from root to tip before mouthing at Wolfe’s swollen head. “Of course it does.”

And then Wolfe groaned, his fingers clenching against his own pant leg, as Eric took him fully into his hot, wet mouth. He leaned back against the wall, letting one hand fall onto Eric's head, as Eric started sucking with purpose.

Even with arousal hot in his belly, Wolfe's lingering annoyance made him more demanding, meaner. He offered no soothing words of encouragement, only demands.

"More tongue."

"Deeper. I want you sloppy, pet."

Still, he sighed with pleasure when Eric gagged, spit soaking Wolfe's cock, before earnestly sucking him down again. "There it is."

This was what he deserved. Eric, flushed and desperate and slutty, all for Wolfe's cock. And he would have it, wouldn't he? All this and more. For an eternity.

When his belly tightened and his balls drew tight, he tugged Eric's hair, catching those green eyes. "Swallow me down, darling. Every drop."

Eric nodded with a garbled sound, and Wolfe watched, breathing harshly with his release, as that Adam's apple bobbed with each swallow.

When Wolfe finally pulled him off, Eric looked stunning: teary-eyed, spit-soaked, heavy-lidded. All the meanness drained out of Wolfe's body in an instant.

"My perfect darling," he crooned, cupping Eric's cheek.

Eric's answering smile was beatific.

Wolfe started unbuttoning his vest, his shirt soon to follow. "Now strip, pet. I need you naked."

Eric eyed Wolfe's softening cock with raised brows. "But..."

Wolfe smirked at him. "Don't worry. Your hole won't be empty for long. I'm nowhere near done with you yet."

Eric flushed beautifully before stripping with an eagerness that would be amusing if Wolfe weren't feeling so beastly with as-yet-unsated desire. As perfect as Eric had sucked him, it hadn't been enough.

Would it ever be enough?

"Do you want a pillow for your knees?" Wolfe asked, feeling magnanimous after his orgasm. However Eric answered, Wolfe would be taking his mate here and now. On the floor.

Eric shook his head, his eyes on Wolfe's bare chest. "No. But you need to be naked too."

"Do I?" Already back to giving orders. Spoiled indeed.

But there was no reason not to comply. Wolfe stripped himself of his trousers, loving the increased attention he received in return, Eric's lustful gaze traveling over his form like a caress.

When they were both naked, Eric's magnificent cock leaking copiously with his arousal, Wolfe waved his hand. "On all fours, pet."

"Jesus."

Wolfe fetched the lube he'd hidden away in the side table. He took a moment to appreciate the sight: his mate's muscular ass presented to him, his strong legs trembling not from effort or fear but anticipation. It must have been torture for poor Eric, not to touch that swollen cock. But he was being good for Wolfe, his hands planted firmly on the floor. Giving him his reward.

Wolfe knelt behind him, stroking the smooth skin of Eric's hip. "All right, pet?"

"'m perfect," Eric mumbled.

"You are." Wolfe pressed a kiss to Eric's lower back, tracing a lubed finger over Eric's hole, delighting in the way it fluttered at the attention. He was such a treasure to work open, the way he whined and moaned and pushed back against Wolfe's fingers.

Wolfe lost himself in the pleasure, pressing kisses along Eric's spine, mouthing at the skin of his shoulders. A feast all for him. By the time he had three fingers in, Eric was a writhing, mewling mess, and Wolfe's cock was back to full hardness.

He lined himself up, breath catching as his swollen head passed the tight restriction of Eric's rim. This was as close to heaven as he'd ever get. This tight, hot grip, the pulse of Eric's pleasure dancing along with his own.

He barely gave Eric a moment to adjust before going hard, his hips rocking back and plunging in deeply again and again, covering Eric's broad back with his own. He felt beastly. Undone. He wanted to plant his seed as deep as he could in this frustrating man, fuck him into oblivion, rut into him until all he knew was Wolfe.

Eric keened with every thrust. "F-Fuck. Fuck. *Fuck*."

His cries were desperate, his skin hot.

Wolfe wanted him closer.

He found himself wrapping his arms around Eric's chest, sitting back on his knees and pulling Eric with him, onto his lap. He paused there, panting. He'd meant to be mating him—conquering him—but here he was holding him. That was fine. He had certain things to say.

"Listen closely, pet."

Eric whined.

Wolfe licked a stripe of sweat off his neck. "Are you listening?"

Eric gave a dazed nod, even as his hips jerked, trying to work himself on Wolfe's cock. Insatiable. But Wolfe held him firm.

He tugged at his mate's ear with blunt teeth. "I can be good to you, pet. Good *for* you. Always, if you ask me. But you will never, *ever* leave me. Do you understand? You are *mine*. And if you run, I will catch you, and I won't hesitate to burn everything down in my wake."

"Fuck. You fucking psycho." Eric laughed breathily, but he didn't withdraw from Wolfe's touch. His ass was still grinding back against Wolfe, as if to tantalize him into moving.

"Do. You. Understand?"

Eric slumped against him, his head finding its way to the crook of Wolfe's shoulder. "I understand." He mumbled the words into Wolfe's skin. "Now fuck me, asshole."

Wolfe pressed a kiss to Eric's temple. "Poor, slutty thing."

But he obliged, rocking his hips once more, sliding his hand over Eric's weeping cock, jerking him in time with each thrust. He could feel his beast yearning to come out, to take their mate for his own.

Have a taste? Please.

So Wolfe let it reap its reward, his fangs dropping with a sigh, biting into Eric's neck.

It deserved this too. For finding their mate, for claiming him when Wolfe wouldn't.

For loving him first.

Twenty-Two

Wolfe

"You're obsessed with bathing me."

Wolfe bit back a smile as he arranged the appropriate towel and robe for Eric on the bathroom's settee, his own towel wrapped loosely around his hips. He noticed that, for all his teasing, Eric had made no move to wash the conditioner from his own hair. "It's my right, pet."

"Right." Eric huffed a laugh. He might have been aiming for snide, but he was clearly too relaxed to manage it. "Because you own me now or something like that? Is that what you were saying back there?"

Wolfe had said all sorts of savage, mindless things, in the course of their mating. He'd meant every word. He leaned down to press a kiss to Eric's damp forehead. "You've always been mine, darling."

Eric gave him a half-hearted pout. "But it's weird that you're not in here with me."

Wolfe had showered on his own as the tub filled, tending to Eric from his place on the bathtub's ledge. "I like to be able to see all of you."

"Perv," Eric accused happily, splashing water out of the tub like an overgrown child.

Wolfe moved to return to his place behind his mate and wash out the conditioner, but he stopped as his wrist was taken in a hard grip.

"But it goes both ways, right?" Eric's gaze was no longer petulant or playful but shockingly serious. "You're not leaving either. right?"

Wolfe smoothed a hand over Eric's blond hair. Such baseless insecurities running around that intelligent mind. It would take a long, long while to iron them out. Luckily, they had an eternity. "Why, darling, are you going to leave a wake of terror if I flee?"

Eric pursed his lips thoughtfully. "I'll terrorize *you* that's for sure. You're not allowed to—to get me used to all this. The pampering and the reassurances and the dicking me down like a champ. And then just *leave*."

Wolfe planted a kiss on Eric's damp shoulder, mouthing at the drops of water, before turning him back around so he could rinse the conditioner. "As if I would ever."

"Good."

Petulant thing. Wolfe smiled, delighting in his ministrations, in the loose, contended feeling pulsing off his mate despite his surface worries. So easily reassured. So easily treasured.

Their companionable silence was shattered by the strident ring of Eric's phone.

Wolfe slapped lightly at his reaching hand. "Leave it."

Eric slunk back against the tub. "I have to call her back eventually, you know. It's been over a week. And the texts I've sent her have *not* been received well."

"Leave it," Wolfe repeated, running his hands along Eric's shoulders, soothing him back into the appropriately relaxed position. "I'll handle it..." And, because he could, because Eric *did*, he added, "Trust me."

"You're going to be relentless with this 'trust me' thing, aren't you?"

"Of course I am."

Wolfe took his time, making his way around the tub to wash every inch of his gorgeous mate. He prolonged the experience by drying Eric with the towel one limb at a time, ignoring his feeble protests of being capable of drying himself.

When his mate was clean, dry, and already well on his way back to an aroused state, Wolfe pressed a final kiss to his neck. "Into the robe with you. Meet me in the sitting room. You'll find a selection of books for you on my desk."

Eric shrugged the robe on carelessly, turning to leave.

Wolfe cleared his throat. "Ah. Leave the phone."

He was rewarded with a supremely suspicious look, but Eric left it nonetheless.

Wolfe waited until he heard Eric's steps into the sitting room, then secured his own robe before taking hold of the gadget and dialing the offending number.

The voice that answered was cold as ice. "Finally. You better be dead or close to it, Eric Monroe."

Wolfe closed the bathroom door gently, turning on the phone's speaker as he made his way to the mirror. He hushed the beast inside him, newly restless with rage at the woman's words. "Mrs. Monroe, I presume?"

"Who is this?"

"I'm Eric's fiancé." Wolfe grabbed his comb from the counter and began attending to his hair. Having a task was always helpful in controlling the temper. "You may call me Wolfgang."

"My son doesn't have a fiancé," Mrs. Monroe said, voice laced with suspicion.

Wolfe grinned at himself in the mirror. "I assure you he does."

"Put him on the phone."

"Well, that's the problem, my dear Mrs. Monroe." Wolfe clucked his tongue, his reflection the picture of regret. "I'm afraid Eric won't be speaking to you again, not for some time."

"Excuse me?"

"We'll have a trial period of three months. If during that time you can communicate via text civilly—no more than once per week, mind you—I could consider reopening the lines of communication."

He had no doubt she'd fail, based on the messages he'd seen before. And he had no problem extending the communication embargo each time she violated the agreement. With any luck, it could be years before she earned the right to speak to his Eric—that was, until the day came they faked human Eric's death. Then this monstrosity of a mother would be out of their lives forever. But for now, due to whatever sentimental pull Wolfe would never understand, Eric wasn't ready to let go. So they would do this, with stipulations in place to protect his mate's peace.

His mate's contentment took priority. Always.

"You have no right to—"

"I have every right," Wolfe cut in. Rude of him, but sometimes one had to meet people at their level. "Your husband's quite the businessman, isn't he, Mrs. Monroe?"

He was met with silence.

Wolfe used the tines of the comb to create a neat part in his hair. "A number of peculiar investments over the years. I can see why you wanted young Eric to earn his living in medicine. A much more stable profession. But wouldn't it be embarrassing, if all your high-society friends got word of your husband's errors? And then there are the regular transfers from our dear Eric's account."

"That's *family*—"

The woman's panic was palpable. Wolfe reveled in it. But he kept his voice even. It wouldn't do to gloat at this stage. "Eric *is* my family, Mrs. Monroe. And if you want to continue living in the manner to which you've become accustomed, you'll listen to what I say. Your trial period starts now. If you try to call again, I'll burn everything you love to the ground."

"I—"

Wolfe hung up. He stared at the phone for a good minute, waiting to see if the offending ringing would begin. But there was only blessed silence.

He found Eric curled up with one of his books on what he was sure to claim was an uncomfortable love seat. He looked absolutely fetching, his blond hair and dark-blue robe setting off the maroon of the furniture's fabric.

Eric raised his brows as Wolfe entered the room. "You know I could hear that, right?"

"It wasn't a secret." Wolfe tugged the book out of Eric's hands to peruse the title. His lips quirked; Eric had chosen one on the brutality of nineteenth century surgeries. An absolutely bloody choice.

Eric was studying Wolfe's face in turn. "You know it's neither reasonable nor healthy to expect me to be happy every second of every day, right?"

Wolfe shrugged, placing the book back into Eric's hands. "Luckily I am neither reasonable nor particularly mentally sound, so we'll simply have to do the best we can."

He wasn't sure what else to say on the matter. A certain lack of empathy had always meant he didn't have to—or care to, in truth—feel others' emotions as his own. But now he did, in the most basic sense. He felt Eric's distress, his discomfort every time that dreaded phone rang. He *knew* how anxious those calls from his mother made him.

And it was horrible, really. If this was how the general population felt, running around with everyone else's emotions tangled up with their own—well, no wonder the world was as mad as it was. But Wolfe was a practical man; he'd simply do everything he could to keep the unhappiness to a minimum.

Why should his mate ever bear such suffering when he had Wolfe to protect him?

He settled himself in a corner of the love seat, smoothing out his robe and patting his thigh as he did so. "Lay your head on my lap, pet."

Eric gave him a dubious look. "You know I've never actually cock warmed before?"

"Did I *ask* you to cock warm?" Wolfe smirked at him, ignoring the way his cock did twitch at the thought. "I'm only asking you to lay your head on my lap. To stretch out, read, and relax. Let me run my fingers through your hair."

"Petting your pet?" Eric quipped. But he did as Wolfe requested and lay his head on Wolfe's thigh, curling up his knees to fit his broad frame on the love seat.

Wolfe didn't miss the little sigh of pleasure as he settled in. He was a very tactile creature, his mate. He would require plenty of physical attention outside of the sexual, Wolfe was sure.

And Wolfe would be more than happy to oblige.

"Enjoying the presence of my beloved," Wolfe corrected, tangling his fingers in Eric's freshly washed strands.

A catch of breath at the word. "Is that so?"

It was. Wolfe hadn't known love before; he hadn't been lying to Johann there. As a rule, he wasn't sure how much he understood it, or how comfortable he was throwing the word about. It seemed to him one so overused by the masses that it had lost all meaning. Except, perhaps, when it passed Eric's lips. But whatever depth of feeling Wolfe was capable of, he knew enough to know it all went to Eric. His passion. His obsession. His care.

Eric rubbed his cheek against Wolfe's thigh, fingering the fabric. "I can't believe we're wearing matching robes right now."

Wolfe had no idea what the issue was. They made a fetching pair.

They sat in companionable silence for a while, Wolfe running his fingers through Eric's hair while Eric pretended to read his book, barely ever turning a page.

Eventually Eric tilted his head up to catch Wolfe's eye. "So I'm your fiancé?"

Wolfe tried to contain his smirk. He'd been wondering if his clever mate would bring that up. "We'll keep it simple. A civil ceremony, I think. You can choose which of the rabble you'd like as your witness, but I'm sure Johann in particular would jump at the chance."

Eric barked an incredulous laugh. "A civil—is this your idea of a proposal?"

"There's no need. It's a fact. You're mine. We're eternally bound as it is. And you love me." Wolfe couldn't help but inject an incredible amount of smug satisfaction into that last bit. It pleased him so, when Eric said those words. "And there's the fact that you, as a doctor in a small town, are a public figure. I'd like my claim to be public as well."

"What if I wanted a big wedding?" Eric was wide-eyed, but whether in disbelief or consternation, it was hard to tell.

The bond didn't lie though.

"You don't," Wolfe pointed out.

Eric kept the wide-eyed act up for a long moment before he relaxed back again with a happy sigh. "That's true."

Wolfe's lips quirked. His mate was remarkably complacent after sex and a hot bath. He would have to keep that in mind.

There was more companionable silence, more absent-minded page turning. Wolfe was sure there was something more on his mate's mind—something beyond their pending nuptials—but he was willing to wait it out.

He didn't wait much longer before Eric spoke, his voice deliberately light. "I might not want to go back to work."

There it was. Wolfe wasn't exactly surprised. Eric had been remarkably unhesitant about his forced vacation. He clearly didn't live for his work, not like others Wolfe had met in his profession. He'd followed his family's instructions in forging his career, he'd found security in the identity, but it didn't give him any joy.

And now Wolfe's beautiful, clever man perhaps wanted to stretch his wings in other directions. Wolfe would have applauded had he thought it welcome. Instead, he kept his voice as even and carefree as his mate's. "As I've said before, you don't have to."

Eric ran his fingers around the edge of his book. "I think I'm done being Dr. Monroe for a while."

"Then you'll simply be Eric."

Eric smiled up at Wolfe, a sharp spike of happiness piercing through the bond. "Your Eric."

Wolfe smiled back, uncaring how foolish he might look. "All mine."

"And then I could do research down the line."

"If you like."

Eric could never work another day in his extremely extended life, and Wolfe would have no qualms. His mate didn't have to prove his right to existence. Not to him.

Eric cast him one last sidelong glance. "You really don't care if I never do anything at all?"

"I want you content," Wolfe said firmly. "I want you near me. That's enough."

"I really do love you."

"I know."

"Even though you're kind of an asshole."

"Read your book, my darling."

"Your beloved," Eric insisted, opening to his most recent page.

"Yes. My beloved."

Twenty-Three

Epilogue

Eric

Eric's fingers clawed into the leather cushions, his breath punching out of him with each harsh thrust of Wolfe's hips.

"How does it feel, darling?"

Eric could only moan in response. It felt too fucking good. True, his belly was digging into the arm of the couch, all the blood rushing to his head, but who could focus on the vague discomfort when arousal had his cock tip leaking like a fountain, Wolfe's satisfied grunts ringing in his ear?

When he didn't answer, Wolfe flipped him over bodily, Eric's back now arching over the couch arm. He gasped as Wolfe pulled his hips up with one smooth jerk.

He tried to take advantage of the brief reprieve to form a coherent sentence. "I was supposed to be reading for my book club."

"And you were." Wolfe leered down at him. It was unfair how sexy he looked, his hair mussed and his sharp cheekbones flush with color. "And then I interrupted. That's the deal. You get your hideous man cave; I get to fuck you senseless in it."

Senseless was right. Eric tried to organize his mushed-up brain waves to keep complaining, partly out of habit and partly because he knew it amused Wolfe to no end. "How—how is it my hideous space when you set yourself up a whole workstation in the corner? You're in here just as much as I am."

"I like to be close," Wolfe answered easily, his hands digging into Eric's thighs, lifting his legs practically over his head.

"Codependent," Eric accused, trying to reach for his dick and pouting when Wolfe batted his hand away.

"As if you aren't the neediest little cock slut in all the land," Wolfe countered, lining up that beautiful cock and pushing into him.

"Oh fuck." Eric keened at the renewed stretch, trying not to come at that feeling of fullness combined with Wolfe's filthy words.

He said stuff like that sometimes, and it had no right to be as hot as it was. It didn't feel like before, when people in town had thought Eric was an unrepentant sleaze (and wasn't it amazing what a wedding band did to change people's minds about that?). There was no malice or judgment in Wolfe's dirty little accolades. Only appreciation. He *liked* Eric needy. He adored him desperate.

And it was all truth. Because Eric *was* a fucking cock slut for Wolfe, no doubt about it. Their bond may have been stable now—it didn't physically or mentally wreck Eric to be apart from him—but he somehow always wanted to be close anyway. He wasn't content unless they'd had some sort of sexual contact at least once a day. And since leaving the hospital—his life just up to the brim with unending stretches of free time—it was often much more than that.

Wolfe renewed his merciless rhythm, and Eric let his head fall back on the seat cushions, giving into the mindless, brain-numbing pleasure of it all. "Oh fuck. Oh fuck. Oh fuck."

"Come for me." Wolfe growled the order. Eric didn't have to look at him to know he was staring. He always was.

"Touch my fucking cock, you asshole."

"No."

But Wolfe did lift Eric's hips even higher, punching that bundle of nerves with each forceful push. Psycho fucker wanted Eric to come untouched. It was his favorite thing, Eric's obsessive mate.

And he'd get what he wanted, wouldn't he? Eric could already feel the electricity building at the base of his spine, his toes curling up in the air.

"Coming. *Coming.* F-Fffuck."

It went fucking everywhere. His belly. His chest. The couch underneath him. Wolfe groaned in appreciation, and then Eric was his sex-blissed rag doll, limp and sated, as Wolfe sought his own release, bending over to cover Eric's body with his as he did so.

They lay panting afterward, contorted in what would have been the most uncomfortable position had Eric not been so fucking drained. Eventually Wolfe rose, puttering about and cleaning Eric up, as he always did.

Caring for his most prized possession.

When Wolfe had righted him to standing, Eric stared down morosely at the new stain on the couch. "You're just trying to ruin this thing so you can replace it with one of your pretentious numbers, aren't you?"

Wolfe pressed a warm kiss to Eric's bare shoulder. "Alas, my evil plan has been all figured out."

"Yeah, I'm onto you."

Wolfe tugged him out of the den and up the stairs, presumably to get dressed in clothes that hadn't been torn to pieces in a lustful haze. "Have you grown bored yet?"

"Of marriage?" Eric asked.

He was given a vicious look for that. "Of your retirement, pet."

"No. Should I be?" For a brief moment, familiar insecurity plagued him. Was it bad, that he didn't mind not being a doctor anymore? His mother certainly thought so, although the one time she'd had the nerve to say it in a phone call Wolfe had calmly grabbed the phone from Eric and hung it up, and then come tax season, she and his dad had been mercilessly audited. Apparently it was a minor miracle they hadn't gone to jail.

But the insecurity didn't last long, not with Wolfe's clear delight at Eric's answer.

Eric tried to frown at him. "Don't look so smug. At some point, I *will* get tired of reading all your weird nonfiction books and actually want to do something."

"Perhaps I'll take you fishing," Wolfe mused, stepping into their closet and selecting clothing for them both, tossing items at Eric seemingly at random.

"You'll have to anyway," Eric teased. "Jay's threatening a camping trip. He wants to wait until Luc and Jamie can swing it. Now that the Tucson debacle's all settled."

"Took them all long enough."

Wolfe began dressing. Eric held his own clothes in his arms, holding off for himself. He liked to watch the process with Wolfe. Because it *was* a process. Undershirts and vests and pocket squares having to look just right.

That was, until Eric caught a glimpse of the ornate clock on the wall. Then he hurried to the dresser, tossing Wolfe's selected items aside and fishing out his athletic wear. "Shit. I'm late meeting Gabe. We're supposed to go running."

Eric could feel Wolfe rolling his eyes behind his back. "You know romping in the forest isn't actually conditioning you, don't you, pet? You can't go far or fast enough for that."

"I know, I know." Eric threw his clothes on in record time. "But we like it anyway; it still feels like exercise. Plus, the beast enjoys it. Soren wants us to try yoga, but Gabe's resisting, I think just to piss him off. That's, like, how they flirt or something."

"You and your friends," Wolfe muttered darkly.

"Aw." Eric sidled over to give him a goodbye kiss. "You're still my number one, babe."

When he turned to leave, Wolfe grabbed his arm, his eyes flashing red in the bedroom light. "Tell me."

Eric didn't have to ask what he meant. It was always the same. "I love you," he said, voicing each word clearly.

That warm, sweet feeling pulsed through the bond, even as Wolfe's lips quirked, fighting his smile. "More than your friends," he pushed.

"More than anyone," Eric agreed.

"And you'll never stop."

And he thought *Eric* was the needy one? But Eric stepped close anyway, pulling on the ridiculous paisley tie Wolfe had chosen until their faces were only a breath apart. "And I'll never, ever stop."

Now Wolfe did smile. "My perfect darling."

And Eric felt perfect. He always did these days. Like he was good. Like he was wanted. Like he was enough.

"Yours."

The end.

Author's Note

Thank you so much for reading book five! I hope you enjoyed this pairing as much as I enjoyed writing them.

Oh, Wolfe. You all can blame both my obsession with Onley James' Necessary Evils series and watching way too much Hannibal for my interest in writing a vampire psychopath. I wanted to explore what it would be like for a vampire to find their mate and have zero guilt or remorse for taking away their humanity. And Wolfe told me right away he was up for the challenge!

These two together had me kicking up my heels and giggling like no other, which might be surprising, considering they're neither of them depicted in the best light in previous books. But I had so much fun with their dynamic—Eric's deep need to be cared for, Wolfe's effortless way of providing. And I just love their acceptance and appreciation of each other's flaws, and the way they soften each other's rough edges with that acceptance.

What's Next?

I have two smaller projects in the works, and then I'll be returning to the series (and to Tucson) with the final installment. Book six—the last book in the series— is going to be (some of you have already guessed this)... Colin and the Tucson twins!

They've all been in my head together since writing Lucien, and I can't seem to shake this romantic combo no matter what I do, so they're going on the page! I have a deep, deep love for Colin and his curmudgeonly ways, and I can't wait to see him cherished by not one but two mates ;)

If you want to stay in the know, you can sign up for my newsletter for updates and news on upcoming releases. And I can always be reached by email if you just want to say howdy. I love, love, love hearing from my readers!

graebryanauthor@gmail.com

I also now have a FB reader group: Grae Bryan's Reader Den
Join us for updates, teasers, and first looks at covers and character art!

Thank you all for reading!

About the Author

Grae Bryan has been reading romance since she was far too young to know any better. Her love for love stories spans all genres, and while her current series is of the paranormal variety, she knows she'll be exploring other worlds further down the line.

She lives in Arizona with her husband, who graciously shares space with all the imaginary men in her head. When not writing, she can generally be found reading more than is healthy, walking her monster-dog, or cuddling her demon-cat. She loves anything and everything gothic, strange, lovely, or cozy.

Find her online: graebryan.com
Join her Facebook reader group: Grae Bryan's Reader Den
Facebook: @GraeBryanAuthor
Instagram: @authorgraebryan
Sign up for her newsletter: graebryan.com/contact

Made in the USA
Columbia, SC
26 January 2025